IF MY LIPS CONFESS

IF MY LIPS CONFESS

A Monk's Story

A Novel

Luis Nixon

iUniverse, Inc.
New York Bloomington Shanghai

If My Lips Confess
A Monk's Story

Copyright © 2008 by Luis Nixon

All rights reserved. No part of this book may be used or reproduced by any means, graphic, electronic, or mechanical, including photocopying, recording, taping or by any information storage retrieval system without the written permission of the publisher except in the case of brief quotations embodied in critical articles and reviews.

iUniverse books may be ordered through booksellers or by contacting:

iUniverse
1663 Liberty Drive
Bloomington, IN 47403
www.iuniverse.com
1-800-Authors (1-800-288-4677)

Because of the dynamic nature of the Internet, any Web addresses or links contained in this book may have changed since publication and may no longer be valid.

This is a work of fiction. All of the characters, names, incidents, organizations, and dialogue in this novel are either the products of the author's imagination or are used fictitiously.

ISBN: 978-0-595-44724-4 (pbk)
ISBN: 978-0-595-89045-3 (ebk)

Printed in the United States of America

For out of the abundance of the heart
the mouth speaketh.
King James Version, Matthew 12:34

CHAPTER 1

My Candidacy

My connection from the Long Island Rail Road to the Amtrak train in Manhattan went off without a hitch. By the time the train got into Washington DC, the weather had gone from sunny and bright to windy and rainy. Brother Andrew, the headmaster of candidates to the monastery, met me at the station entrance. With his long black cape covering the habit of the order, it was not hard for me to spot him in the crowd of about two hundred people. Brother Andrew and I met twice before on vocational retreats. He is one of my inspirations in joining the order. He has a good spirit about himself. Once I got closer to him, he shook my hand and said, "Welcome." As I looked at the station wagon, which should have been retired years ago, Brother Andrew explained, "I have to give the passenger door a real tug for it to open." On the drive to the monastery, he mentioned that I will be entering with two other candidates who seek admission to the monastery. I stopped myself from asking him to tell me about the other two candidates, mainly because it is not well received if you ask personal questions about people, where they are from, how old they are, what schools they attended, and so forth. Our lives are about prayer and work. Personal friendships and hanging out with those you like can destroy community life. So states the holy rule of the monastic order.

We arrived at 5:46 PM. Brother Andrew led me away from "the old tank," my nickname for the station wagon. We entered a long hallway leading to the inner cloister of the monastery. I could hear the organ music from the chapel playing softly and slowly. He introduced me to Brother Mark, who informed me that my bags would be carried up later and directed me to the robing room to prepare for the welcoming ceremony, which was to be held at 6:00 PM, before evening prayers. Entering the large room, I gazed at the pictures of past superiors. It is here I met my fellow candidates, Phillip and Ryan. As we began to introduce ourselves, Brother Stanley, who looked all of two hundred years old, sternly told us not to speak because it was the Grand Silence. The Grand Silence in our monastery is an hour of prayer and meditation when all members must be quiet, speaking only when absolutely necessary. In most cloistered orders in the church, the Grand Silence lasts from late evening until after breakfast the following day. Since we are not a cloistered order and deal with the public in our mission houses, we strictly observe it just one hour a day, between 5:00 PM and 6:00 PM, as stated in our constitution.

Pointing to our left, Brother Stanley showed us a table that had three cowls on it. I was glad the material was light, since I hate to sweat under layers of clothing. We placed the cowls over our heads; the material stopped at our waist lines. Brother Stanley tapped the table and motioned with his right hand for us to follow him. Leaving the robing room, we headed down a long hallway to the chapel, where the community awaited us. The superior-general would formally admit us to the candidacy program, our first step in becoming members of the Order of Saint Matthew. As we approached the chapel, Brother Stanley raised his left hand and motioned for us to kneel in front of the grill that separated us from the community. As the organ stopped, Brother Andrew appeared on the opposite side of the grill and opened it for us to enter. All eyes were on us as we walked down the center of the chapel toward the superior-general. I quickly noticed that everyone was separated by rank in the order. Novices were seated to the left near the grill, professed members to the order on the right, and senior members up front near the altar. And of course our area, the lowest of the low, will be a small area behind the novices in their simple dark gray robes.

The Cowl

As we walked closer to the altar, my eyes were attracted to the large fresco of Christ above it. Lowering my eyes I saw the superior-general standing in front of the altar with his hands over his belly. He was a short, stocky, smiley man with a full beard. He motioned for us to take our temporary seats up front. Looking out into the crowd of monks and priests assembled, Father General began his speech.

"Dear brothers, on this day we welcome Phillip, Ryan, and Luis as new candidates to the monastery. Our order is now in eight countries, with 210 members in various works of clerical, missionary, and social services. Soon we will celebrate the 286th anniversary of our founding, marking the day when blessed Father John Finnelli, our founder from Verona, Italy, was called by the Holy Spirit to start a new order in the church dedicated to caring for the poorest of the poor in our society. We have here in our presence three new candidates to the Order of Saint Matthew who have answered the call to take the vows and adopt the lifestyle of our monastery. We don't know if these men will stay with us, but we pray God will help them decide. Whatever the case may be, we pray for God's will to be done in all things. Amen." Taking his normal seat near the altar, Father General began evening prayer.

Once grace was said before dinner, the Grand Silence was lifted. The refectory is quite large. I counted forty-five of us living here. Now that we were able to speak openly, Phillip, Ryan, and I were eager to discuss the paths that led to our joining the monastery, where we are from, and what works we want to do in the order. Phillip, about six feet tall and thin, was from Martinez, California. Ryan, also about six feet tall and thin, with red hair, came from Corpus Christi, Texas. Philip looked up from his bowl of soup and asked, "What are your vocations, priest or brother monk?" We both responded by saying monks. He again looked up from his bowl of soup and said, "Priesthood's for me." Our conversation turned toward music artists like LL Cool J, Sting, James Brown, Eric Clapton, and of course my favorite, Madonna. One by one we noticed Brother Stanley sternly looking at us from a nearby table, giving us the impression we were too loud or our conversation was not acceptable for a monastery atmosphere. Whatever the case may be, Phillip mentioned, "You know guys, Brother Stanley was born to be a monk. You can tell by his constant observance of rules as well as by the way he carries himself when he walks."

After dinner Brother Andrew approached our table and instructed us to get settled in by unpacking, for tomorrow we were to begin our studies in theology and philosophy, which would supplement our spiritual training for becoming a religious monk or priest. Brother Andrew sternly reminded us, "Your day starts at 6:30 AM with morning prayers and mass. Remember, lateness is not acceptable when serving God or for prayers." Before leaving he remembered to tell us our schedules were in our rooms.

After waiting until Brother Andrew was out of sight, Phillip said, "I have an idea. Instead of going to our rooms, let's hang out a bit, maybe roam around the grounds and check out the surroundings." I could tell Phillip was an adventurer.

Ryan, on the other hand, was more into upholding the rules. He reminded us, "Roaming around and having private visitations are against the rules of the monastery. And it's not something I want to get caught doing my first night here."

"It's also late," I said, "and we have to be up before six." So Phillip backed down from his idea.

At the top of the stairs leading to the bedrooms we met an older member of the monastery who introduced himself as Father Patrick. His Irish accent was so thick I could barely understand him. Pointing past my left, he informed us our bedrooms were down the corridor next to the novices' bedrooms. Our assigned bedrooms had cute welcome signs with our names on them attached to the doors. The room was what I expected: a bed, writing table, chair, small dresser, and a bathroom shared with my neighbor next door. After unpacking, I undressed and got into bed, where I silently prayed and thanked God for my vocation.

In my haste to unpack for my first full day in the monastery, I forgot to set my alarm clock. What woke me the next morning were the bells announcing morning prayers. Jumping out of bed, I dressed quickly and ran down three long hallways to the chapel. As I took my place with my fellow candidates, Phillip and Ryan were trying to hold their chuckles back while stealing glances at me. Ryan, who was closest to me, let me in on what was so funny, whispering, "Hey, your cowl is on inside out." Father General was looking right in my direction from the altar. I didn't dare turn my cowl around in front of him during prayers.

After mass I was sure Brother Andrew was going to chastise me for being late. But he simply passed me and whispered, "It's cool. I was late my first day too."

Our classroom was in the large basement of the monastery. Brother Andrew wrote on the blackboard "custody of the eyes" and explained, "This means not looking at things that can lead us into sin."

Phillip chuckled and asked, "Brother Andrew, can you elaborate on that?"

Brother Andrew didn't beat around the bush. "You shouldn't stare at a woman's chest or legs, at people kissing, or look at billboards with naked people on them. And if you are sexually attracted to someone, you may catch yourself looking at them." After pausing a moment, Brother Andrew said, "You have to always be aware of your surroundings and your frailties. It can be very embarrassing if you are caught looking at someone or something inappropriately."

It rained most of the next day. It was very hard getting used to and maintaining quietness. That evening during the Grand Silence, Phillip assembled the novices in the hallway with Ryan and then knocked on my door. In silence he motioned for me to come out into the hallway. We were all curious. Phillip took off his shoes, leaving his socks on, ran really fast, and then stopped, sliding down the hallway as if he were ice-skating. Apparently the marble floors had accidentally been overwaxed. The rest of us wasted no time in taking our shoes off. When it was my turn, I raced down the hallway. As I began to slide, I realized I couldn't stop. And what's worse, I collided with Father Patrick as he came out of his bedroom carrying a load of books. We both landed on the floor, with the books spread everywhere. As I helped Father Patrick off the floor he noticed my shoes were off. Shaking his finger at me, he sternly said, "You did not join a college frat house. Put your shoes on."

As I helped gather his books off the floor I could see that my fellow candidates and the novices had split the scene. My apology at the time meant nothing to Father Patrick, since he wanted to be about his business. Later I met up with Ryan and some of the novices in the monastery gardens. I acted as if nothing was wrong and said nothing about my run-in with Father Patrick. Phillip rummaged through a Washington newspaper and finally handed me a section. Looking down I noticed the headline read, "Drag Racing." Phillip said, "If you're interested, you have to learn how to stop first." I was not amused, and as they laughed I almost walked away, but then I broke down and laughed, seeing how funny it was now that I thought about it.

The novices of the monastery left us to go to one of their meetings. We continued reading the paper. As he read the entertainment section, Phillip got another of his great ideas. He held up a picture of Madonna—the pop star, not the Virgin Mary—and excitedly suggested, "Hey, let's stay up late and see her new erotic video on MTV. The article says the video will premiere tonight on MTV at eleven." Phillip, to keep selling the idea, reminded Ryan and me, "Everyone's in bed at that time."

Ryan sucked his teeth and asked, "Phillip, do you really want to be a priest? If they find us watching a Madonna video, what will our excuse be? And yes, I would leave with her if she knocked on the monastery door."

Before Ryan could continue, Phillip cut him off by apologizing. "I'm sorry if I offended you. I just thought it was a cool idea to see the video."

Listening to the two of them, I said I'd like to see it myself. Ryan now knew I was on Phillip's side, so I stood side by side with Phillip. As we both stared at Ryan, he finally gave in and said, "Guys, if we're caught, it's every man for himself." Looking past the large statue of Saint Michael, we noticed Brother Stanley coming our way. Immediately Ryan placed the sexy picture of Madonna back among the other articles. After dinner we arranged to be at the top of the stairs leading to the cloister by 10:45 PM. We agreed not to wear shoes or anything that would make noise and give us away. I looked both ways when I left my room, feeling as if I was in my parents' house doing something wrong.

We met at our appointed spot. Phillip was very hyped up, and Ryan was afraid of getting caught. As we made our way through the refectory, we heard someone coming in our direction. We quickly hid under one of the tables, hoping not to be seen. Peeping up over the table, Phillip whispered, "It's Brother Stanley double-checking to see if the doors are locked up for the night." For all of six seconds we thought it was clear to stand and proceed to the television room. But we dove back under the table as Brother Stanley came back looking for another exit. His path took him right past the table we were hiding under. Ryan totally freaked out. But we sat still, seeing the lower part of his robe as he passed, dangling his set of keys.

It would have made Brother Stanley's day if he could have caught us up to no good. But after he passed the table and left, we continued our Madonna mission. We nearly ran to the television room, with Ryan leading the way. It was now 10:58 by the clock on the wall. "For an order that's so frugal and strict about the poverty rule," I said, "don't you think it's maybe a little strange that aside from everything else we have cable television with MTV?"

Looking pale and nervous, Ryan said, "Shut up and just watch the damn video." Phillip found the remote and tuned into the MTV station we were looking for. I could tell the song was going to be good by the beat. Ryan, who was now totally into the video, reminded Phillip what he said about Madonna knocking on the monastery door. After successfully slipping into the inner cloister and back to our rooms, I laid out my clothing for the following day. I hated looking for the different pieces when I was in my morning daze at 6:15. The next morning after breakfast Brother Andrew informed us that we were to meet with Father Peter, headmaster of novices, at 1:00 PM sharp in the classroom, as it was nearing time for us to be accepted as novices into the monastery community.

Father Peter, like Brother Andrew, was among the youngest members of the community. Father Peter looked to be in his early thirties. At ten minutes after one, he entered the classroom with his bike. "The old tank," he explained, "was not working, so I had to ride my bike to see a sick parish member." After he got settled, he sat on the desk in front of us and got serious. "As novices," he said, "you will have to study intensely what it means to be religious men of the church." The real blow came when he reminded us of another rule. "You are not to leave the mother house during your time as novices in the order. For this is not only the time of intense prayer and study but also the time to really give thought to the lifestyle you are entering. Next Tuesday, after your class on canon law with Father Peter, the monastery council will meet to discuss whether each of you is to be accepted into the novitiate." We were nervous. We knew this meeting could send one or all of us back home. We remained silent when Father Peter asked if there were any questions before he left.

Tuesday arrived. Our big meeting would occur in six hours. We will go in one by one as they call us. We stood outside the superior-general's office whispering to each other and feeling very anxious about a meeting that just could send us home if the council feels religious life in the Order of Saint Matthew is not right for us or them. Ryan thought we should have all the basic answers down so that there would be no hesitation when we answered them. Some of the questions are: Why are you here in this monastery? What do the vows of poverty, chastity, obedience mean to you? What work attracts you in the order? Has the candidacy program been what you expected it to be?

As Ryan was whispering, Brother Andrew entered the hall from Father General's office telling us we three could go in all at once. This was the first time the order had had all candidates evaluations at one time. I'm sure we looked stunned. I suppose we all thought that if we were called out on our shortcomings, it could be very embarrassing; on the other hand, this was the first true step toward true humility in the order. Entering through the large oak doors of the office, I could see all the members of the council: Father General; Father Peter, headmaster of novices; Brother Stanley; and Brother Andrew, master of candidates.

Sitting on a rather uncomfortable chair in front of them, I placed my hand in my cowl to grasp my rosary for good luck, but instead I found the granny apple I had taken from the table at lunch. It would have to do as my good luck charm. As I shifted in the chair, I felt my rosary in my back pocket. To take it out now would be too obvious. I wished it were in the front pocket of my cowl where no one could see me holding it for good luck. After all the commendations from the council on our studies, work, and attentiveness to a strict prayer life, Father General now said that if we had anything to say, now would be the time to speak. Phillip, Ryan, and I looked at each other and then back at Father General. One by one we responded that Father Peter and Brother Andrew had answered all of our questions. Looking at the council and pausing a few seconds, Father General raised his voice and said, "Welcome to the novitiate, my brothers. On the eighth of June, the anniversary of the founding of the order, you will be installed as novices." Relieved, we said our thank-yous to the council as they nodded at us and smiled. Brother Andrew came over to shake our hands and said, "Brother Mark will fit you for the novices' robes tomorrow at 2:00 PM." We left the office, and standing in the hall, we raised our hands upward like three musketeers and gave a big sigh of relief.

When we entered the robing room the next day, we saw the dark gray fabrics laid out on the table. Brother Mark, who was standing near the sewing machine, invited us to come closer. Hanging behind him were robes that must have been used by novices in years past. Brother Mark brought out his measuring tape to take our sizes to see if any of these robes would fit us. If not, he would have to make new ones from the gray material on the table. One by one, he found our sizes and laid them on the tables for us to try on. As we tried them on, Brother Mark went to the dresser at the back of the room to pull out dark navy blue belts for our waists. As we moved about in our robes to get used to them, Brother Mark put name tags on the robes so that the father general would know which one to give to us at the ceremony.

CHAPTER 2

The Clothing of a Novice

I couldn't sleep most of the night, but I made sure I was in full form for Father Peter's instructions by having a cup of black coffee at breakfast. When we met in the chapel, Father Peter instructed us where to enter and where to kneel. After his sermon, Father General would call us one by one to him to make our profession of temporary vows of poverty, chastity, and obedience. The instructions were simple, but Father Peter also provided written guidelines of the events.

Napping a little, I woke up on my own and quickly became afraid that I may have missed the ceremony. But then I noticed it was only 1:36 PM by my bedside clock. My emotions ran high as I sat on the side of the bed. I could hear the footsteps of Brother Stephen, Ryan, and Phillip approaching my room. I stood up and opened the door before Brother Stephen knocked. Brother Andrew came along to escort us to the chapel. Our trip through the cloister was silent. We could hear the organ as we approached the chapel. We peeped through the doors and saw members of the order who lived in the mother house. Some were at prayer and others were coming in to take their seats. Ryan's and Phillip's proud parents sat in the front row of the guest pews. It upset me that my own parents were not present, but then again, their interest in my life has never been terribly great.

The Clothing of a Novice

Dreadlocks No More

The music of the organ grew louder, and the priests of the community started in procession down the chapel aisle. Ryan, Phillip, and I took our places on a bench behind the grill in back of the chapel. When all the priests had entered, the grill was closed and would remain closed until it was time for us to enter and make our way up to the altar. After all the regular prayers were concluded, Father General delivered a sermon on the history of our order and our work. "We did not choose God," he said, "God chose us for this ministry. If we look around, there are those whom we would not pick as friends if we lived in the outside world. And yet we are here for the same purpose, to love God and serve his catholic church on earth."

After his sermon, Father General returned to his seat, which had been moved out in front of the altar. With the organ now playing slowly, my emotions remained intense as we moved closer to the grill. Brother Stephen reopened the grill, motioned to us, and nodded as each of us entered, one behind the other. We walked up the center of the chapel and stopped at three kneelers about twenty feet in front of the altar and knelt.

"What do you ask, my brothers?" asked Father General.

"To be admitted into the novitiate," we responded.

Father General now looked at the monastery council and said, "Do you, my brothers, accept these candidates for the novitiate?"

The council responded in unison, "We do."

Now calling us up one by one to kneel in front of him, Father General asked, "Do you promise to live in poverty, chastity, and obedience to the church and my authority? Do you make this choice of your own free will?" To each question, we replied, "I do."

And as the three of us stood together and bowed to Father General, he stood to bless us with the sign of the cross, saying, "May what God has begun in you come to full fruition." After blessing our robes and handing them to us, Father General led the choir in singing "Veni, Sancte Spiritus" ("Come, Holy Ghost").

Standing at the altar, Father General gave each of us leave to put on the novice's robe. I was amazed at Brother Stanley's show of emotion; he smiled at us and nodded as we passed him on our way into the sacristy. Phillip also noticed Brother Stanley's reaction and whispered, "I guess he does have blood in his veins after all." Before we put on the dark gray robes of the novitiate in the sacristy, Ryan, Phillip, and I had to face a sacrifice of vanity. Anyone who reaches the rank of novice or professed member in the order must submit to one of our order's oldest rules, the tonsure. In our order, the tonsure consists of having your hair cut low to the scalp as a symbol of humility and renouncing the world and the vanities of worldly pride. Before and even after I entered the monastery, my mind blocked it out that my thin dreadlocks would be cut. Vanity was definitely in my mind. I was so proud of the shoulder-length dreadlocks that had taken me so long to grow out and groom on a daily basis. Walking farther into the sacristy, I told myself it was only hair. If I am to be a monk, then this is not only a sacrifice for myself but also to God and the order I wish to live with. While I knelt in the sacristy, Brother Brian untied my dreads from behind. Brother Vincent held a large pair of scissors, lifted my dreads from my left side, and proceeded to cut them slowly. I hated to hear the crunch of the scissors removing them. I managed not to look at the tray to my left holding my former dreadlocks. It was soothing, however, to see the eight brothers who accompanied us to the sacristy area pull back their hoods and show their heads, as if to say they too had sacrificed their hair in joining the order, and so must we. Walking in procession back into chapel to the sound of loud organ music, we bowed to Father General in front of the altar as he said the final prayers. At the conclusion, the assembled brothers applauded our new rank within the order.

Taking our regular seats in the classroom, Father Peter entered and stood in front of the teacher's desk. "This is the time when your formation becomes real to us," he said. Pacing up and down the classroom aisle, he continued. "Sexuality is not the concern of the order. Whether a man is gay or not is not our concern. Our main concern is that he live his vows in union with Christ who suffered on the cross, a life he willingly chose at the altar before his brothers and before the sacrament. Some brothers have more problem areas than others. But remembering why we came here to begin with helps us in our struggles to abide by the vows of poverty, chastity, and obedience.

"There are forty-five men in our community, with forty-five different personalities that can clash at any time in our work and fellowship. Father General said yesterday that if we look around at our brothers, there are some here whom we would never be friends with in the outside world. Our vocation has yoked us with others who are here for the same purpose, to consecrate our lives to God and his church on earth. The period of your novitiate may or may not be hard for you, but it is designed to educate you as a member of a religious community." Father Peter closed by saying that our novice class schedule and new work schedule would be in our rooms.

From Novice to Professed Member

The time we spent as novices was hard, both in terms of manual labor and observing the Grand Silence, which Phillip had trouble with many times. All three of us were caught twice in one month laughing aloud in the library. We would make each other laugh by whispering stupid jokes to one another or by sliding down the banisters in the cloister. During our last stage as novices, Father General sent us by train to Garrison, New York, for a four-day retreat at a house run by the nuns of a semicloistered order. When we returned, it would be time for the post-novitiate ceremony, in which we would receive the official habit of the Order of Saint Matthew consisting of a dark navy blue robe with a black scapular. The scapular is a long band of cloth that goes over the head and hangs from the shoulders in the front as well as the back, reaching down nearly to the ankles. A large hood is attached to the scapular, and a black belt goes under it to hold the robe close to the body.

The retreat house was high in the mountains and had lots of paths to hike around. To pay for our room and board we worked each day in a small soup kitchen for the local people. On the last day of our retreat Ryan suggested we forego our novice robes after lunch and check out the area of Garrison. It was a cool idea, since we'd prayed and meditated until we'd nearly made ourselves crazy. We were also somewhat nervous with anticipation, for we were about to become full members of the monastery. We set out wearing T-shirts, jeans, sneakers, and our backpacks. First we headed along some trails and then to the village area. It felt so good to get out into the world. Ryan was the first one to bring this thought up as we stopped at a small coffee shop in town. Sitting outside the coffee shop, two girls about twenty-two or twenty-three years old passed by us smiling and looking directly at Phillip. It was obvious to Ryan and me that he was their type. Looking a little bashful, Phillip continued drinking his coffee while Ryan and I chanted from the sacred rule book of our order, "Custody of the eyes, Brother, custody of the eyes."

Shaking his head and looking up from his coffee, Phillip said, "It's hard, brothers."

Ryan never missed a beat as he looked at the girls, now a little ways down the sidewalk. In a perverse manner he deepened his voice and said, "It's hard alright."

We finished our coffee and were drawn back to the wooded trails. But Phillip led us off the trail and we ended up getting lost. After about twenty-five minutes we arrived at a peak that overlooked the trees and houses in the distance. Looking about in all directions, I spotted the orange roof and cross of the retreat house about a mile away.

We were out of breath when we reached the top of the retreat house's steep driveway. One of the nuns who was planting flowers at a small shrine gave us a message. Father Peter would meet us at the Amtrak station in Washington DC at 4:15 PM, close to our arrival time. If this changed, we were to notify him as soon as possible, and if not, we didn't need to call; he would just meet us.

Knowing our little excursion was over, we packed our things and prepared to head back to the mother house on the next day. On the train, Ryan and Phillip slept while I took in the scenery through the train window. After a while, I dozed a little myself. The train whistle, along with the announcement, "Washington DC, last stop," woke us up.

While we were standing and stretching, the train's rapid swaying caused two women to bump into Phillip on his left side. As they made their apologies, we noticed it was the two women we had seen outside the coffee shop in Garrison. Remembering us and suddenly noticing our robes, they quickly walked away. As they did so, all three of us, and maybe a couple of other passengers, could hear one of them saying "What a fucking waste."

Ryan and I couldn't help laughing at the woman's comment. "Brother, what a waste," we teased Phillip as we handed him his bags.

Nodding and welcoming us back as we walked toward him, Father Peter said, "My brothers, the monastery has been very quiet without you. Father General would like to see you one by one after dinner, mainly to discuss your post-novitiate studies and the ministries you will be doing in the order."

I was none too pleased to see the monastery's tank of a station wagon again. I pulled so hard on the passenger door that it hit me in the knee. Although I badly wanted to curse, I kept to the role of the good monk and shouted "*Freaking freak!*" instead. The others stared at me, stunned, and I congratulated myself that my training as a monk was paying off. In class we were told to always be aware of our surroundings, especially when in public. If this had happened two years ago, my surroundings would not have mattered; I would have shouted "*Fuck!*" seven times over—or until the pain went away.

We arrived at the mother house just in time for the Grand Silence, and Father Peter led us into the chapel. The smiles and nods of the brothers welcomed us back as we knelt before the altar. After the Grand Silence and before leading the community in evening prayer, Father General welcomed us back by name, asking the community to pray for us and our vocation, for tomorrow we would receive the official habit of the order and then be transferred to the different ministries we had chosen.

CHAPTER 3

Give Me Manhattan

On our own, Ryan, Phillip, and I visited Brother Mark in the robing room to see how our new garb was coming along. Brother Mark had our measurements from when we entered the novitiate and were fitted for our novice robes.

Brother Andrew visited the robing room to let us know that Father General wanted to see us in his office. We were surprised that Brother Andrew knew where to find us, but, in fact, most brothers about to be professed in the order make a last trip to the robing room to see their new garments.

Father Daniel, Father General's assistant, instructed us who was to be first—me—as he pointed to a bench where we could wait to be seen. I already knew Ryan and Phillip wanted to work in parish ministry and live in a church rectory. But as for me? I really didn't know if the order had a mission house where I could live and work with street people in a homeless center. Though our order has such facilities abroad, I'd rather work in this county before considering working abroad. Father Daniel called me in first. I entered to see Father General at his desk with his thick-rimmed glasses on, looking over some papers. Waving his hand, he said, "Come in, my brother. I've been looking over your application to the order, and I see you want to do serious work with the homeless and soup kitchen services. Our order," he continued, "only has parish outreach services that run food pantries. But there are various mission houses in the United States that have nuns, priests, and brothers from different orders living together in community. Many of these are doing the kind of work you seek."

Standing and coming around his desk holding a green booklet, he showed me the different programs I can work in with the poor. Some are secular, and others non-secular, in their living arrangements. Waving his hands enthusiastically he said, "Brother, please read through the booklet tonight and come to me tomorrow and tell me which programs best fit your interests." After receiving his blessing I departed and passed Ryan and Phillip on the bench. Before I continued to the refectory to satisfy my craving for a green apple, Father Daniel handed the three of us a paper that outlined the next day's ceremony. Father Peter will be in the chapel at nine tonight to go over everything. Just like with the entrance to the novitiate ceremony, I found it simple and directly to the point. Looking up from my paper I asked Ryan and Phillip to catch up with me in the television room when they're done with Father General. I used this time in my room to go over the booklet Father General had given me. One program that called out to me was a mission house in Spanish Harlem called Austin House. It was run by a Catholic priest named Father Doug Robbins. As I read more and more on the program in Spanish Harlem, my excitement grew. This is where I wanted to go. To me Manhattan is the greatest city in the world. Aside from wanting to live and work there, I was attracted by the museums, live concerts in Central Park, the Knicks games at Madison Square Garden, as well as street fairs in the late spring and summer.

Bishop Millen from Chicago, a friend of our order, presided over the ceremony. Stopping twenty feet in front of the bishop and Father General, we began the profession of promises. One at a time we kneeled before the bishop saying, "I promise to God my life and work in the Order of Saint Matthew for a term of six years before taking perpetual vows in the order."

After each of us signed his name and entered the date in the book of professed names in the order, Bishop Millen blessed us and our new robes. Father General proudly gave us leave to go to the sacristy to change. When we returned to the chapel, the bishop gave us his final blessing. Our monastery brothers stood from their pews and applauded while the organ loudly played the Alleluia. Later that same night at eight I met with Father General to tell him what ministry I preferred to work in. Happy with my choice, Father General shouted, "Great! I will get in contact with the priest who's in charge of the program in Harlem to see if there is room for you to live and work there. I will get back to you in a day or so with an answer from him." Having grown up on Long Island, I knew what cultural riches Manhattan had to offer. If I don't get this assignment, I told myself, it would be a great disappointment. I doubt that I could have found another program in Manhattan that was as good.

Father General surprised me in the corridor outside of the library. My wish had come true. Father Doug had an opening at Austin House. He faxed over the needs of the program in Harlem. Father General handed me the list. Reading over the list of program needs, it seemed to me I could do more than one job on the list: volunteer director, soup kitchen staff, outreach clothing room organizer, and new member to work on a future project for housing homeless people with HIV and AIDS.

At the end of his fax to Father General, Father Doug added that I could come as soon as I wanted and to please inform him of the day I planned to arrive. Walking along the corridor with Father General I received his blessing. "Luis," he said, "remember our founder's wishes. We must always serve the poorest of the poor and be willing to go where even some religious men and women of the church refuse to go. You will have two days to prepare to leave for Harlem. Father Daniel will call Father Doug in New York to tell him of your arrival date." As we entered the gardens of the inner cloister, his demeanor became very serious, and he began to warn me about what I was about to enter into. His advice and words were drawn from experiences he had when he was younger. "When you go out in the world, there will be people who just want to hurt you or even people who hate God. You will be the object of all their hostility and anger about the church's stance on issues of abortion and contraception. You must try not to let these issues overburden your vocation. Our first mission is to help all in need, no matter if their belief system is different from ours or not."

While I was packing my things, Phillip and Ryan visited my room. I'd left the door open a crack. Ryan tapped on the doorjamb and said, "Well, well, Brother, what did Father General have to say? We saw you two speaking near the library."

Holding my shirt and then lifting it in the air, I shouted, "Harlem is mine, my brothers." They instantly congratulated me, but Brother Stanley, who was passing by, cut them short with one of his famous stares. We guessed this time it was to remind us of the order's rule prohibiting members of the community from visiting other members' bedrooms. Phillip, who could still see Brother Stanley out of the corner of his eye, whispered, "He's standing at the end of the hall looking in our direction." At this we agreed to talk more at dinner time.

At dinner Ryan asked Phillip and me for our addresses and phone numbers where we will be living. As he ate his beef stew, Phillip was the first to remember another rule: no friendships in community, for they can destroy community life if we only hang out with those we click with. "We have two mandatory community retreats every year," I said, "along with various community events where we will see each other. Phillip is studying for priesthood, and we will be too busy in our ministries. And besides, it will give us more to talk about when we finally do meet." Ryan was leaving for Chicago the next morning after mass, around 7:30 AM, and I was to take the 11:45 AM Amtrak train to Manhattan. Phillip stayed in the mother house for his intensive studies in theology for priesthood.

After mass Phillip and I said our good-byes to Ryan in the front entrance to the cloister. Rushing toward us, Brother Andrew interrupted us and turned to Ryan, quickly saying, "Brother, we have to leave now for the Amtrak train. I have a 9:00 AM council meeting, and then I must go back to Amtrak to drop Luis off for his 11:45 AM train." Ryan put his bags in the station wagon, and instead of saying good-bye, he just said, "See ya around." Later, when it was my turn to climb into the old tank, I extended my right hand and wished Phillip well. At the end of our short conversation, he said sincerely, "Peace, Brother." In the car Brother Andrew handed me a letter from Father Doug and more literature on the mission Austin House.

Once settled on the train, I began to read the detailed papers on the history of Austin House and its mission to the poor. Austin House was created in 1946 in London, England, after the Second World War to help the poor and homeless rebuild their lives in a community setting, living together and growing their own food as well as making and repairing furniture to help them survive. Some of their principles of living were taken from the Amish communities. The name Austin comes from Nancy Austin, who lost her husband in the war. She decided to band together people who had lost all hope of living after their homes were destroyed by bombs. Her hope was that they could support one another in rebuilding their own lives. Austin communities exist in only four countries: Italy, France, England, and the United States. The other countries each have two houses, but there is only one here, the one in Manhattan. As time went on, the needs of the poor changed, so Austin House changed as well. People who are coming out of prison or trying to get off the streets may now come to Austin House to live in community. To help with the transition, Austin House provides GED programs, job training, counseling programs, and a system for getting a job outside of the community before leaving it. Austin House helps homeless people with HIV and AIDS make and sell goods so that they can buy buildings where terminally ill people can live as a group and die with dignity.

Before I read the last paragraph, I felt my eyes getting tired, so I purchased a black coffee with one sugar from the lady vendor at the end of the car. That usually does the trick. Sipping my coffee and looking out the window of the train I saw children's baseball games as well as businesses with New Jersey in the name. That let me know Manhattan wasn't far off. I looked back down at my paper to read the last bit of information on Austin House. It went on to say that volunteers as well as those coming out of prison or getting off the street all live together in a four-story building that has offices and a soup kitchen on the lower levels, with dormitories for the community on the upper floors. The residents receive free room and board and a stipend of forty dollars a week, which mainly comes from donations since the program receives no government funds. When I first looked at the other mission houses in the booklet, I noticed that a lot of mission houses for the poor offered room and board along with the stipend of thirty to forty dollars a week. This is totally cool with me, but like many nuns and monks, I knew that if I needed extra cash for an emergency, my monastery would help.

Finishing my reading and then my coffee, I looked out the window to the east and saw the Manhattan skyline in the distance. I put my Austin House literature away and pulled out the subway map. To get to Harlem I'd take the 1 or 2 train uptown from Penn Station to Times Square–42nd Street, then the shuttle to Grand Central–42nd Street, and from there take the uptown local to 116th Street and Lexington Avenue. Transferring from the Amtrak train to the subway system was very easy for me; the fast pace and rudeness of some didn't faze me a bit. As I traveled on the train uptown, I got some brief stares; others nodded to me with a smile of reverence. For the first time I really felt out of place because of my religious garb. Many of our brothers do not wear habits except when in the mother house or for special occasions. Feeling the way I do, this will be the case for me too.

I got off the train and took the south exit out of the subway. Emerging from the subway, I now entered a world that always gets my juices going. The hustle of the streets, the smells of food, and the sounds of salsa music energized me. Looking ahead, I could see street vendors as far as my eyes could see, selling clothing, toys, food, and body oils. I realized I was finally here in Manhattan, not as a visitor but as a resident. Since I didn't know the numbering system of the buildings, I ended up going in the wrong direction. Before I turned around to walk in the right direction, I noticed the large outdoor market under an overpass that carries the metro north trains to and from Connecticut. Fruits and vegetables are what I saw first; the green apples at the end of the table were ripe and good for the taking.

I found Austin House standing near the East River. I made my way through the small but tough crowd in front of the building and came to the security desk. His name tag said William Brooks. He stood almost seven feet tall, with the build of a football player. Raising his voice before I could speak, he said, "Hello. You must be Brother Luis from Washington DC. Welcome." William looked to another security guard whom he addressed as Peter. Peter introduced himself to me and offered to take me and my small suitcase to Father Doug's office. The old building has four levels and no elevator. Peter led the way to the third floor, turned left, and walked to the end of the hall. Before Peter had a chance to knock, a tall, stocky Hispanic guy in his early to mid-twenties threw open the door so quickly that it hit the wall hard. Peter and I both heard the guy say, "I don't think so, old man." He passed us holding his leather jacket in one hand and a soda can in the other.

Judging by Father Doug's reaction, William, the security guard downstairs, had not called ahead to tell him we were on our way to his office. Peter shook my hand, gave me my suitcase back, and left quickly, as this little episode was uncomfortable for all three of us. "Welcome, Brother, welcome," said Father Doug as he stood up from his small couch. And with open arms, he proceeded to hug me. My foot hit a small picture frame on the floor that must have fallen when the door hit the wall. I picked it up and passed it to him as he sat in a wooden chair near his desk. I took a seat on the little couch facing him. He smiled at me and said, "So, Brother, tell me about yourself."

I then began to tell him of my vocation, where I was from on Long Island, along with the history of the order of priests and monks I belong to. After I spoke, he told me about his background, how he was a Catholic priest born and raised in Quebec, Canada, who ended up in Harlem. He seemed to love Manhattan as much as I did; he went on to say he was sixty-five years old. Expressing his excited feelings, he said, "I've been in Harlem for almost twenty-five years, ever since my ordination. My vocation is to help the poor. When I heard of the mission of Austin Houses in England, the idea of opening one in my favorite city was an easy one."

As he continued to talk about the homeless of the city and his future hopes for the programs of Austin House, I began to judge him in my mind, feeling there was a sloppiness about him. Father Doug was quite obese, but that is not a problem for me. It was the faded small blue T-shirt he squeezed into that showed his lower belly, and the way he kept pulling it down every couple of seconds that distracted me. Not only was it too small for him, but I also could make out ketchup stains on the right side. His black sweatpants looked like oversized bell-bottom pants, with long strings that needed to be cut. It all reminded me of the old saying that first impressions mean everything. As I tried to stay focused in the conversation, Father Doug proudly showed me some framed photos and went on to say, "Brother, from Monday to Friday we serve about three hundred a day in our social services office downstairs and our soup kitchen."

He paused and looked at my religious garb. "Do you intend to wear it all the time? I think it will make the prostitutes and drug dealers of the area feel uncomfortable. If they come into the building to get help, gloom and doom are their first thoughts. In my experience, in years of interacting with the locals, I think regular street clothing may be best."

Standing and going to his desk, he picked up the key to my room on the fourth floor, room 4E. As I took it, I said, "The issue of clothing was on my mind coming here. And I feel the same way you do."

"Where would you like to work?" he asked.

"I think the outreach office and soup kitchen would be ideal for me. Having two jobs instead of one to keep me busy will help me get to know people in the building as well as the locals who come into the outreach office."

Handing me a schedule of times for prayer, meals, and work, Father Doug said, "I think you should rest. I'll show you around the building after dinner."

After the tour that evening I couldn't help but feel amazed at how all the different departments functioned with such little space. Making his apologies, Father Doug left for an interfaith council meeting on West 96th Street. I took this time on my own to get to know some of the people living in the building. It was a little rough at first. I got the impression that some suspect that anyone who's too nice or wonders about them and where they are from may want something from them. I found a lively group in the large community room, listening to the sound of Queen Latifah's hit "Just Another Day." Hair braiding and board games like dominos were going on. I went over to a gathering at a small card game to introduce myself. They had the impression that I was a guy who'd just gotten out of jail. I almost laughed out loud when asked where was I incarcerated. Before I had a chance to respond, William came in to let me know there was a phone call for me at the security desk.

It was Father General on the other end of the phone just checking to see that I had arrived okay. He directed me to report by phone or letter twice each month, a practice required of all members of the order who live outside the confines of the monastery. After hanging up the phone I went back to my room. As I walked up the stairs I could see light coming from the roof door, which must have been opened to let in some fresh air. I stepped onto the tarred roof. The view was awesome. The evening was clear, and the sun was going down over the buildings in the west. Looking south I could make out the slanted roof of the famous Citigroup Center, and to the east I could see that the lights of the Triborough Bridge had just come on. As I leaned on the side of the building facing east, I could hear Queen Latifah's "U.N.I.T.Y." coming from the building across the way. Enjoying the music and the good breezes of evening wind, I found myself not noticing time. It was not until my arms and back were sore from leaning on the side of the building that I decided to go to my room to unpack, pray, and turn in.

Father Doug introduced me to the community of about forty people at my first mandatory morning meeting; these meetings are held every morning, Monday through Friday, to discuss any important issues a department may have. I stood and gave a brief personal history. I got strange looks when I talked about my vocation as a monk. After speaking I received a lot of welcomes and the meeting came to a close. Father Doug introduced me to Robert, who works in the outreach department. Robert will orientate me to the running of both the office and the soup kitchen. As Robert led me to the office, I couldn't help but let him know that I felt some people acted a little strange in the meeting when I talked about being a monk. He turned to me when we reached the office and said, "I feel a lot of people maybe never saw a black monk or priest. We have priests and nuns that visit and work here, but none have been black until now. Father Doug, who is white, may or may not bring it to your attention in the future." Robert showed me the desk that would be mine. It had a good view of the clothing room and soup kitchen area.

Austin House is open to anyone wanting to get help, and I had a good idea what I was getting into from reading the background on the Austin House in Harlem program. But it would take some time to get used to hearing men and women prostitutes as well as transvestites express themselves using words like *fuck*, *bitch*, and *nigga*. Everyone was invited to stay for mass or the interfaith service in the chapel on the first floor if they chose to. The bizarre actions of a homeless woman named Sandy one evening at mass left some in horror and others laughing. It seems that Sandy, who didn't speak much, was an alcoholic. When it came time for communion, she decided she was going to take the whole chalice of wine and drink it. While about a dozen of us looked on, Father Doug tried to get the chalice out of her hands. Father Doug called me to his side and made it a rule to use grape juice from now on. In this way no one will be tempted in their programs of recovery in Austin House.

It's about a month since I've been in Harlem, I thought, and every day has been a good one. I've made good friendships in the Austin House community as well as with our neighbors in the buildings to the right and left. The street people know my name, but usually they just call me brother. I do thank God for my relationship with both the homeless and the prostitutes. They are respectful when they see me in my religious garb on Sundays. They don't shy away from me. As a matter of fact at times, they've given me advice on where to walk at night and who not to talk to. I actually have them looking out for me, not as a religious man but as a friend. As I'm sure they must know by now, I don't approve of their professions, but I see them as God's people, as my brothers and sisters who need God as much as I do.

I came into the building after helping volunteers in the soup kitchen bring in crates of donated vegetables. William gave me the message that Father Doug wanted to see me in his office. When I arrived at Father Doug's office, the door was open and he was sitting on the couch, looking at some papers on his lap. I tapped on the door frame. He looked at me and put down his papers on the edge of his desk. "Come in, Brother. How's it going?"

"Good," I responded. I made a move for the wooden chair, but he invited me to sit on the couch next to him on his left.

He starting off the conversation by telling me why he wanted to speak to me. "Brother, I see and hear you're doing good work in the community. It's been hard for me to get permanent men and women of God to work here. Our work is very hard and stressful at times. Believe me, I know. I've written your monastery superior a good report on you. Thank you so much for being here with us as we journey with the poor." Father Doug, having gotten all the compliments out of the way, now switched the conversation to gay men in the community and the male prostitutes who come in for outreach services. "Brother, if you have problems with any of the gay guys harassing you in any way, please let me know."

I quickly thought to myself, why should I? I can take care of unwanted advances by myself. I began to get very uncomfortable as his body shifted more toward me. Lowering his voice and looking at me in an unpleasant way, he said, "Luis, you're a very good-looking young man. I'm just protecting you." When he gave me an unexpected hug, I pulled away, and he quickly added, "Austin House is blessed to have you." I politely excused myself, saying I had more kitchen chores to do before working in the outreach office. As I walked away from his office, I couldn't help but feel I'd just been hit on. I hoped it was a mistake on my part; perhaps he's just an old priest who's very affectionate.

I had to face my sexuality head-on from the first day I arrived at Austin House, from meeting the muscled, good-looking prostitutes that come into the outreach office to the male ad models in the safe-sex literature handed out on the streets or posted on billboards I see when walking to the store. I've always known I was gay and never had a problem with it in my religious vocation, not until the day we had four men come from a program called New Start in New Jersey. According to the state, there were too many people in their program, so some needed to be relocated as soon as possible. Later that morning, as I was pushing boxes of clothing across the floor of the outreach office, Robert let me know the four men would arrive between 2:00 and 2:30 PM.

CHAPTER 4

In One Look

Julia was twenty-eight. She and her nine-year-old son Roberto lived two blocks over from Austin House in a small one-bedroom apartment. Both of them have visited our pantry services many times before. Julia's husband left her and the boy about two years ago. On this day of using our pantry services, Julia had lost another job because she lacked a babysitter. As Julia and I sat and talked over possible jobs in the area, I gave her a reference to All Saints Church up on East 128th Street. They needed a church caretaker as well as some clerical help in the church office. Our conversation was interrupted when William yelled to me and Robert that the new intakes from New Jersey had arrived. I gave Julia my full name and the address of Austin House and the assurance that I would give her a good reference for any job. William led the men into the office just as I was handing Julia and her son two bags of canned goods. I went to my desk to get the list of the men's names, while Robert led them to the bench on the opposite side of the room where they could wait to be seen.

At first glance I could see the men were well dressed with the good smell of men's body oils. Robert came over to my desk, and we split the names up two and two. I did the intake for Frank Vasquez and Carlos Mendez, and he took Roberto Harris and John Pellum. Custody of the eyes became a very real issue for me now in a way it had never been before. While getting situated with the blank intake forms, I got a better look at Carlos Mendez. My feelings got the best of me. Before ever thinking of joining the monastery, I'd had a mental image of what the perfect boyfriend would look and act like. I'm mystified by what I saw in his tough-guy looks, his low-riding baggy black jeans with red boxer shorts peeking out, and his tank top showing off small tattoos on his biceps. His mannerisms gave off the vibe, "Don't fuck with me." To get a better hold on my attraction to this guy, I took Frank Vasquez's information first. During the intake with Frank, I fumbled in not hearing certain information and had to ask him to repeat his family contacts and where he was born.

Seeing that Frank's intake sheet was nearly finished, my heart raced. The office was not a good place for me. I made an excuse to Robert and the volunteers in the office, saying I needed a five-minute bathroom break. But instead I found myself in the chapel asking God to help me with my attraction for this man. Maybe in the back of my mind there was a feeling that my vocation and my religious garb would shield me from the attractions of the world and my human desires. I secretly hoped someone like Robert or one of the long-time volunteers would do the Carlos Mendez intake. But when I returned, Carlos was still sitting there. I took a deep breath before calling him over.

I introduced myself. "Hi. I'm Luis."

With a firm handshake, he introduced himself. "Hey, man, Carlos Mendez."

I decided not to ask him the questions on the intake sheet but instead had him fill in the answers himself as I went for coffee in the kitchen. While I was getting my large cup of coffee, black one sugar, Mabel and Debbie openly expressed their smitten feelings for Carlos. They'd gotten a good look at him waiting in the outreach office. Carlos had not been here an hour and yet he was already creating a buzz with the girls—and I suspect in another hour he'd create a stir among the gay guys living in the community.

Returning to my desk with coffee in hand, I pushed my newspapers aside as Carlos handed me his completed intake form. As he went over it in detail, I maintained eye contact, since to look away when talking to someone would be rude. His eyes were big and dark brown, almost blackish in color. It was killing me. I had the overwhelming feeling he knew what I was thinking. As he leaned back on the wooden guest chair at my desk, he slowly fondled the buttons on his leather jacket. When he was reading over the intake information, I couldn't help but notice his dark pinkish lips looking so full and kissable. I'm not an actor, but I think I did well in not giving off any vibes of attraction. At least I think I did.

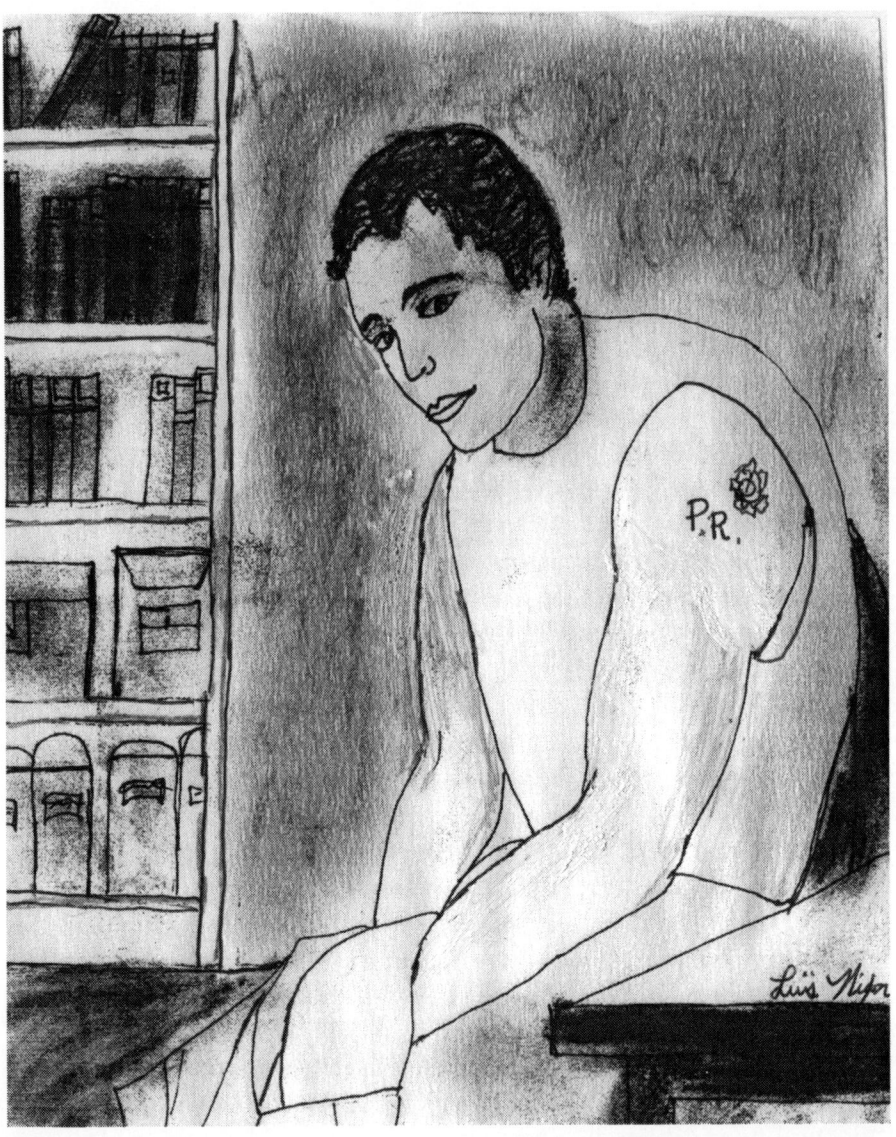

Now that everything was in order with the intake paperwork, Ben, one of the long-time volunteers, came in to assign the men their beds and to give them the schedule of work, required job training, and group counseling that would become effective the next day. I got a thank-you from Carlos as he picked up his one piece of luggage and followed Ben as he led the new intakes to their bed assignments. I looked at the clock opposite the outreach clothing room. It was almost 5:00 PM, evening prayer time in the chapel. I changed into my religious garb and went to the chapel to light the candles. Coming down the stairs, I bumped into all four new intakes. Ben was showing them around the building. From the corner of my eye I noticed that Carlos was silent while the other men with him were very talkative, asking questions about the program and its history in Harlem. Since Carlos wasn't asking me questions, I asked none of him. After I explained chapel services, the different times, and the fact that it was not mandatory, Carlos stepped forward.

"Are you a priest?" he asked.

Turning to my right to face him, I of course replied, "No, I'm a monk."

Smiling at me, just as I'm sure I was at him, Carlos asked sarcastically, "Do you pray a lot?"

I made my way toward the chapel door, and looking over my left shoulder at Carlos, I said, "Yes, indeed."

After giving his final blessing at evening prayers, Father Doug said he wanted to see me after dinner, around 7:30 PM, in his office. I was already hungry before I entered the dining room, but the smell of roast ham and sweet potatoes made me even more hungry. By the time I'd gotten my plate of food, there wasn't a place to sit. All the way in the back of the cafeteria there was a small area that I was sure I could squeeze into with a folding chair, but a resident in Austin House got to it first. As I held my plate of food with nowhere to go, Frank and John offered to make room at their table. I took a seat, not knowing Carlos was also at the same table. He came back to the table with the salt he'd just gotten out of the kitchen. Carlos was now right across from me. I wished I was somewhere else, anywhere but that table. Frank and John were in their own conversation about getting construction jobs and saving money to get an apartment. Taking the first move in conversation, I asked Carlos about his life in Philadelphia and his one sister and nephew. I remembered these things from looking over his intake form earlier. He was a little hesitant at first, but as I found out during dinner and afterward, he opens up.

Gesturing toward me, he made an up-and-down motion with his hand and said, "So, what's with the getup? What's all this about?"

Glancing at the cross on the wall, I opened up about my love of God and serving in a place like Austin House. Carlos, I discovered, is up front about what he feels about monks and priests. "I don't think it's right for the young to enter a monastery. It's fine for someone old like Father Doug," he said, motioning in Father Doug's direction. I quickly realized he might be about to ask me how I do without sex. Ed didn't realize it, but he saved me right at that moment. He came to the table to remind the guys of their AA meeting at seven. I changed the subject after Ed left and asked Carlos about his mother and other family members in Philadelphia. Carlos gave me what I would describe as a smirk and gave the no-sex talk a rest for now.

Eating and talking over dinner and then coffee, I could see some of the women in the community glancing and smiling at Carlos as they passed the table. The time went fast as we talked about Manhattan versus Philadelphia colleges. I was totally won over. Just like me, Carlos was into books, daily newspapers, and movies. We noticed we were the only ones left in the dining room and his AA meeting was starting in five minutes by the clock on the inner kitchen wall. We were engrossed in talking over the New York Knicks versus the Philadelphia 76ers as we stood, and without realizing it, we both reached into the fruit basket at the same time. I discovered he loves green apples just like I do. Of course, now that I think about it, everything else I liked about Carlos fell into place, so why should I be surprised by his love of green apples? For three seconds our hands touched as we grabbed the last green apple. He gave it to me, but I split it between us.

Yelling to one another is normal at Austin House. Up and down the stairways, from one end of the hall to another, as well as out the windows. William yelled, "Yo, Brother Luis. Stop at the security desk when you get a chance." As I came out of the kitchen to the front security area, William was reading his logbooks. He looked up and gave me a message from Father Doug asking if I could possibly see him a little earlier. As he ate his half of the apple, Carlos extended his right hand for me to shake and said, "Later, man. Thanks for the apple."

On my way to Father Doug's office I had a bad feeling that something wasn't right. Walking up the stairs, Ed passed me in a hurry, not speaking as I said hello. The door to Father Doug's office was already open and he was sitting behind his desk. He was telling William at the security desk not to let Ed back in the building until he calmed down. Noticing I was in his presence, Father Doug quickly said, "Lock the door, Brother," and went on talking to William on the phone, leaving me to wonder what kind of situation I had just walked into.

I stood in front of his desk as he hung up the phone and asked, "Father, is anything wrong? What's going on with Ed? I've never seen him as angry as he was when he passed me on the stairs just now."

Father Doug didn't look at me or make eye contact while he shuffled his papers on the desk and started his explanation. "Well, Brother Ed is doing some things and saying things to guys in the building that are sexual in nature, and I had to confront him about the situation."

As Father Doug went on to talk of complaints about Ed's flirtations, we suddenly heard Ed beating loudly on the office door and yelling, "Open up the door, you fat faggot motherfucker. I know you're in there. You have messed with the wrong one. Open up!" I was surprised by all this and didn't know what to do, so I just stood there. Father Doug immediately called security to have them come right away, explaining that Ed was kicking the door of his office. Before security arrived, Ed succeeded in getting into the office. He ran toward Father Doug and slapped him again and again in the head while knocking him to the floor. Father Doug tried to protect himself on the floor as Ed kicked him in the head and stomach.

I couldn't wrestle Ed off Father Doug by myself, but the two security guards and I managed to get him out the office. I lifted Father Doug to his office chair and looked over his wounds to see if he was okay. In a forceful, rude way, and I guess with some embarrassment, he kicked me out the office saying he didn't want to talk. I paused to catch my breath and then walked to the stairwell, where I caught a glimpse of Ed talking to William and Frank and yelling, "That bastard just don't want me hanging out with Angelo. You guys know the birthday gift I gave Angelo of small heavy handballs? You know, the ones used to exercise the hand? Well, Father Doug said it was of a suggestive sexual nature and I should watch myself." William wasn't able to calm Ed down or even get him to sit in a chair. As I stood eavesdropping by the stairwell, Father Doug's office door opened, so I quickly returned to my bedroom and went to bed around 9:30 PM.

The next morning I was drinking my coffee while walking up the stairs for the mandatory morning meeting. All I could hear was whispering about Father Doug and Ed's episode last night. Passing the gossipers on the stairs, I noticed how it got quiet as I passed them. At the meeting I thought for sure Father Doug would mention something about last night, but not a word was said. The meeting was all about the daily schedules and one or two problems the kitchen team was having with the stove. No one at the meeting shed light on last night's events. As he left after the meeting, Father Doug pulled me aside to tell me that the reason he asked me to his office last night was to offer me the position of volunteer director because I have good organization skills. Austin House deals with volunteers who come from here in America and also from European countries. I jumped at the offer, knowing it would expose me to many people and cultures. I expressed my gratitude and walked down to the outreach office on the lower level. Carlos wished me a cheerful hey and a quick nod as he scrambled to the kitchen for work.

Putting my coffee on my desk in the outreach office, I could hear voices from the clothing room. I made the voices out to be Debbie and Sally, who have been in Austin House for three years. Curiosity occupied my mind. I knew, just knew, it was about Father Doug. I moved a little closer to the clothing room door to hear a little better.

"The power of dick is just too hard for the old man not to have," said Debbie.

Sally turned toward Debbie as she folded some sweaters for a box on the floor and began to talk about some script that Father Doug repeats over and over again. "Debbie, I tell ya, girl, the script never gets old for him. He calls who he likes in to that office of his, tells them they are good-looking and to please let him know if any of the gay guys bother them or disrespect them."

Helping Sally fold the sweaters for the box on the floor, Debbie purposely lowered her voice to confirm her feelings. "Hey, girl, all those men that have been through our program didn't even know each other. There's no way they could keep repeating the same script unless the whole thing was truthful. Let's be real."

Having had my fill of listening, I pretended to walk in the office again, but this time I made some noise by moving some folding chairs around, letting them know I was there. It seemed to work, as both of them quietly exited the clothing room. Sitting at the two desks that are opposite me, Debbie and Sally both said "Good morning" just as Robert rushed in to tell us we would have two hundred donated canned goods coming in later, around 2:30 PM. "Our pantry is nearly empty, so this is the blessing we needed," Robert couldn't help but say.

Sipping my coffee, I can see Julia and her son are back. Before I could even speak, Julia broke into a wide smile and yelled, "I got the job, man!" All Saints Church had agreed to hire her. "It's perfect," she said. "I can bring my son if I don't have a babysitter. I really feel your letter of reference did the trick and just wanted to stop by to let you know." We offered her some more canned goods to tide her over until she got her first check. But after that, she felt she could buy her own food instead of coming to us.

One of the work rules of the Austin community is that from time to time everyone may move from one job to another if they so desire. Since I have my hands in so many areas of work in the building, it was only a matter of time before I'd be working with Carlos. I got to know him better when we worked together in the soup kitchen and from helping him phone his mother back in Philadelphia. We have so much in common; it was not lust that made him the object of my affection. I think the average person looking at Carlos with his rough edges and tough-guy mannerisms would never think he was an avid reader of philosophy and history or that he kept up to date on daily news. Out of curiosity, I wanted to know more about areas of his life he keeps secret, such as why is he in AA and how he ended up in New Jersey if he came from Philadelphia. But I didn't want to push him away. When the time is right, I thought, he will talk about it.

CHAPTER 5

❀

Uh Oh

Up at 3:56 AM to use the bathroom, I looked down the hall from my bedroom toward the bedrooms of Father Doug and the other live-in volunteers. A short muscular Puerto Rican guy, maybe in his early twenties, was carefully and quietly leaving Father Doug's room, not noticing me at all. Half asleep, I was in the bathroom before what I'd just seen fully hit me. Then I remembered that twice in the past I'd seen the same scenario, a guy leaving Father Doug's room in the early hours. I must have blotted out those events, probably because I'm not fully awake when I go to the bathroom so early in the morning.

Alert and back in my bed, I came to the only possible conclusion: Father Doug was not only gay, he was actively having sex. There was no concrete proof, only gossip and my seeing guys leaving his room at different times. But these men weren't from our community program at Austin House, and visitors were only allowed to enter the building after 11:00 PM with the permission of Father Doug. And I also made the connection with what Debbie and Sally were talking about in the clothing room, about how Father Doug called in men he was interested in by asking them to tell him if the gay guys in the building bother them. As my eyes were opened, I saw more clearly how Father Doug had used his script, as Sally called it, with me, along with the uncomfortable hug from him in his office. Even though I had romantic feelings for Carlos in my heart, I couldn't violate my vows to God, not even if I had the sure chance of having sex with him. But here was a priest, Father Doug, most likely having sex with other men.

"Oh fucking shit!" was what I heard as I left chapel the next morning. Frank, John, and a volunteer were reading a note posted to the left of the front door of the building: "Ed no longer lives here in the community. He is not to enter the building at all. Security must be alerted if seen. Father Doug, administrator." Everyone fell quiet after reading the note. When I turned to go into the kitchen, my now closest friends in the community, William and Debbie, confided in me.

William said, "The reason Ed is no longer here, aside from beating up Father Doug, is over some faggot shit. Debbie, honey, I remember by name a few guys in the past having arguments and leaving because Father Doug was meddling in gay relationships." I listened to William as I walked slowly into the kitchen for my morning coffee. He reminded me of the night Father Doug had the fight with Ed and how he kicked me out of his office, not wanting to talk. "This is the way it is around here, Brother Luis. Never question. It means trouble."

I was pouring my coffee as William and Debbie fixed theirs when Robert came rushing in with a flyer in his hand. At first he refused to show it to me, but after some horsing around I grabbed it out of his hand. I was shocked at the contents. The flyer read in bold letters: "Faggot priest. Don't go to Austin House. If you are gay he may want you or your lover. Quick cash can be had, gentlemen." And to put the cherry on the cake, a small photo of Father Doug was also on the flyer. Unable to speak for the moment, Robert paused and then lowered his voice, since people were beginning to come in for breakfast. "Guys, this is some crazy shit. Father Doug discovered them when he went out for his morning paper." Appearing wide-eyed and excited, Robert explained that Father Doug had him sweep them up. I thought to myself, Father Doug hadn't acted as if anything was wrong in chapel for morning prayers. As I sipped my coffee, I noticed two priests in their clerical garb asking for Father Doug. The tall young priest called himself Father Jim and said he came from All Saints Church. The shorter chubby red-haired one was from Saint Paul's near 116th Street. Their demeanor was quite serious.

Later at lunch in the dining room Sally told us she'd overheard some of the conversation outside Father Doug's office, almost spilling her ham sandwich and punch over this hot gossip. She whispered, "Yo, Brother Luis, the flyers were posted or found outside the visiting priests' churches."

Ben came to our table, pointed to me, and said, "Did you tell him the scoop?"

Flipping her braids over her shoulders, she nodded and said, "Yes, mystery solved."

Ben sat at our table, excited about a much-needed furniture donation from East 86th Street that was coming in today. He needed extra muscle and said, while looking in my direction, "Brother, I asked your friend Carlos to go on the truck to pick it up with Juan and Marcus."

Sally put her right hand to her breast and let out a big sigh, saying, "Brother, man, hook me up with Papi," meaning Carlos.

Giggling, Ben turned to her and said, "Hey, what about your boyfriend Nathan?"

Standing with her lunch tray while Ben sat giggling, she looked in his direction, said "Fuck you," and left the table. Everyone knew her boyfriend was a real player with the ladies. Sally knew it, too, but wasn't yet able to let him go. From the little bit of time I'd known her, I could tell her self-esteem was low and that she made bad choices in men.

Slurping his potato-leek soup, Ben offered his opinion of Carlos. "He's quiet and a hard worker, but not one you can approach easily in general conversation."

"Well, he's not reticent with me," I said to myself.

Carlos sought my company, as I did his, but the recent flyers and the gossip about Father Doug had me feeling very paranoid that there might be rumors that I was after Carlos or that we were in a relationship. The fact is, we all live and work here. People see almost every move or meeting you have. After work I went to confession at Saint Francis church, seeking spiritual advice about Carlos. Depending on the priest, I may not make it out alive, I thought, considering the church's stand on homosexuals and homosexual feelings. Taking advantage of the warm, but not too hot, sunny day, I walked from East 116th Street to get the West 116th train down to 34th Street. The richness of the Puerto Rican and African American cultures, the art, the street vendors, the smells of our cultures' foods—all this put an extra slowness in my walk. As I soaked it all up, I thought I'd never had this feeling before, not when I lived on Long Island or in Washington DC. White people were always the majority, even when I entered the monastery. I have no racial issues with white people; I can appreciate all cultures. But Harlem for me is a Mecca of good black and Hispanic cultures.

Some people, however, can be really stupid when they think of Harlem. Harlem, like any other place in America, has good and bad areas. It has its little secrets, spots where the rich may live. Harlem has an area up on 138th Street with beautiful town houses inhabited by doctors, lawyers, and successful businessmen and women. Anyone walking around Harlem can clearly see the different levels of living here, from the upper middle class to the nicer areas of town houses. But the only images some Americans have of Harlem are the bad drug areas and their abandoned buildings. Now that rebuilding of some problem areas has taken place, the comment I hate with a passion is "Ah, Harlem is getting cleaned up now," as if the whole of Harlem was a big burned-out war zone.

As I walked down the steps to the lower level of Saint Francis church, I could see confessions going on. I moved toward the shorter line on the left side of the church. When it was my turn to enter, I made the normal blessing of myself and stated how long it had been since my last confession. "What's on your mind today, my son?" asked the priest. He sounded like an older, soft-spoken man who was resting his arm on the small ledge of the confession window. I told him who I was and my vocation in the church as a monk. I briefly stopped before letting him know I was in love.

As I took a deep intake of air and released it he could tell I was uncomfortable. Speaking softly, he said, "Go ahead, my son, take your time. Go slowly."

Gathering courage, I blurted out, "I'm in love, Father, in love with a person in the live-in program where my order has stationed me."

Calmly he asked, "Tell me, son, have you had sex with or spoken of your interest to this person?"

"No, Father, I have not gone that far. It's not just his physical looks that attract me. It's also his attentiveness and good daily conversation." As I spoke I looked down and noticed his fingers tapping on the ledge of the confession window.

He cut me off as I continued to speak, saying, "I'm sorry, did you say her or him?"

My heart slowly sank. "Yes, Father, I said him."

He paused and grunted twice. I had a feeling this type of love wasn't acceptable to him. The gentle soft-spoken priest raised his voice a little and was very blunt with me. Before he dismissed me to do my penance he put two fingers up and gave me two options I must pick from. "One, if you are to remain a monk, this attachment could hurt you in the future. You must break all connection to him, otherwise you will always have a conflict between him and your religious vows. Two, you must consider whether celibacy is too hard for you. If so, you must leave the order." He then asked me to pray aloud and make the act of contrition. The now abrupt priest gave me leave to pray as my penance the sorrowful mysteries of the rosary in the church.

While riding the subway back up to Harlem, I had a lot to think about. I'd waited a long time to come to Harlem to do the work that I was doing at Austin House as a monk. What was important was my vocation as a monk. It was going to be difficult. Of the two options the priest had given me in confession, I chose the first, to distance myself from Carlos and to focus my attentions elsewhere.

As I came up the sidewalk, I saw Carlos and Frank with three volunteers from Saint Paul's Church. They were leaning up against the building, smoking and hanging out. I wasn't strong at all. I hung out with them for a bit, talking over basketball. When I did leave the group, Carlos followed me into the building. He wanted to know where I'd been. I lied and said I was doing errands downtown.

Carlos said he wanted to see if his mother could send money for some things he needs, like new shoes and shirts, but the pay phone on the second floor was out of order. I offered him items from the outreach clothing room, but he wasn't interested in that style of clothing. So even though it was against the rules, I let him secretly use the outreach office phone, as I had done twice before. Speaking in Spanish, which I don't understand, he made the arrangements with his mother.

Carlos got off the phone just as Father Doug approached the door. Carlos was telling me that the money comes out of an account he and his mother jointly have in Philadelphia and that some could be used for me and him to go to the movies or explore the city, when Father Doug opened the door to the office. Father Doug gave us a strange look and handed me a list of some new referral places, some new shelters in the city as well as pantries in the Bronx. He then reminded me that it was almost 5:00 PM and evening prayers and the Gospel readings had to be set. Carlos left without saying "Later" as he always does or looking at Father Doug.

"He's trouble, that one," said Father Doug, shaking his thumb in Carlos' direction. "Be careful, Brother. He's a gang member and he sells drugs. And I doubt, judging by his stand-offish attitude, that Austin House can help him." As we both walked toward the door, Father Doug let it slip, perhaps intentionally, that he'd seen Carlos and me together many times and suggested I encourage him to be more outgoing with the other members in Austin House.

We were interrupted by William, who came to give Father Doug his messages. I cut the conversation short and went to the chapel. At dinner I made the first move to distance myself from Carlos by turning to my left to sit at a different table with Julio and Cindy. But Frank and Carlos waved me over to their table. I was in serious trouble here, trying to distance myself from him. I wasn't going to do it. He was my friend, and I would just have to deal with it. My prayers and faith in God will help me deal with my feelings, I thought. During dinner I noticed Father Doug giving me looks from time to time, looks that I ignored. They reminded me of Brother Stanley's famous looks in the monastery that let you know you were doing something wrong.

If Carlos was or is in a gang, that would explain his tough behavior and the small tattoo of a closed fist on his upper right shoulder. Not that I thought all people with tattoos are in a gang. This information didn't faze or scare me. I always felt there was more to him. But it might be a reason he always shied away from talking to me about his life back in Philadelphia. Shortly after dinner I found out I wanted to know about Carlos and his sexuality. I already knew the few feminine gay guys in the house eyed Carlos just like the girls did. He was never offended if someone said, "Papi, come over here," or when he would pick up a heavy box if someone asked, "Hey, Papi, wanna marry me?"

I went up on the roof, as I did most evenings, to listen to the sounds of Harlem. The view of the Triborough Bridge and house music coming from the building next door relaxed me, especially after dealing with the crowds in the soup kitchen and the outreach office.

Carlos found his way to the roof one evening, discovering my hiding spot. He and Timothy were trying to find Frank to tell him he had a call from Puerto Rico. Carlos moved toward me from the roof door and asked shyly, "So this is your hiding spot. You want to be alone?" I wanted to pull him even closer to kiss him, but I turned in the direction of the Triborough Bridge. "No, man, you can stay," I responded, trying to imitate him and not appear too soft. I could see the fascinated look on his face as he took in the beauty of the scene. And while we both leaned over the side looking east, he shook his head slightly and said in a low voice, "This is cool. Man, you can see far."

I was not prepared for what came next. We both stood quietly, listening to the music from the building next door. It was LL Cool J's song, "Mama Said Knock You Out." Lowering my eyes and looking in his direction, I could see him moving his hands to the beat of the music. It came like an unexpected punch when he said, "Are you gay, Luis?" I was wide-eyed and couldn't even look at him. My mind was quick to wonder what had made this an issue. "Well, man, we've talked over a lot of things," he said. "This is something we haven't touched on in our friendship. Have you noticed that we don't even joke about sex and girls, Luis?"

I turned toward him after he spoke and said, "Well, Carlos, I'm a monk and we are friends, but the topic of sexuality or even sexual desires would be uncomfortable for me."

Not pleased with my answer, he moved back a little, shook his head, and said, "Yo, it's just you and me here. Just be real." Lifting his arms over his head, he raised his voice. "Just say it. Are you gay or what?"

I looked back at the bridge and gave an uncomfortable giggle. "My being gay or not shouldn't matter in our friendship," I said, "mainly because sex is not an issue for me."

Flipping the script, so to speak, his boldness helped me to be bold, and I said, "So, Carlos, what? Are you gay, or what?"

He shook his head and again raised his voice. "Now we're talking. Well, Luis, I love women, but I have had encounters with guys."

Even though I was nervous about this conversation, which after all could get me ousted from my order, I looked back at him and asked, "So, you're bisexual? You like both? Are you attracted to the guys downstairs?"

"No, man. I'm not into feminine guys. If I want a girl, I'll be with one. I've had a few encounters with guys, but it's not a regular thing." The possibility that Carlos might be attracted to me was making me increasingly nervous. Moving back toward me, he said, "My philosophy is this: if you find someone attractive, it's an insult not to compliment them."

This was a comment I didn't know how to take. Is he conceited because he knows he can have just about any guy or girl? Or is he just giving me a little push to come right out and ask him if he's interested in me? Or what, I wonder. I knew he thought the lifestyle of a monk was not appropriate for young people. I remembered that I was one. I pushed myself back from the roof wall and said, "Hey, thanks for the conversation and friendship in confiding in me, but I gotta go look over some papers for being volunteer coordinator." I wanted to just leave, but Carlos extended his right arm for a handshake. That was okay, but then he suddenly gave me a bear hug. He knew what he was doing. I didn't have to ask. I knew. I just knew he had to feel I was romantically interested in him. But monkhood held me back.

CHAPTER 6

❀

Our First Outing

I had weekends off. Today was Saturday. I wore my baggy faded blue jeans with a Bob Marley T-shirt and comfortable old sneakers. My backpack had seen better days, but it held all my flyers about art openings and premieres as well as the subway map. I picked up my messages from the security desk on the way out. Father General had called to say hello and remind me that my monthly report to the mother house was due.

Carlos, who was reading his newspaper and listening to his Walkman, saw me as I was about to leave. "Hey, man, where're you going with the backpack?"

"I'm heading to the Metropolitan Museum of Art. There's an exhibit of Egyptian art," I replied.

He put his paper down and walked with me in the direction of the eastside subway at 116th Street. Taking a green apple from his baggy black jeans, he took a bite and said, "I've never seen the city, not since I came from New Jersey to Harlem." At the station he gave me a half hug while grabbing my right hand and then we parted.

Without thinking too much about it, I called him back. "You know, your opportunity to see the city could be now if you've got nothing planned for the day." Without a word he handed me his Walkman and went to the token booth.

As he got some money out of his jeans for the subway fare, I suggested he call Austin House to let them know where he is. My paranoia took hold when Carlos made the call at the entrance to the subway. I tapped on his left shoulder and whispered, "Just tell them you're visiting friends." Holding his change

- 43 -

in his right hand and staring at me with a smile, he shook his head in agreement and did as I said.

I started to explain why I told him to do that, but as he put his change in his pocket, he stopped me. "Hey, I get it, okay?"

I didn't want to give it a rest, because it's important to me that he doesn't take it the wrong way. He took his Walkman back as we waited for the train. "Look, Carlos, the fact that we hang out in groups or just the two of us is one thing, but if we are seen going downtown it could lead to gossip, just like the gossip about the old priest, Father Doug." He just smirked as he put on his earphones.

When we arrived at East 86th Street, we got out of the subway and walked west to the museum. While I was wondering if this was classified as a date, Carlos said, "How about getting lunch in Central Park after we look at the Egyptian exhibit?"

The excitement of the city always makes me want more of what it offers. As I walked up the stairs to the entrance of the museum, I felt as if it was my first time again. Some of the Egyptian pieces in the museum I'd seen before, as well as other exhibits that were on display. I just wanted to see if more had been added to the collection. After spending an hour and a half talking about the art of Ethiopia and Egypt, we went outside to find a vendor for some hot dogs and drinks. Coming up in front of us was the Great Lawn of Central Park. With the great weather and the warmth of the sun, we opted to sit not on a bench but on the grass of the Great Lawn. As in the past, I liked the fact that Carlos and I didn't have to speak every moment we were together. We ate in silence, watching the people go by. His company gave me such a good feeling.

After about twenty minutes we gathered up our garbage and looked for the receptacle. Carlos fixed his shoelaces and I took a stretch. After deciding to get lost in the park, we headed south from the museum and ended up walking all the way to the zoo. Sometimes I think Carlos can read my thoughts and I his. I watched his reaction to the animals and thought, here he is again, trying not to show his sensitive side. Just looking at his face I could read a lot of what I felt he was thinking. But he tries to hang onto his tough-boy image in all situations.

The large information board to my left caught my eye as we entered the zoo. I looked for the penguin exhibit, since penguins have always been my favorite; when I was a child I loved drawing them and watching documentaries on them. I asked Carlos if he has a favorite animal he would like to see. I tried not to stare at him. He looked so cute standing beside the fence with his hands in his jeans pockets and his Walkman earphones around his neck. He suggested we see as much as we could. The penguin house is a small building next to the polar bear section. The strong smell of fish really took some time to get used to, but we were so impressed as we watched the penguins swimming from the right to the left of the tank that we sat for nearly twenty minutes and watched as the zookeeper fed them fish from his hands. We moved on with our tour of the zoo. As we passed the large round seal pool in the middle of the zoo, Carlos thanked me for letting him hang out with me.

Leaving the zoo at the south exit, I obtained his approval to make Saint Mark's Place our next stop. Getting out of the subway at Astor Place, we both noticed a Starbucks on the corner. Carlos offered to buy me an iced coffee. I suggested we walk around with it as we take in the sights. Saint Mark's is one of my favorite places to go. The people express themselves freely. Some have blue, green, or purple hair, wear leather pants, or have nipple rings connecting to actual earrings. This was Carlos' first exposure, and it seemed to bother him. He kept calling it a freak show. We debated whether people should be able to wear what they want. The conversation got a little heated. I said he wasn't sensitive to some people being different from him, but he was unwilling to bend to my train of thought and waved me off as we came to a music store.

I was about to put a cassette tape back because I didn't have enough money when I got to the register, but Carlos laid a twenty on the counter so I could buy it. Right away my irritation from before just disappeared. But I said no. Unlike the people in line in the store, I knew that Carlos needed to save his money so he has some when he gets out of Austin House. I asked a stranger for the time. It was 4:35 PM. Evening prayer starts at 5:00 PM, so I would never make it back to Austin House in time. I let Carlos know I needed to call Austin House. He left me at a pay phone and went to look at some hats a few stores down. I made my call. William had to take my message because Father Doug was not answering his pager. I hooked back up with Carlos after the phone call, feeling tired. He didn't want to go back to Austin House, but I managed to convince him that we could do this again. He gave me a firm handshake and said, "Cool, man," and then we headed for the uptown subway at Astor Place.

Since I'd missed evening prayers, I had my own personal prayer time in the chapel when I returned to Austin House. On my way back to my room, I was shocked to hear someone ask, "How was your hot date?" I turned to see who spoke to me. It was Father Doug, who now gave out a sinister laugh.

Thinking quickly I said, "Excuse me?"

"I saw you and Carlos getting out of the subway from my office window."

I put him in his place about us. "It's not what you think. We're just friends."

As Father Doug went on to ask me if I'd looked over the volunteer list of people along with orienting myself on policy and procedures, I had a strong feeling that after we talked over volunteer stuff, he may want to talk about Carlos and our outing, so I cut the uncomfortable conversation short by telling a lie, saying I had stomach problems and need to lie down.

At our morning meeting the next day, Father Doug talked about our financial situation. "We are badly in need of funds, but don't lose hope. A miracle has happened that will help us get more names for our mailing list. Somehow literature about Austin House made its way to the National Conference of Bishops. Bishops from Connecticut, Chicago, and Boston have agreed to let us use their mailing list to supplement our mailings to solicit funds. In all, it's a total of almost forty thousand names, which is all we can handle for now. It will be a lot of work, stuffing envelopes and putting computer-generated address labels on the outside of the envelopes."

At Father Doug's suggestion, we split into groups of fourteen, each with a team captain. This kept us from being scattered and not knowing what to do. For about a week and a half our little community worked not only on the mailing but also at our normal jobs in the building, making it very crazy day and night. The groups worked four- to five-hour shifts and sometimes more on their own free time. Carlos and I were not on the same team, so when we saw each other we would simply wave or nod or say a quick hello in the halls. Each team had different break times and meal times in the dining room, and that prevented us from having a good conversation for almost a week.

Father Doug announced the completion of the mailing list at a morning meeting. I noticed amid all of the big cheers and sighs of relief that Carlos was not in the meeting. But when it was over I caught up to him at the community information board on the second floor. When I approached, he handed me a letter to read. The letter, which had come with some spending money from his mother, gave Carlos the news that she was not doing well. She had a diagnosis of multiple sclerosis from her doctor. It was now past 9:00 AM, and I was supposed to be in the outreach office working, but my full attention was on Carlos and how to help him emotionally get through this news. I reread the last section of the letter. His mother seemed happy that the doctors caught it early enough to control it with medication. Using this information helped me comfort him. For the first time I could actually see his sensitive side out in the open, with no attitude of toughness between us. His sister and brother-in-law would do their best to make sure she got the best care in Philadelphia. The letter ended by telling Carlos not to worry.

Carlos said very little before heading to the kitchen to work. As we were about to part, Carlos took a small bag out of his pocket and handed it to me. He said he found it on the street and thought I'd like it. Unwrapping it I saw it was the cassette from the music store on Saint Mark's Place that I hadn't had enough money to buy. He must have purchased it when I was on the phone trying to tell Father Doug I couldn't make it back in time for evening prayers. I was impressed but also a little annoyed, since I thought he should be saving his money. I accepted the gift. I guess he could see how pleased I was with the tape, which, by the way, was Bob Marley's greatest hits. After hearing about his mother's illness, the half smile on his face spun me into a little better mood. Swallowing the feeling that I wanted to kiss him, I offered to buy lunch the next time we went out. As I was speaking I noticed a sudden strange look on his face. Carlos cut me short and looked over my right shoulder. I turned and saw Father Doug coming down the stairs just as Carlos exited to the kitchen.

When I visited Father Doug in his office later that morning, I found him in very good spirits. He was sitting behind his desk holding the reply envelopes that had just arrived that day. I looked down at his desk. There must have been sixty envelopes, and I could see checks spread about the desk. "The fruits of our labor, Brother Luis. Our work paid off. Just look. The total is sixteen hundred from today's mail alone." As he went on to tell me we could now pay the phone and electric bills and meet the other needs of the community, Julio entered the office with more reply envelopes. As we could all see, the extra names from the bishops helped greatly.

My main reason for going to Father Doug's office was to let him know I was going downtown after work. As soon as I said this, he gave me his full attention and put the checks to the right side of his desk. "By yourself, or …?" he said.

From then on it was obvious to me that he was curious about who I was hanging out with. "By myself, Father," I stated, "to unwind and maybe visit a couple of bookstores."

Father Doug asked me to sit on the small couch to the right of his desk. "I'm concerned," he said. "Are you okay? You have so many duties in the outreach office, the soup kitchen, and as volunteer director. It all can be overwhelming," he said.

"I'm fine," I assured him and proceeded to give him my personal schedule of prayer outside of the small prayer group at Austin House, as well as my work breaks and the times I take off to go downtown to take in some of the sights.

He seemed pleased that I was taking care of myself. "Father General and I had a nice conversation about you. May God grant you many years of service in the church." Again I found myself trying not to look at the ketchup stains on his shirt from the hamburger on his desk. I stood and thanked him for having me live in Austin House, and then I offered to walk up to 125th near Lenox Avenue before 5:00 PM to deposit the checks into our community account at Citibank. Father Doug quickly explained, however, that he and Julio have to log each check before depositing them, mainly to see who donated from the list of names the bishops gave us.

After chapel I poked my head into the dormitory where Carlos was staying and saw him napping. It'd been awhile since we had some time alone because of the mailing and our jobs in the community. But I never wake people up from sleeping unless it's very important, so I returned to my room to gather my backpack and some money for the subway. I walked down the stairs to exit the building and it was just perfect: there was Carlos, up from his nap, stretching his arms and looking at the community board of entertainment events. He grabbed my right arm to stop me while rubbing the sleep from his eyes. "What's going on?" he asked, giving me my arm back and following me downstairs. As I walked out the front door with Carlos, I pulled out a green apple and split it with my pocketknife for us. He took a bite of the apple. "Hey, man, what about that offer to buy me lunch?" Looking at the evening sun, I reminded him that it was almost dinnertime. He put one hand in his jeans and walked with me toward the subway. "Okay," he said, "then let it be dinner instead." When I stopped and looked at him, he gave me the cutest look. I decided to let him come along. We agreed to meet in the subway on the lower platform in ten minutes so that no one would see us leave together. He's mindful of my paranoid attitude about Austin House members or Father Doug seeing us together all the time.

As Carlos ran back to tell security he'd be out for a while, I noticed Eric, who came to us from prison. He stands about six-two, with muscles he brags about and says he got in prison. He's a ladies man and, like Carlos, the girls and some of the gay guys eye him up and down. But there is something about him that makes me uneasy when I'm around him. He's leaving our community in a couple of days and I for one am happy. My instincts tell me he's up to no good. I've caught him a couple of times talking to some of the guys I know to be head drug dealers over on Park Avenue here in Harlem. As I walked past Eric and his friends, he said, "Hey, what's up, Brother Luis?" I just nodded to him and continued on to the subway.

While I was studying my map in the subway, Carlos came rushing down the stairs. As he got his tokens at the booth I reminded him we had all day, so rushing was unnecessary. He didn't ask where we were going. I could tell by now he remembers what I said in our first outing about just allowing the mood to take us, no matter where we might end up. Bowling Green station in lower Manhattan was our first stop, and as the sun set over the harbor with New Jersey in the background, I felt riding the Staten Island Ferry would be a good idea on this warm evening. "Where the fuck are we, man?" Carlos asked. We walked up the subway stairs and through the small park near the ferry terminal. On our right we could see the Statue of Liberty. Judging by the line in front of us, it seemed every tourist in the city shared my idea of riding the ferry to Staten Island and then back to Manhattan.

Carlos and I stood in line, slowly moving with the other people to get on the boat. "When we are on the boat," I explained, "we will see Ellis Island, the Statue of Liberty, and parts of Brooklyn and New Jersey." Carlos gave me that pleased look on his face. We stayed at the end of the boat facing the pier. The end that faces the pier always turns around and leads the boat when it actually gets out into the harbor, so by doing this we would see things as they approached us on the water. This was another of those special times when we neither of us talked. We just took in the sights and enjoyed one another's company. Intimacy, I've learned, can also be just the quiet moments. Like a postcard, the sky at sunset was blue and purple and the sun was a big bright orange ball. The sunset was perfect as we passed the Statue of Liberty with its torch lights on. With the warm strong wind blowing in our faces, I pointed out New Jersey on our right and the Staten Island Bridge in the distance to our left. Making a U-turn and paying our toll to go back to Manhattan, we rushed to beat the crowd.

Heading back to the city, the skyline and lights were something to behold. At first everything was a little blurry, but as we got closer I pointed out the Brooklyn Bridge on our right. Getting off the ferry, we walked north to the famous South Street Seaport. By now it was almost nine, so we stopped and ordered a couple of gyros from a street vendor. While Carlos ate his messy gyros, with extra tzatziki dribbling all over his chin, he pointed up at the Brooklyn Bridge at South Street Seaport. Looking at the Watchtower Buildings of the Jehovah Witnesses across the river, I talked about walking the bridge. Carlos was more than just eager and up for the task of doing it, but he became irritated when I reminded him of his Austin House. I told him we could do the bridge some other time.

We arrived back in Harlem just ten minutes before his curfew. Carlos joked about my paranoid feelings about people seeing us together all the time, so he suggested he go into the building before me. Taking this time to myself, I walked to a small park near the East River for some prayer time. My eyes would hardly stay open, so I found my mind was too tired for any long period of prayer. After praying one Our Father, ten Hail Marys, and prayers for the homeless and poor, I returned to my room at Austin House for a good night's sleep.

The following day I accepted three volunteers from our sister community in England. While sightseeing in Manhattan, they will also work four hours a day for room and board. Marie, Allen, and James appeared to be in their early twenties; all had long hair and tie-dyed shirts. They seemed eager to work for us the four weeks they are here. I put Marie and James to work in the outreach office pantry and Allen in the kitchen. While I was giving orientation to them in the library, Father Doug came in to introduce himself. All three knew Father Doug from his trip to England two years ago. Letting them all get reacquainted with each other, I returned to the outreach office.

I found Carlos holding a small envelope of money from his mother. "Can I give you this to hold for safekeeping?" As he passed it to me, he said, "If I keep it in the safe, I can only take out small amounts at a time."

"The house has this rule," I explained, "so that when you move out into your own apartment you will have money saved up." I made sure I got my point across. "Also, you can't ask me every day for money."

Robert walked into the office, so Carlos shook his head in agreement and lowered his voice. "Hey, I would never make you uncomfortable with this," he said sincerely. "I trust you to hold the money," he assured me, "but if you need to use some in an emergency or for something you want, just do so." We heard Mike call him to help out with a delivery, so Carlos rushed off to the kitchen.

In the envelope wrapped in red paper I counted out two hundred dollars. I didn't feel comfortable holding the money on me, so I returned to my room on the fourth floor to hide it. Eric caught me unlocking my bedroom door and announced that he was leaving today. I already knew this because I could see his suitcases standing in the hall outside his room. I felt uneasy around him, as I've often have. Eric gave me the news that tonight he was going to ask his girlfriend to marry him over dinner and asked if I could help him pick out a shirt to wear for dinner. This shocked me at first. This is a man who is always well dressed and who knows what to wear for any occasion. And I'm just a monk who every day wears jeans or slacks with a T-shirt. I asked him to hold on two minutes and went inside to hide the money from Carlos in my room.

When I arrived in his room, Eric motioned for me to quickly enter, saying he didn't have a lot of time. What was about to happen has taken me some time to get over and I've never told a soul. Eric had placed five selections on his bed. When I walked to the bed to get a closer look at them, I heard the door slam behind me. Instinctively I turned. I saw Eric charging toward me. Both of us landed on the bed. I struggled to get him off of me, but Eric is taller and stronger and a bodybuilder with muscles. I was no match for him. As he turned me on my stomach, I pleaded for him to stop playing around. "This isn't funny," I said. But he knew I was no match for him and refused to let me up off the bed. He put his right arm over my back to hold me down and his left hand squeezed my neck to keep me quiet. Then he started humping me from behind while trying to lower my pants. The voices of two people passing outside his room caused him to slow down a little.

I was horrified. I lay there with my right hand on the wall and my left clutching the mattress, unable to move. Eric ejaculated on my lower back. Then he got up and said, "The Puerto Rican guy," meaning Carlos, "must be very happy hitting what I just got." Eric tossed me some tissues to clean myself. I just lay on the bed, unable to speak at all. I was just glad what he did was over. He acted as if it was all just nothing to him. He pulled me up by my arm. "Now get up and leave so I can make my date with my girlfriend downtown for our special dinner." Guys like Eric don't think of themselves as bisexual when they're with men; to me it seems as if gay sex is just temporary relief until the feeling to be with a woman comes again.

Apparently I wasn't moving fast enough for Eric, so he slapped me hard on my left shoulder twice as I sat upright on the bed. As I stood and walked to the door, he said, "Ya know, that fat old priest has always been on my stick. But old men aren't my thing when I play around." As I stood at the door with my head down, Eric took the liberty of putting his hand under my chin and raising it. He looked me in the eye and said, "Keep this in mind, Brother. Reporting to any other person that a man forced you into a sexual act is more demeaning in society than if a woman got raped by a man in some back alley." Then he opened the door and looked both ways down the hallway to make sure no one would see me leave.

I stumbled back to my room. Feeling nasty and dirty, I prepared to take a shower and put my clothing into the big garbage drum in the hall next to the bathroom. Hate doesn't begin to describe what I felt after what happened in

Eric's room, though I'm positive I will move past these feelings of anger and disdain and not hate Eric. At some point my faith and religious beliefs will give me the grace I need to forgive him, but not now. After showering I went to the roof, where I often go to unwind.

As I leaned over the roof facing the street I could see Eric and what looked like his girlfriend saying good-bye to people on the sidewalk. Shielding my eyes with my right hand from the strong evening sun, I looked down. I also saw Carlos near an alley talking to some guys I knew to be drug dealers. Later, while he was doing his laundry in the basement, I approached Carlos about what I saw from the roof. For the first time I saw a side of Carlos I'd never seen before. He exploded with anger. "Who are you," he yelled, "to question me about doing what's right? Stay out of my fucking business!" He started to leave, but turned and said, "Listen, there are personal things about me that are just personal and mine alone."

I took two steps in his direction and said, "Remember, we're friends. If you ever want to talk, just let me know." When he was gone I couldn't help but wonder if anyone had ever said that to him before. It may have sounded a little soft to him, given the rough outer attitude apparent in his facial and body language.

Three days went by without Carlos offering to spend some time to have even a general conversation. I must have hit a serious nerve, I thought, when I questioned him about the guys near the alley. This not talking was more than upsetting to me. I could tell that I had more than just feelings of friendship for him. But the first chance I get, I thought, I'm going to speak my mind and just walk away. How else can he know what I'm thinking or how I feel unless I tell him? I've always known there were gray areas in his life that he didn't discuss with me, such as why he left Philadelphia and suddenly ended up in New Jersey and his past drug dealing and run-ins with the police. My information came by way of Father Doug and the program Carlos came from in New Jersey. But even after all the time we'd spent together in deep conversations about life, he still hadn't been totally open with me, the one who was supposed to be his homeboy, his friend, and his confidant all in one. One thing I knew for certain: I'd never bring out information I know to his face. These are things he himself has to bring into the open, if and when he decides to do so.

Before the soup kitchen opened, Mike came over to outreach to ask for additional volunteers. Not having anything else to do, I volunteered myself and Sally, leaving Robert and the two volunteers from England to hold down the office until the soup kitchen was done serving and we'd returned. Mike handed me and Sally an apron to wear. Madonna's "Rain" was playing in the background. The kitchen team clapped for us as we entered because feeding three hundred and fifty in a soup kitchen is hard work. Having sufficient people to work can do a world of good.

CHAPTER 7

❀

Not Wanting to Leave Harlem

Carlos worked behind me and Sally as we dished out the day's meal of beef stew, steamed vegetables, and water or juice to drink. Carlos made little eye contact as he handed salads to me and Sally to place on the serving trays with the main meal.

One of our regulars is Old Jake. Jake is eighty-seven years old and a legend in the area for his tap dancing and singing at the Cotton Club. I'm told by the locals that he's been homeless for the past six years. No one knows why Jake won't accept some type of housing or shelter. Jake is always helpful to us. He volunteers to clean the kitchen after soup kitchen closes and bring in deliveries of food. As he stood in line to be served, I could see that Jake and one of his buddies were drunk and acting hostile to the kitchen workers. Apparently Jake and his friend wanted more juice and beef stew.

I stepped forward to explain to Jake and his friend that there just wasn't enough to go around twice. But this only made them more hostile. The situation started to get out of hand and turned into a pushing match as the security team tried to get them out the kitchen area. When my back was briefly turned, Jake's friend took out a small pocketknife and began threatening to cut me and anyone else who tried to get them out of the busy area. Carlos rushed in my direction and grabbed the knife out of the man's left hand before he had a chance to cut my right arm. I was stunned for a couple of seconds, and then I thanked Carlos for his actions. He just tossed the knife into the garbage in the inner kitchen and went back to work.

After the soup kitchen closed, I started toward Carlos, who was sweeping the floor, but Sally handed me a letter. It had the return address of the mother house on it. I chose to read the letter and not bother Carlos, so I grabbed a folding chair and headed outside. It was Father General's annual letter to members of the order living outside the monastery. Our order's mandatory community retreat in Washington DC was only four days away. I'd made a mental note that the retreat was coming up, but I was disconcerted by how soon it was.

Putting the garbage out to the street, Carlos could clearly see me sitting and reading the letter. He came up to me and hit my leg. "Good news, I hope. Who's it from?"

Looking up at him as he stood in front of me holding his apron, I quickly decided to play with him for a moment. Giving him a staged surprised look, I said, "Oh, so you're talking to me now?"

Carlos took a step or two back and lifted his apron in front of his face. "Man, you gotta forgive my outburst in the laundry room. But you have to understand that there are things in my life and people I know that I don't care to talk about. I felt you pushed the issue a little too strongly."

"I don't feel I should apologize for being honestly concerned for you," I said. I stood up from my chair to reinforce my point. "True friends look out for one another and don't shy away when the person could be fucking up, going backward instead of forward in his life."

Carlos looked both ways down the sidewalk to see if anyone in Austin House could see us, then gave me a bear hug. I was the first to back away. As we walked toward the entrance, I glanced upward. I didn't tell Carlos, but I saw Father Doug on the fire escape looking down at us. I knew Carlos had looked around before giving me a hug. Telling him he should have looked up would have pissed him off. Plus, I just didn't care. He's my friend. It's nothing sexual.

"I'll be going away for a three-day weekend. My religious order has mandatory retreats …," I started to explain. I thought it was cute how he cut me short and asked when I'd be back for us to hook up again. Looking east on 116th Street, I replied, "Three days." I felt I didn't want to separate myself from him and the Harlem community for a monastery retreat.

I changed the subject to the money from his mother that I'd hidden in my room. "It's important you tell me now if you need some before I leave for the weekend."

Turning to face me, he lit up a cigarette, which is the first time I'd seen him smoke. "I'm cool for the weekend," he said. "Are you cool with going away?"

He seemed to sense that I'd rather not go. I didn't reply as I entered the building for evening prayers in the chapel. I invited him to go. With the cigarette still in his mouth, Carlos shook his left hand holding his lighter and said, "I'm Christian, but I'm not too much into organized religion." He slapped me on my right arm. "But say a prayer for me, especially my mother."

Nodding, I answered, "You betcha." I turned back to Carlos and said, "You smoke? I didn't know you smoke."

He took the cigarette from his mouth with a gangsterlike attitude. "Is that a problem, Brother Luis?"

"Oh, no, but it's not good for you."

He took another a puff and said with some pride, "It's just a once-in-a-while habit. I don't smoke every day."

That Thursday we stayed up late in the community room watching Godzilla movies, which is another interest we have in common. "I'm leaving in the morning around nine," I reminded him. With a hand slap from him, I turned in.

Lying on my bed the next morning, I glanced at my habit hanging on the back of the bedroom door. The voice of the priest from the confessional came to me again. "There will always be a conflict between Carlos and your religious vows." With my backpack and small suitcase I made my way to Father Doug's office to say good-bye. I tried not to be too obvious in rushing to say good-bye to Carlos. I just stood by the front security desk and waited. I figured he had to pass the desk soon because the kitchen is next to the security desk and breakfast was being served. While I waited, I said my good-byes to most people in Austin House and some who were visiting the building for outreach services. But I didn't see Carlos.

Disappointed, I made way to the train station, stopping only to buy a green apple for my trip. As I stood at the booth in the subway looking for change to buy a token, I heard a voice screaming at me from behind. "Yo! Yo, mista. Do you got a quarter? I'd really appreciate it, man." With the apple in my mouth and coins in my hand, I turned to this person behind me. It was Carlos. I almost dropped the apple in surprise, but Carlos caught it and took a bite. Looking at him as he stood there holding my apple, I had those same feelings I'd had when I first met him. I suddenly felt warm and nervous, my hands twitched slightly, and I wasn't able to look him in the eye for fear he might not like me or what I look like or who I am as a person. Anyone with any sense would say, if he doesn't like you for the way you think and look, then it's not worth getting all bent out of shape or going on an emotional roller coaster.

"I know you're paranoid at times about what people think of us, because of the actions of Father Doug and gossip about him, so I thought it would be kinda cool to meet you in the subway to say good-bye. Hey, guess what," he said excitedly, "I've got a new job working outside Austin House at a sneaker store in the Bronx. It's at 149th Street and Grand Concourse. And what's very cool, my uncle and two cousins I haven't seen in nine years live near the area."

My stomach took an unhappy turn. "I'm saddened by the news. I think it's great you're moving forward and making a life for yourself and all. But the fact is, this is the beginning of you physically moving away from me, and that means fewer daily conversations over meals or looking at the sights of Harlem from the roof of Austin House. I'm glad the news came now, 'cause I'll have time away in the monastery to get used to the idea."

Hearing the train pull into the station, Carlos grabbed my backpack and helped put it over my shoulders. Holding my small suitcase in my right hand and the subway token in the other, I looked into his eyes. Even though I was upset, I was completely sincere when I said, "Congratulations on your new job. It's great that you'll meet members of your family again." I tried hard to show some enthusiasm. I felt at this point I shouldn't give him any inkling that I wasn't supportive of him moving forward with his life.

Carlos clasped my right hand in a firm handshake and put his right shoulder in front of my right shoulder in what I call a half hug. "Man, be cool. See ya soon." He waited until I was on the platform to play a very public joke by yelling not once but twice in front of all the Harlemites, "Man, what are you worried about? The test came back negative." The looks and snickers from the other passengers made me chuckle. Watching him stand there looking back at me as I sat on the train, I had to take custody of my eyes by not staring at him too long. He looked so cool in his baggy blue jeans and red T-shirt. As he placed a cigarette in his mouth and gave me the peace sign, the train pulled off.

I hadn't called ahead because I didn't want to bother anyone in the monastery with giving me a ride from the Amtrak station. I took a taxi instead. The driver was maybe in his early twenties, with very fair skin and red hair. I guessed he was Irish by the four-leaf clover dangling from the mirror. Even though I was a stranger and a customer, he started talking about big breasts and sex with women after we passed some women on the street. And then he continued to give me an inside look at women, along with his expert advice on how to handle them. When I got in, I hadn't used the word monastery; I'd just given him the street and house number. So when he turned into the monastery's drive, he said, "Shit, I must have taken a wrong turn."

As we pulled up and saw brothers unloading food and others doing garden chores, I said, "No. This is the right place."

He became quiet for a couple of seconds and then said. "It's $9.50. Say, I gotta ask you. Are you one of them? You're not wearing a habit or nothin'."

Handing him ten dollars and two dollars extra for a tip, I said, "Yes, I'm one of them."

"Hey, I'm really sorry about all the sex talk." Taking the money and shaking my hand, he said, "Thanks. By the way, I'm Bill McKinney."

"No problem," I said. "After all, if the whole world were made up of celibate nuns and monks, there wouldn't be any more people."

It felt like returning home to walk through the large open doors of the monastery. I had arrived shortly after five, during the Grand Silence. Brother Mark silently pointed to a paper on the desk directing me to one of the guest rooms. Before entering the cloister to change into my habit, I chanced to meet Ryan and Phillip leading new candidates into chapel to be presented to the community. We nearly stopped to exchange greetings and hugs, but remembering the holy rule, we simply nodded as we passed each other.

I quickly settled in and joined my spiritual brothers in chapel for evening prayers. Once grace was prayed at dinner and the Grand Silence concluded, Ryan and Phillip and I excitedly began to talk over our various mission works, all three of us trying to speak at the same time. But we managed to calm ourselves. Phillip told us all about his religion classes for the priesthood and his volunteer work at Martha House, a home for homeless teens. He seemed burdened by a hectic schedule but was looking forward to ordination down the road. While we ate our meal of fish fillet and mixed vegetables, Ryan filled us in on his work in Chicago. It was similar to mine, but he lived apart in a church rectory, whereas I both lived and worked with the poor. We discovered that both of our programs had new outreach services to people with AIDS and started exchanging ideas on how to get more funding for our programs. We soon realized, however, that we were leaving Phillip out of the conversation.

Phillip was happy that his grades at Catholic University pleased Father General. The order, after all, was paying his tuition. It's the practice of most religious communities in the church to pay for the education of their members. The income earned by priests or brothers who work in churches or mission houses goes directly into the order's accounts to pay for food, upkeep of buildings, as well as college tuition for its members. Each of us receives a small weekly stipend of twenty-five or fifty dollars, perhaps even a hundred dollars, depending on our needs and where we live. In this way we maintain our vow of poverty. I'm pleased my fellow post-novitiate brothers are doing well. Trying to keep our laughter down at the dinner table was hard at times, especially when Ryan told us of an article he'd read dealing with a bishop in Ireland who was on a personal crusade to stop rock groups and hip-hop singers from simulating masturbation while on stage wearing crosses. In a very low voice Ryan went on to say that the bishop wrote letters asking for private meetings with such groups. Ryan paused and said, giggling, that some of the artists wrote back saying if the bishop wanted to see them, he could come to one of their shows.

After we finished our meal, Father Peter visited our table to welcome us back to the mother house. As we gathered our dishes for the sink in the kitchen, Father Peter informed me that Father General would like to see me in his office at 7:30 PM. Jokingly, Ryan and Phillip said, "Ooh, Brother Luis is in trouble. He's being sent to the principal's office." Overhearing their taunts, Father Peter insisted, "It's perfectly normal for Father General to have private meetings with brothers who live outside the mother house to see how they are doing in their mission work." Shaking his finger at them, Father Peter quickly added, "And you two are on the list to be seen tomorrow." So Father Peter had the last laugh.

Since any meeting with Father General can be intense and might concern your future in the order, I returned to my room for some quiet time to rest and prepare for it.

CHAPTER 8

❦

The Monastery Retreat

The novices were leaving Father General's office as Brother Andrew waved for me to enter. Some would consider it a sin, but I pride myself on reading people well. When Father General stood up from his desk to greet me, the stern, motionless look on his face and his piercing eyes gave me the feeling this was going to be a serious and perhaps unpleasant meeting. I made a small bow in front of him and nodded my head. Father General blessed me by making the sign of the cross on my forehead. As he led me to the guest chair in front of his desk, he welcomed me back to the mother house. Father General was not one to tiptoe around issues. He cut right to the chase. It seems that Father Doug had been doing a lot of talking with him on the phone about me and Carlos. Naturally, I was shocked. I knew the two had talked about my vocation to Austin House, but I thought there hadn't been more than one or two phone calls. Father General, however, tells me that they have talked regularly. "Brother Luis, Father Doug has not told you himself, but he feels you are spending too much time with this young man Carlos and not enough time with other members of the community." With closed fists hidden under the long cuffs of my robe, I listened as Father General continued, now speaking in a low tone of voice. "It is important, Brother, that you not give the wrong impression by your actions."

It was all I could do to refrain from saying I'd seen guys leaving Father Doug's room in the early morning hours, guys who didn't live in the building and guys who didn't know each other. Something within me told me to keep silent and not be overly defensive. I was afraid that using the information about what I'd heard and seen in Harlem might lead Father General to believe that I was just combating what Father Doug had told him of me and Carlos. My best choice, I felt, was to act surprised. I said, quite truthfully and wholeheartedly, "Father General, I converse daily with many residents of Austin House as well as many street people, all of whom I know by name and whom I consider my friends." I went on to discuss my vocation. I reaffirmed the dedication of my life to God and thanked Father General for helping me work in Harlem.

"I am pleased to hear you say these things, Brother." And with that he dismissed me and gave me a final blessing. Closing the office door behind me as I left, I was convinced that what William and Sally told me had some truth to it. Father Doug will try to destroy any relationship at Austin House that he thinks is gay; but as far as I could see, the straight couples were of no interest to him. And why? I think it's jealousy. He studied for the priesthood and lived in churches. From what I've read, if he wanted to meet men in those days, he would have to meet them in secret meeting places such as alleys or movie houses. The things we take for granted today, like gay pride day, openly gay bars, and gay resorts, travel cruises, and recreational clubs—to a man like him, who is sixty-five years old, these were unheard of when he was younger. I think it must disturb him when he sees young gays who are fully out with their sexuality. One even wonders whether he feels cheated out of having these opportunities of gay expression when he was discovering himself.

My first thought was to talk to Father Doug about everything he discussed with Father General. But it was going to take some true humility on my part to deal with him. Father Doug, as I've witnessed, strikes back with quick force if he gets his feathers pulled. And as administrator of Austin House, he has the power to remove me and any others with a blink of an eye. My position in Harlem is very valuable to me. I will feel no guilt if I have to always stay two steps ahead of Father Doug. After my talk with Father General I now saw Father Doug as a threat to my friendship with Carlos. I'm no longer sad that Carlos is moving out. We can meet somewhere in the city, away from Austin House. Everything I felt was now working out for the better.

In the community room of the mother house I saw my fellow spiritual brothers from India, France, Haiti, Africa, and Italy, all of whom were here for our order's annual mandatory retreat. They were engaged in catching up with each other, sharing news of the various mission work they were involved with, be it social work, parish ministry, or social justice programs. Our order is diverse not only culturally but also in its work. When I saw Brother Alex from the Sudan in Africa, my first response was to ask for more information on our order's work in Africa. As we sat on the uncomfortable couch in the community room, Brother Alex said our order in the Sudan had only three members, who worked with the poor and people with AIDS in a small hospital. He pointed to Brother Sam, who was originally from California, and Father Bill, from Buffalo, New York, as the two who were stationed with him in the Sudan.

Before I entered the order I'd wanted to go overseas to the missions. But after I thought it through, I decided traveling and living in another country didn't appeal to me, so I chose Manhattan, one of the greatest cities in the world, as the place to do my mission work. It's also good to know that if somewhere down the line I want to go overseas, the order is open to that. While I was talking to Brother Alex, I looked up and saw Phillip and Ryan coming toward us. I could tell by the expression on Phillip's face that he had one of his exciting ideas for us. Sure enough, when we three met in the middle of the community room, Phillip said, "Hey, I've had enough of the crowd. I need a break, and so does Ryan." Looking around the room, Phillip said, "Let's beat the heat of the room and chat outside in the garden." Putting a hand over my mouth to stifle a yawn, I declined the invitation, as did Ryan. Sleep was the priority.

Images of Carlos flashed through my mind as I lay in bed. I remember what the priest told me in the confessional. For years I'd scoffed at poetry and people who talked of true love. I found it all overly sweet at times, the way people expressed themselves. But now that it's happened to me, I could for the first time in my life say I understood. My heart races, and I have to look away from him. My hands tremble, and I need to make fists and stuff them in my pockets. His eyes have the power to break me down and yet build me back up again. His physical beauty, his masculinity, his mind and intellect, the way he genuinely attends to me —it scares me at times, this power he has over me. My "truth being real moment"—that's what I call the times when I cannot lie to myself. The truth is, I am just plain upset that God and the universe didn't allow our paths to cross before I entered the monastery. I turned onto my left side to get more comfortable and saw the shadow cast by the cross on the wall above the desk, a quick comfort and reminder of why I entered the order and why I stay.

After breakfast the next day, Phillip, Ryan, Father Paul, and I looked over the retreat schedule. Our first talk was by Father General on the act of forgiveness at eleven. Father General spoke about how we can't move forward in our lives or even heal ourselves until we forgive those that have hurt us in some way. This has always been an issue for me, and the fact that I am a monk does not shield me from this feeling. What Eric did to me in his room at Austin House has made it difficult for me to start moving forward. I'm haunted by his comment about how demeaning it is for a man if I tell someone he's been raped. I'm too embarrassed to talk about it, it's true. Even in the confessional I can't talk about my bad feelings toward Eric, even though I know I did nothing wrong. And to be totally honest, I may not ever tell anyone and just keep it a secret.

This was Saturday, the first full day of our retreat. It is a custom of our order to maintain total silence for retreats. And just like at the retreat house in Garrison, New York, Ryan, Phillip, and I were going crazy from too much quiet and meditation. It is readily apparent that we share the same need to talk and can't stand to be confined for days. None of us would have made it this far if we belonged to a cloistered order, where quietness, group prayer, and meditation happen five or six times a day. Some people are called to this type of life, but it wasn't for us. Even one weekend of maintaining silence and constant reflection was driving us crazy. Most of us knew the orthodox temperament of the father general and would not even dream of asking that the format of our mandatory retreats be revised. I happened to be preparing a salad for dinner with Brother Andrew. I confessed to him that I was going crazy from the strict rule of silence. He paused a couple of seconds, looked around, and whispered, "Priests of the community have gone down this road with Father General before. And as we can all see, the requirement of total quietness on retreats remains and will not change in his administration."

In the gardens of the cloister I lay flat on my back on a bench with my eyes closed, enjoying the sun. Ryan and Phillip sat across from me, whispering to one another. Phillip suddenly smacked his hands together. He had another one of his famous ideas. "I think we should steal the monastery station wagon and go joyriding after everyone is asleep. I have the keys," he whispered. "Brother Mark and I went out earlier for donated canned goods." I sat upright, pressing both palms onto the bench. Ryan and I are speechless. Ryan was looking down, motioning no with his head. "But there are some real cool areas to visit, like Georgetown." I tried to cut him off by waving my right hand. But Phillip spoke a little louder. "We can just drive by these places. We don't have to get out of the car."

I reminded Phillip about the rules. "Moreover," I said, "taking the car out for a joyride would not be to the liking of Father General, especially on a retreat. And as it stands now, no member is allowed out after 9:00 PM except in special circumstances, and joyriding is not one of them." Sometimes I think

Phillip has the attitude of a used car salesman. He has the ability to smooth talk you into his way of thinking, whatever it was.

Standing and pacing in front of us, Phillip said, "Listen, it'll only be for an hour or two." He stopped pacing and leaned against the large statue of Saint Michael and stood there, looking directly at us, and waited for an answer as the bells rang for evening prayers. Ryan and I looked at one another as we stood up. Ryan's face showed he was in agreement, as did mine. We walked past Phillip, slapped him on his left shoulder to let him know we were in, and followed our fellow brothers into the chapel. We agree to meet at 11:45 PM at the stairs leading to the cloister. Phillip stopped us and whispered as quietly as he could, "Don't make the mistake of wearing your robes. If we do stop for a soda or snack in Georgetown, we don't want to look out of place among all those college students."

Later that night Phillip met us at the appointed spot. He shook the car keys in front of us and whispered, "Let's rock onward, my brothers." We headed for the back door of the kitchen. Since none of us had keys to any monastery doors, we made sure Brother Stanley had made his final rounds of locking up doors before we left. That way we could leave a door unlocked for us to enter later.

I searched the radio for some good music, stopping when I heard LL Cool J's "Mama Said Knock You Out." Ryan reached over the seat to turn it up louder. He and I knew the words, so we sang along, off-key, while Phillip joined us on the refrain. This moment was classic—monks breaking rules, out for a late-night joyride, rapping to rap songs, while looking at the sights of Georgetown. We all agreed it was good to be out and about. But driving through Georgetown was an eye-opener. The crowds filled the sidewalks and spilled into the streets, which had us wondering if it was some special occasion or holiday. The lines for some of the clubs and entertainment spots wrapped around the corner. As we drove along watching the people, Phillip broke the silence. "Hey, I got a question. Have you ever wondered what it would be like living like these college students, going out on dates and going to clubs?" Before we could answer, Phillip pulled into a 7-Eleven. We got some decaf coffee and then piled back into the station wagon and sat for awhile in the parking lot. Like the students around us, the three of us were in our twenties. This was another "truth being real moment." Yes, we could lie to each other, but we couldn't lie to ourselves about our real feelings about celibacy.

Ryan was the first to comment. He began hesitantly, saying, "Guys, look, celibacy's been a big issue for me in the last four months. Things have been very difficult between me and a coworker named Marissa. Even though she knows I am a monk, she's given me the green light to pursue her."

Phillip instantly screamed, "Oh shit, man. What?"

Ryan continued. "Yes, guys, she's asked me to dinner and even gave me her phone number and address."

Phillip and I turned around to face Ryan in the backseat. Phillip became very excited and vocal at this point and wanted to know many things at once. "Are you going to leave the order? Has there been any physical contact?"

Ryan took a deep breath and broke the news. "I'm leaving the order, but not because of Marissa. My true vocation is not in the order but outside of it. I feel the confines of the monastery limit my ability to be happy. All is not lost, and maybe God called me to do good works in the order, using it as a stepping-stone to get somewhere else."

I felt like I was losing a blood relative. "Have you given yourself some time to think this over?" I asked.

After sipping some of his coffee, Ryan said, "Yes. Father General and I have been talking about this for five months. After the retreat is over, I will inform Father General of my final wishes."

Total silence filled the old station wagon. There was nothing much Phillip or I could say. But we wished him well in his new life outside of the monastery. He seemed to have given his thoughts time and wasn't confused at all.

Phillip now turned the spotlight on me. Raising his voice a little, he asked, "So what's up with you, man?"

I paused. Like many gay men, I was hesitant to let it be known that I was gay, especially to someone who's straight and may or may not accept the news. But this fact had to come out if I was going to be honest with them and talk about Carlos and me in Harlem. Putting my coffee into the cup holder, I looked first to Phillip and then to Ryan. "Guys, look. We are friends, and it's like this: I'm gay. But don't worry, I'm not attracted to either of you."

I got blank stares at first. Phillip was the first to speak. Actually, he first let out a yell. "Well, man, I kinda knew that. Every time the three of us are together and I comment on a girl or something, you never added anything, nothing about past girlfriends or whatever, man."

Finishing his coffee, Ryan nodded in agreement and commented, "I kinda felt the same way, but you never made me uncomfortable in any way. Father Peter did say sexuality is nothing to us, because whether you're gay or straight, celibacy and living your vows is the goal."

This conversation made me feel even closer to Ryan and Phillip, mainly because in the past we had discussed just about everything, but not gay sexuality. Perhaps it was fear on my part of not being accepted because of being gay.

So I started to tell them about me and Harlem. I looked to my left at Ryan. "What I'm going through is similar to you living in Chicago," I said to Ryan. Not wanting to bore them, I gave them the basics about my feelings for Carlos. I even filled them in on Father Doug and the various gay things happening in the Harlem community, from the flyers to the men leaving his room late at night, as well as how he treats gays or relationships that seem gay to him in Austin House.

Phillip turned to me at one point and voiced what I'd already felt. "Hey, Luis, you ever thought this guy was gay himself and not able to handle those that are out with their gayness?" Before I could answer, Phillip asked, "Are you leaving the order too?"

"No," I replied.

He then put the spotlight on himself and his life in the mother house. "Well guys, unlike yourselves, I have no love interest. I've broken the Grand Silence in the mother house twice by joking around with the novices and was caught by Brother Stanley. My penance from Father General both times was to clean the shoes of the senior members." Ryan and I laughed and hit him on his right shoulder. Then he became serious. "Studying for the priesthood is harder than I first thought it would be. What's even more messed up is my keeping up with my cleaning duties in the mother house. And on top of those duties and my studies, Father General has me volunteering in a homeless shelter." Ryan and I reassured him his hard work will all pay off in the end.

Ryan glanced at his watch. It was well after two in morning. We decided to head back. Confused and not used to driving, Phillip made the mistake of thinking the car was in reverse when it was actually in drive. The car lurched forward. The front bumper hit the cement base of a light pole. We got out to inspect the damage. The dent was very noticeable, and the screws on the left side of the bumper had been loosened. It wasn't right, but like teenagers fearful of what their parents would do after they found out the teens had stolen the family car, we made an oath not to tell anyone of the accident. We'd seen some of the tough penances Father General had handed down to our fellow monastery brothers for not following rules. One of the more outrageous was when a novice spoke loudly during the Grand Silence. Father General made him clean the back stairway on his hands and knees, not just to help him be repentant for breaking the holy rule but also to show him true humility in serving God. So we were quite definitely in agreement: we knew nothing of the car or what had happened to it.

The second full day of our retreat was much better for me. Talking honestly and openly on the outing the previous night was more refreshing than the experience of the retreat. And judging by the attitude and smiles on Ryan's and Phillip's faces, they had had the same experience.

Father Victor, who is from Puerto Rico, gave a lecture on meditation and prayer at eleven in the conference room. His accent was so strong you really had to listen closely to what he was saying. It was a very good lecture, but much of what he had to say about the art of focusing your thoughts and positioning your body while meditating I'd already read in books or heard in sermons. The meditation that works for me is to walk on the beach or look at a sunrise or sunset along with my personal prayers. If I sit in one spot for any length of time, my thoughts are all over the place.

After the lecture, Phillip and I walked in the cloister gardens. It hit us even more so than last night in the station wagon. We couldn't believe Ryan was leaving us to live in the outside world, free of his vows. For once I was the first one to have a good idea, and not Phillip. I suggested the three of us have a farewell party for Ryan. Of course, this would break another ancient rule of the order. Anyone who chooses to leave the order may not inform his fellow members of his choice to leave. He simply packs his bags and leaves quietly without being seen. And so the only way we know what happened is simply that we no longer see them. There is no continuing contact; he is now detached from the order. The only real reason I can think of for making this a rule is to prevent the influence of the world, with its money-making and material goods, from diverting any member away from his religious vocation.

At lunch everyone heard Father General give a little speech about the dent in the car. "My brothers, whoever went out last night and dented the car, please come forward and admit why you were out with the car." We sat there nervously, not making eye contact, and continued to eat our lunch. At dinner time we heard another speech, but he sounded more stern and abrupt. "My brothers, the fact is this. Someone was out with the car, had an accident, and did not come to me today to confess. Not being honest is very disturbing to me. My brothers, honesty is one of the virtues to which we aspire. I say to the one who had the accident: You did not join a frat house. This is not like stealing your parents' car for a joyride without permission. We are all adults here, living a consecrated life unto God. Remember that."

Ryan, of course, had no fear of penance because he was leaving the order. He and I encouraged Phillip to just admit that we were all out for a joyride and that he moved the car forward thinking it was going to go backward. We fell into a guilty silence when Brother Stanley passed us in the main corridor of the cloister, looking up from his book long enough to give us one of his stern looks.

I promised Phillip I would go with him to Father General to admit the mistake. But Phillip insisted we stick to our original agreement. I could tell from his body language that if I or Ryan kept pressing the issue he would just walk away from us. I have no right to judge someone's vocation in the monastery, but I wondered if Phillip would ever become a truly humble priest. On the other hand, I thought to myself, we had been with him. He never forced us to go on these little adventures. But I wasn't brave enough to go to Father General by myself. So we never talked about it ever again.

Once we reached the gardens of the cloister, I brought up my idea of having a final get-together for Ryan. We agreed to meet in the bell tower at midnight. I was to bring snacks from the kitchen, Ryan would get some donated cans of soda from the pantry, and Phillip offered to get a bottle of wine from the storage area near the kitchen.

I was fascinated by the view from the bell tower. I looked down on the monastery buildings and then beyond. There was no moon out; a few pale stars dotted the dark blackish-blue sky. Phillip and Ryan arrived ten minutes late. Ryan apologized, saying that Brother Stanley was a little late locking things up for the night, and they were almost caught by him on their way to the bell tower. Taking the wine and snacks from under our scapulars, we sat on the floor of the bell tower. The time we spent in the bell tower was another classic moment. We discussed what was said the night before as well as God and politics, areas of conversation most people would leave alone for fear of angry disagreements.

Eventually we got around to talking about Ryan's decision to leave the monastery and open a new chapter in his life. "I am not leaving the order because of the young woman," he reiterated, excitedly waving his hands. "I'm glad I came and gave it a try."

"What will you do?" asked Phillip.

"Study for my master's degree in social work," said Ryan, "and stay with my parents back in Corpus Christi to save money after I find a part-time job."

I was glad to hear him say this. He seems to know what he wants, I thought, and sounds as if he's well grounded. We hadn't intended to get drunk, but the sips of wine had us all a little light-headed. Although we were pretty diverse when it came to music, Phillip and I ended the party by singing some of the old hits from the singing group The Mamas and the Papas.

After the service at ten, those of us who lived outside the mother house departed, returning to our various missions. Phillip and I were tired and had a slight hangover. As we waited in line to be blessed by our father general, we looked around for Ryan, but he wasn't present. Ryan's quiet exit from the order, we suspected, had happened or was in the process of happening. Ryan hadn't been in the refectory for breakfast, either. When I went back to my room to pack my things, I noticed a note on my floor. It was from Ryan, dated the day before. It was short and to the point.

"Yo, Luis. Man, you're a good guy to be around and a million laughs. If rules change about writing letters to past members, look me up. My family is in the phone book. Just remember: South Corpus Christi, Texas. Ryan Demarco."

Peace, Ryan.

Folding the note and placing it in my backpack, I changed out of my robes and into jeans and a T-shirt. With my backpack and small suitcase I proceeded to leave the cloister. I met Phillip in the doorway of the main entrance. We shared our good-byes, except Phillip prefers to say "see ya later" instead of "good-bye." He says the word good-bye sounds final, like you're never going to meet again. So as I shook his hand that day, I decided to adopt a similar custom and say "see ya later" or "peace, man" when departing from a friend. Walking outside, I saw Father General standing in the crowd of brothers who were about to leave. To our surprise, he had arranged for two vans and the monastery station wagon to take brothers to the airport, bus station, or Amtrak station, saving us both time and money.

CHAPTER 9

❦

Back in Manhattan

I stared out of the Amtrak window. My longing to see Carlos and Manhattan intensified with each stop the train made along the way. Finally, after two grape sodas, a brief nap, and one hot dog from a vendor on the train, I could see the first views of Manhattan as the train passed through parts of New Jersey. That "great metropolis," as it's been called by writers and historians, has always captivated me. It's hard to believe it was just a village 250 years ago. Since today was Monday and my first day off to enjoy the city wouldn't be until Saturday, I took a long detour up to Harlem, taking the west side train to 86th Street. I walked east from the station and stumbled onto Central Park. My plan was to keep walking and walking until eventually I came across the Great Lawn where Carlos and I had eaten our lunch on our first outing that afternoon after museum. Remembering that the Metropolitan Museum was closed, I made a point of checking it the outside calendar of upcoming events. Exhausted and not seeing any exhibits listed on the calendar that I had not already seen, I headed for Harlem by way of the east side 86th Street train, which took me to 116th Street.

 I was received back at Austin House as if I were the pope himself, with hugs and handshakes from the people I lived with and greetings from some of the homeless I saw on a daily basis. Most of the messages waiting for me at the security desk dealt with referrals, but there was a small envelope addressed to me.

William, the security guard on duty, smiled with joy as he said, "Brother Luis, Janet and I are going to have a second child. We'd like you to baptize the baby."

"That'd be an honor," I said, "but monks and religious brothers cannot marry people or baptize babies; only deacons and priests hold that duty."

Janet shot back with a sassy tone in her voice. "There should be changes in the church."

I congratulated the two of them, kissing Janet on the cheek. I agree, I thought to myself, changes should be made in the church as well as in the order to which I belong.

I flipped through my messages as I headed up the stairs. Father Doug wanted to see me when I got in. He was the last person I wanted to see, of course. I discreetly searched for Carlos, but didn't find him in any of the common areas of the building. Every time I heard someone shout "Hey man" or "Good to have you back" I was hoping it was him. Disappointed, I went to look for Father Doug to get that out of the way so I could unpack and enjoy the evening. Father Doug wasn't in his office. After searching most of the first and second floors, I decided he must be in his bedroom. I've made it a point not to visit Father Doug in his room for any reason. It makes me uncomfortable, the way he sits close and his habit of patting your leg when he speaks or remembers something he wants to say. Before knocking on his bedroom door I placed my backpack and small suitcase in my room. I recognized the classical music coming from his room. It was Bach's "Jesu, Joy of Man's Desiring," a piece that has and will always be my favorite. The organist at the monastery often played it during communion. I tapped on the door.

As usual, Father Doug observed his normal laid-back dress code. He wore an old gray T-shirt with a peace sign on it, a couple of sizes too small, and some red shorts that had a ripped pocket in the front. In an effort to be serious and not laugh at Father Doug's clothing, I focused on the family portraits and other objects in the room. I just knew if I don't keep this up, my thoughts would easily be distracted by the way his T-shirt always rises up, showing his flabby belly and belly button. I know one should keep eye contact when speaking to someone, but in this case I let my eyes wander away and then back to him again.

He motioned for me to sit on the edge of the bed, but I chose the chair, picking up the papers and a small box that were sitting on it. I'm not a mind reader, but I could tell he was thinking something about my abrupt way of heading for his chair and not the bed. Father Doug motioned for me to put the papers and box on the dresser next to the closet. He leaned back against the headboard of the bed and asked me to tell him about the retreat and the works of some of the members of the order.

When I was done, he said, "Traditional orders in the church aren't for me. That much formal structure doesn't fit my personality." I looked around his room. Knowing how he keeps his office and how he dresses, I didn't think Father Doug would last in our order, where appearance and a structured prayer life with others are what we are about. While he continued speaking, I thought, too, about his extra activities. It would be harder to have regular late-night visits from guys living outside the building if he lived in a rectory or a monastery.

Father Doug finally got to the point of why he wanted to see me. "Brother Luis, I want you and Robert to be new check signatories. I'm starting something new here at Austin House, and I'd like to have two trusted members who can make deposits and withdraw cash from the bank when I'm not around." I was not comfortable handling any sum of money, large and small, so I pleaded with him to find someone else. But Father Doug remained firm in his plan of having me do this, so in the end I agreed to be a check signatory.

I stood to leave, but Father Doug handed me an official letter from the Archdiocese of New York. I sat down again and opened the envelope. The archbishop's letter was short and to the point. We are a Catholic institution, he wrote. Handing out condoms or any other form of contraception is against Catholic teaching. The letter advised us that if this continues in our outreach programs and street ministry to prostitutes, our programs would no longer receive funding from the archdiocese and we would not be permitted in the future to use the mailing list we'd received from the bishops' conference. This is one of the church's stances that I do not understand. Yes, I believe in valuing life and I dislike late-term abortions, but a large part of our ministry is to people with HIV and AIDS, and we are concerned about the prevention and spread of it in the Harlem community. I slowly folded the letter and put it back in the envelope. Both of us were angry and realized this will hurt us. When we preach or speak one-on-one with people who have AIDS or HIV, we always advocate abstinence or the use of condoms if they must have multiple partners. Sadly, we would have to comply with the archdiocesan office and not hand out condoms. Our only choice was to work around this issue in secret by referring people to the state health van that comes around weekly to hand out pamphlets and condoms in Harlem.

CHAPTER 10

New Things to Deal With

I flipped through the rest of my messages back in my room. One was from Robert who works with me in the outreach office. "Brother Luis, Carlos Mendez has left our program and has moved in with his family in the Bronx. He departed on Saturday after missing curfew on Friday. Robert."

It was normal for Father Doug and the members of the outreach team to write notes like this to keep us all in the loop about what's going on so there aren't any surprises in meetings. I had mixed emotions. I knew he was leaving, but I didn't expect it to be so soon.

I opened the small white envelope that William had handed me. Inside was a small piece of light blue paper. "Hey, Luis, by the time you read this note you will have realized that I'm not at Austin House any more. I'm cool with everything. I just could not stand those rules any more. I came in twenty minutes late from seeing my family. Security and Father Doug punished me by making me sit on the bench near the front door for a half an hour. I'm no kid and have never been late before. Anyway, my job is mad cool, man, and my uncle gave me a small room in his apartment in the Bronx. I will come by Tuesday after soup the kitchen closes, around 2:00 PM to hang a little. Carlos. M."

Why, I wondered, hadn't Father Doug told me anything about this matter or even hinted. I can tell he's always been curious about me and Carlos from his comments and the way he lurks about looking at us. Anyway, I still have the money he gave me hidden here in my room. I'm sure that's one reason he's coming. While I unpacked I played the Bob Marley cassette Carlos purchased for me at Saint Mark's Place.

At Tuesday's morning meeting Father Doug had big news to share with the whole community. Choosing to stand instead of sit, he reflected on the history of Austin House here in Harlem. He talked about how Austin Houses around the world have always been self-supporting, but over the course of the thirty-plus years Austin House has been in Harlem, we have failed to become self-supporting. We have survived the last ten years on grants from companies and private donations. The utility bills and our stipends add up to almost six thousand dollars a month, including the non-donated food we purchase cheaply in bulk. Lowering his head a little and taking a deep breath, Father Doug announced that as founder of the community he had come to the conclusion that if we are to survive we have to take government funds. There was an immediate uproar, many shouting "No! No!" and standing to face Father Doug. Sally, James, and Allen succeeded in calming everyone down. Everyone knows that if we receive any type of funds, the state can tell us what to do. This not only affects our living situation but also the religious aspect of the chapel services because of the separation of church and state.

Once the room was silenced, Father Doug presented the deal he had made with the mayor's office downtown. "We can still have chapel services, but we can't solicit people to attend. We will receive eighty thousand dollars a year, which will help pay the monthly costs of running the building. Instead of stipends, everyone will be paid a small salary. Anyone who is interested will have to apply for the in-house positions—housekeeping, security, maintenance, kitchen work, and outreach clerks—downtown in the human resources department at city hall. There will also be some restructuring of office space and dormitories for people when they first enter Austin House."

Looking around the room, I could see that the mood had lightened quickly, especially when people heard they were to be paid small salaries. Father Doug reinforced to the community the fact that our rule about saving money still stood, since it was necessary to save money in order to have something on hand when you're ready to leave Austin House and live on your own. Stressing that this was not a quick or easy decision, Father Doug asked that we be open and ready to work with the city on some new changes. At the close of the meeting Father Doug approached me and Debbie, who was standing next to me. He had a meeting at the mayor's office for most of the morning, finalizing the contract with the city. Amid the buzz of new changes in the upcoming months, I moved through the crowd of community members who lingered after the meeting. My day in the outreach office was exciting, as always, what with the occasional fighting between prostitutes over clothing and homeless people unhappy with receiving referrals because we lacked space to accommodate them in our building. I made it through knowing Carlos was going to call; I watched the clock, counting down the time.

After lunch William gave me a verbal message that Carlos had called, but knowing I was at lunch, he hadn't wanted to disturb me. He will not be here at two but will call me back then instead. Trying not to show my disappointment in front of William and others near the security desk, I returned to my desk in outreach and looked for things to keep me busy until two. I stared at the clock: 1:30, 1:42, 1:49, 1:56.

I almost spilled my coffee when I heard William yell from the security desk. "Yo! Brother Luis! You got a call on line two. I will transfer it to you in there."

Moving my coffee out of the way of the phone I played it cool, only letting it ring three times before picking it up. "Hello?"

Carlos quickly said, "Hey, what's up? I'm at work. I can't really talk long. Are you free to hang out tonight instead of this afternoon?"

I, of course, still played it cool, so I replied slowly, "Ya wanna go to dinner?"

He paused. I could hear him tell a customer where the restrooms were located. When he put the phone back to his mouth, we both spoke at the same time and agreed to meet at the diner at 86th Street and Lexington near Tower Records.

After a brief nap I arrived at the diner about twenty minutes early. I have a weak spot for music and bookstores, so I crossed the street to go to Tower Records and check out newly released albums. I heard parts of a song coming from the radio of a car that was waiting for the light to change. I could hear the DJ announce the singer's name: Lisa Loeb, with the song called "Stay." New York traffic is no joke, and as the traffic was dense and clogged with people crossing the street, I got to hear the song start off. It was slow at first, and then it picked up a little, with a great drumbeat in the background. I was so impressed with her voice and heartfelt expression that I purchased the album.

Exiting the store, I saw Carlos standing outside the diner near the subway. He spotted me crossing the street and moved closer to the edge of the sidewalk. For about ten seconds or more I thought about how some people would freak out if they saw one man suddenly grab another and proceed to kiss him on a public street. Once we were face to face, Carlos gave me such a sudden bear hug, I hardly had time to say hi or give a handshake.

As in the past, I was the one to back away first. One of Carlos' attractions is that he is his own man. It does not bother him to hug me, another man, in public. As he slowly let me out of the embrace of his arms, I felt his lips brush against my right cheek. I'm a dark-skinned black guy. If I were white, I'm sure my skin would have turned bright red at that moment. Turning in a half circle, I pointed to the diner as he grabbed the Tower Records bag from my hand. Reaching in the bag and checking out the Lisa Loeb album I had just purchased, Carlos was surprised that I liked so many kinds of music, explaining that he mainly chooses to listen to hip-hop and house music. Over dinner we talked about what we wanted for the future in our lives. After I expressed my love of Harlem and Manhattan and that I hoped to work here for many years to come, Carlos said he wanted a family down the road and to be able to help his sick mother back in Philadelphia. Then came the big news. Carlos was interested in a girl named Nancy, whom he'd met through his cousin Maria in the Bronx. As he gave a complete description of her and her personality, I slowly felt my appetite leave me. I had to remind myself again that I'm a monk and also that Carlos is bisexual and I am totally gay.

Knowing of my romantic attraction to him, I had to decide whether to continue our friendship. My mind couldn't let go of what the priest had told me in the confessional. Looking up from my menu, I was so glad the waiter came. Hearing him ramble on about Nancy had me very annoyed. Okay, yes, I was a little jealous. We both ordered the chicken noodle soup and side salad with two Cokes. The one area of Carlos that has me bothered is his bisexuality. Even if I weren't a monk and was just an average guy out in the world who was attracted to him, I'd still have a problem. Whether it's a man or a woman, I'd find it hard to share him with others. But he'd implied that if we were together, he would feel the need for a woman most of the time because he's a true bisexual. I remember that time on the roof when he said that he loves women but had had brief encounters with guys.

Just like I've noticed Carlos' mannerisms and facial expressions, I couldn't help but feel he knew mine. One thing I take great pride in but don't openly express, because it's seen as a sin or stupid, is the fact that I can read people well. About 80 percent of the time my first impressions are right. When our food arrived I had the strong vibe Carlos either wants or thinks a jealous reaction is coming his way. Because of his looks, I am sure this had happened with guys or women he's encountered before. It was as if we were playing a game to see how the other really feels. I made up my mind to play it cool and stepped into the ring, so to speak, to see if my vibe was true or not. Observing my rule of maintaining constant eye contact, I gave an enthusiastic reaction but tried not to go overboard. Taking two sips of my soup, I said, "Great for you! When can I meet her? How many times have you both gone out?" Continuing to ramble on about Nancy, I said, with stress, "This is really what you need, Carlos. Not only me as a friend, but also a girlfriend."

Carlos sipped his soup without making eye contact and glanced out the window as he briefly answered all my questions, but not in an upbeat way. I thought he would be thrilled for us to meet. I felt his surprise when I pushed him to see if he and this girl have something in common. He said she works a lot and if down the road we can meet, that would be cool to him. I brought him back to the other question of how many dates they'd been on. The number two quickly came out of his mouth as he motioned the waiter for more crackers for his soup. I'd gotten the right vibe, I thought.

Carlos switched the conversation by asking about my retreat weekend. Soon he was laughing as I told him about Ryan and Phillip and our monastery adventures. "I've only met you and not Ryan or Phillip, but none of you fits the stereotype of a monk, not with all that laughing, listening to hip-hop, and cracking jokes." Finishing what remained of our dinner and paying our bill, we headed for the subway.

CHAPTER 11

❀

In These Moments

Keeping to our regular system of getting lost in the city without having any real destination, we rode the eastside downtown train from 86th Street. We talked about his job. He loves working in retail stores and hopes to be a manager one day. While I was telling him of the only real job I'd ever had before entering the monastery, a part-time job at a Pathmark food store in Huntington, Long Island, out of the corner of my left eye I could see three girls in their late teens sitting across from us, not looking at me but at Carlos. As the girls whispered and glanced at Carlos, two things struck me. His attention doesn't falter, despite their silly giggles and attempts to get his attention. One girl is even so bold as to ask him for the time. I could see that her two friends had wristwatches. Carlos, as in the past, also remained attentive to me in the conversation. He didn't allow them to take him away from our conversation together. As Carlos told the girl it was 8:26 by his wristwatch, I noticed the train pulling into east 33rd Street, so I put my backpack over my right shoulder and motioned for us to get out at this station. Leaving the train car we heard a whistle from one of the girls. I assured Carlos that it was for him and not me. I could tell he took pride in knowing he is good-looking.

The stairs at the western end of the station gave way to a perfect view of the Empire State Building. There was no question about it, we were going to the top. We boarded the elevator along with tourists from America and abroad. The elevator operator had us swallow to relieve the pressure on our ears caused by the rising altitude of the elevator. We were speechless the moment we stepped onto the observatory deck. This was the first time either of us had been to the top of the Empire State Building, and neither of us had ever been in a plane or atop any other building that brought us up this high in the sky. The night weather couldn't have been any better. It was clear. The light of the full moon was dimmed by fast-moving clouds below it. The constant cool breeze reminded us that fall would soon be over. I pointed out New Jersey to the west, Staten Island to the south, the Bronx and Harlem to the north, and now, to the east, Huntington, Long Island, the town where I grew up, about an hour from Manhattan. We must have spent a good hour on the observatory deck. Intimacy, I've often felt, does not always mean sex or even talking in deep conversations. For me it also exists in the silences that Carlos and I have shared from time to time, standing or sitting side by side, enjoying each other's company and the sights and sounds of Manhattan, watching the taxis, trucks, and cars below, and gazing at the moonlight on the East and Hudson rivers. The moment was so good I didn't want it to end. What pushed us to leave was the announcement from the security staff that we had ten minutes before closing time.

We bought coffee at a Starbucks down the street from the Empire State Building and began walking north up Fifth Avenue, passing New York's upper crust getting in or out of their limousines. And we looked up at spectacular terraces and roof decks with small trees. Living large, that's how Carlos described rich people who want for nothing. We zigzagged our way to Seventh Avenue, walking north on Fifth Avenue, then left onto 38th Street, and right onto Seventh Avenue. We didn't quite know where we were. The further north we walked, the thicker the crowd became. There were billboards with bright lights and large outdoor televisions with ads and newsreels; the pleasant smells of pretzels, hot dogs, and peanuts wafted from almost every corner. Carlos tugged my jacket and pointed to a sign on the side of a subway railing at West 42nd Street: "Welcome to Times Square." After spending a half hour playing war games at an arcade and drinking sodas, we decided this night must end. We both had to work in the morning. It was nearly midnight, and as always our time had been so good that we didn't want it to end. With his tough attitude Carlos will never allow himself to soften too much. His way of making reference to our time together is to firmly shake my hand and say it was cool.

Using the shuttle from West 42nd Street to East 42nd Street, we transferred to the uptown number four local train. Having the train car to ourselves left us free to discuss what was on our minds. Carlos recounted the night he left Austin House and how he was out after curfew. I already knew most of the facts, but he also told me that Father Doug had security bring him to his office that night. Carlos repeated the same script Father Doug had used with me and others, saying that Carlos was good-looking and should inform him if any of the gay guys in the house bothered him. It was instantly obvious that this upset me. Carlos wanted to know if I was okay. I felt a large knot in my stomach as I turned to look at Carlos. I lied and tried to convince him I was just tired but very interested in what he had to say. The knot tightened as he told of Father Doug pressing him about our friendship and what we do when we go out. Carlos said he stood up from the couch at this point in the conversation, thanked Father Doug for letting him stay there, and then said he would take his things and move to the Bronx to be with his uncle and cousins. I did chuckle at the end. Carlos said that as he was leaving, Father Doug moved closer to touch or hug him, but instead Carlos turned and made a quick exit.

"Hey," I said, "next Saturday night at Madison Square Garden the Knicks will be hosting the 76ers from Philadelphia. Wanna go?"

Carlos looked down at my not-so-cool, faded sneakers. "Okay, and if the Knicks win I'll buy you some new sneakers." Jokingly, he hit me on my left shoulder. "So what will I get if the 76ers win?"

I have only a small stipend and no other financial means. "I'm a monk, remember. I don't have a good-paying job. But tell you what, if the Knicks lose, I'll pay all our subway fares the next two times we go out in the city." This was no match for a new pair of sneakers, but I had no other choice. Carlos extended his right hand and we shook to seal the deal.

I'd almost forgotten to return Carlos' money. As the train stopped at 116th, I pulled it out from my back pocket. He took out a fifty for himself and gave the rest to me to use. While I stood there using my body to hold the doors to the subway car open so the train wouldn't leave before I exited, I insisted he take all the money. "Your uncle could hold it," I said, "or maybe you should open up a real bank account." With the train conductor screaming for me to let the doors go, I swung the small envelope at Carlos and waved to him as the train pulled away. On the way back to Austin House it suddenly hit me: Carlos and I were so busy running around that I forgot to ask for his new address and phone number in the Bronx and he forgot to offer it to me.

On my way to chapel for morning prayers the next day, Father Doug pulled me aside on the second floor to chastise me for staying out late, saying that the order would not approve if I continued to do so. Father Doug knew good and well that I normally don't stay out late, because he checks the sign-in and sign-out sheets at the security desk. I lowered my voice and said firmly, "Look, I work hard for Austin House. And if I want to go out to museums or art showings, or just go sightseeing with friends or by myself, I will do so." I could see the anger in Father Doug's face. But I didn't care. I leaned forward and said, "I know why you're this way with me." Nodding my head up and down, I continued, "and so do Carlos and others." After that, Father Doug stopped making comments about me and Carlos. Father Doug wasn't stupid. If the church ever did a full investigation of the allegations against him, he would need a friend who lives in the building and had also taken religious vows. If this ever happened and I were interviewed, I would only tell the truth about what I'd seen and say nothing of what I'd heard from others.

CHAPTER 12

※

Father Doug's Favorite

Assembling for our morning meeting Father Doug introduced Peter Mills, a light-skinned African American who was about six feet tall. He looked to be in his early twenties. Like any other person coming into the community, he would have to work on one of the teams in the building. Father Doug placed him on the cleaning team, which has been short of workers. I grew annoyed as I listened to Peter tell of being from the Bronx and how he got into drugs. I'd seen him somewhere before, but I couldn't place him. It finally hit me when I saw him sweeping the fourth floor hallway later that day. Peter was one of the guys I'd seen leaving Father Doug's room in the early hours of the morning. I was positive of this.

The past two weeks with this man in the Austin House community have been an injustice to our program, and it was Father Doug's fault. Everything began when the city added a provision to the final contract giving Father Doug the last word on who gets hired for the in-house positions. One day, not long after the contract had been finalized, I entered the dining room for lunch. I could see something was wrong with Sally, Debbie, William, and Mark, who were standing near one of the tables. They fell silent when I approached. Usually this meant there was some conflict with Father Doug.

"What's wrong?" I asked.

Mark was the first to speak. "Peter Mills has won Father Doug over in a way that's not fair to the rest of the community. Father Doug has given him three salaried positions: weekday security supervisor, weekend security supervisor, and weekday house manager."

I took a seat and said, "Look, this is all a big mistake or a bad rumor. I'll straighten it out."

William said angrily, "Man, I'm entitled to at least one of the security positions. I worked in clothing stores doing this work, and I've been in Austin House much longer than Peter Mills." William was the hardest of the four to calm down.

I dashed to Father Doug's office and found him eating a club sandwich at his desk. I apologized for intruding on his lunch break. Father Doug was eager to know what the emergency was, since I was slightly out of breath. I wasted no time in asking, "Did you give Peter Mills three of the in-house positions?"

Without looking directly at me, he paused and put his sandwich down. He then motioned for me to close the office door and have a seat while he proceeded to hand me a lot of bullshit about how Peter wanted to get on his feet as soon as possible.

"I'm not convinced," I said. I noticed he was a little nervous and made very little eye contact. I got the strong impression that Father Doug had gotten himself into a bad situation with Peter Mills, probably a situation of his own making. But I felt I had to step forward on behalf of the community. Trying to keep my voice down, I said, "This is a slap in the face to those who are here looking for a job. Giving one person three paid positions is an injustice. You're not thinking of the men and women who live with us, men and women who need a job or else they won't get their kids back from city social services."

I waited, hoping for a response to my liking, while Father Doug played with the papers on his desk. He then paused, slapped his desk hard, and raised his voice. "I make all the decisions and no one else."

There was nothing else to say after that. I returned to the dining room. Sally, Mark, William, and Debbie knew by the look on my face that everything was now set in stone. Peter Mills would be getting three weekly paychecks of a combined total of twelve hundred dollars. We knew this because the positions and salaries had been posted on the community bulletin board.

Father General telephoned me this morning from Washington DC to inform me that he received the newsletter about the recent changes at Austin House and the city funding. Father General encouraged me to apply for one of the clerical positions in outreach. I was then getting a weekly stipend of forty dollars and free room and board. The mother house provided all members with health benefits. Austin House also donated two hundred dollars a month to the order for my services. Father General surprised me a little when he said that he and Father Doug had talked it over. All that was needed was for me to fill out the city's application.

The position would pay twenty-five thousand a year and the city would provide health benefits. This would relieve the order of having to make monthly payments to Blue Cross and Blue Shield for me. In keeping with the holy vow of poverty, my stipend would be limited to a hundred dollars a week, with the rest of my salary going to the mother house. I detected a note of excitement in Father General's voice. This would, after all, bring in considerably more money for the order. I have to say that I, too, was excited, since this would give me some more money to roam around Manhattan.

The month of November was a downer for me as well as a real eye-opener. I'd always known the church's views on gays, but until now I had never taken them personally. There were some outbursts during mass at St. Patrick's Cathedral. Various gay groups stepped forward to denounce the church for not showing a more Christian attitude toward gays. And then there were the newspaper reports about bad priests who were involved with sex or other scandals. I was also saddened by the church's view on condoms. In dealing with prostitutes who come into the outreach office of Austin House for help, I've found it hard not to advise them to use condoms. The church's view is that condoms stop procreation and that the gift of life is sacred and comes from God alone. This is true, but if people have a terminal illness like AIDS and they still insist on having multiple sex partners, in my view it is better to give them condoms in order to stop the spread of AIDS and other illnesses.

I often wanted to reach inside of the television and strangle the Catholic priests and Protestant ministers who preach intolerance toward gays, using scripture to justify their feelings of disgust. My eyes were now open to the fact that for years child-molesting priests were moved around from diocese to diocese by bishops who preferred to move them out of their jurisdiction rather than provide them with counseling. I felt sick and confused. How could the church protect bad priests and yet speak with such vengeance against gays? One Saturday afternoon when I was by myself in the community room, I saw a priest on television who was speaking to a mostly Catholic audience about the church's views on homosexuality. "It's not a question," he said, "whether the gay person is a good person living a good life. For any gay person to get into heaven, he or she must abstain from gay sex for their entire life, as homosexual acts are sinful. The Catholic church and other religious organizations are now starting support groups for gays who want to have better Christian lives." My mind filled with curses as I switched the television off. Even if they attend these groups, men and women cannot turn their sexuality off. Some call it a defect, others call it a lifestyle choice. I say we were born this way and that it's not a choice. No one in their right mind would choose a life that can bring such hardship, engender so much hatred, or lead to the loss of friends and family. You are what you are. Human nature is what it is. And at some point the participants in these support groups are going to be attracted to one another and want to date. If some gays want to come forward in these support groups, then more power to them. I know for myself this would not be an option if I were not a celibate monk.

My conflicts with the church's views have me doubting for the first time if being a part of the Catholic church in the role of a monk is right for me in the long run. Self-examination, I've learned, can be painful and difficult. Besides giving myself time to explore my doubts in meditation and prayer, I'm also going to give it some time before I speak with Father General on the matter. Despite all this, my spirits were lifted when Carlos paid a surprise visit to Austin House on Thanksgiving Day, a day I thought he would be spending with his family in the Bronx. The kitchen staff and I were standing in the inner kitchen by the stove, instructing six volunteer students from Fordham University to make sure everything would go right when we opened the doors for the homeless to come in. I was making a point of always wearing gloves when serving the food when I noticed Carlos standing in the doorway, causing me to stumble in midsentence. I hurriedly finished my instructions and reminded everyone we had ten minutes before serving.

Carlos wanted to lend another pair of hands and volunteered to help us out. I took his leather coat and placed it safely in a locked cabinet in the outreach office. With less than four minutes to go, I pulled him aside. "Why aren't you with your family?"

He explained, saying, "They're not eating until six o'clock. It's only noon now, and since I'm not working, I thought I'd see if you needed some help." I put him to work slicing turkey.

We were told by many of the homeless that this was one of the best Thanksgiving meals ever at Austin House. We had an impromptu performance of "This Little Light of Mine" by a volunteer named Chris, who had brought his guitar with him.

Carlos stayed an extra hour to help me clean the large pots and pans, leaving him only an hour to get up to the Bronx. Following me into the office to get his jacket, he reminded me that I had won our bet when the Knicks beat the 76ers and wanted to know what color sneakers I wanted. I begged him not to buy them, but he insisted. I had turned my back to him to take his leather jacket out of the locked cabinet and didn't realize how close he was behind me.

When I turned quickly to give him his jacket, I almost knocked him into my desk. Instantly I grabbed his arm and pulled him toward me. We'd had moments before when we looked at each other, but this one was more intense. We seemed only seconds away from actually kissing. But something stopped us. I really can't say what it was, maybe a noise or people talking outside the office. I hastily thanked him for his work, and he tried to hug me good-bye. I ran into him a few minutes later at the security desk. As I thanked him again, I again had the awkward feeling that came over me when we almost kissed in the outreach office, so I ran to my favorite place, the Austin House roof, to have my "truth being real moment" and confront myself about Carlos. I came to the conclusion that I needed to have an honest and open talk with Carlos.

Three days passed. I again kicked myself for not getting his address and number. Once again we had been too involved in talking about things like work, sports, world events, and sightseeing. Carlos finally called on Monday and asked if I wanted to hang out this coming weekend. Saturday was the best day. We decided to meet in front of the Metropolitan Museum of Art at eleven in the morning. I inquired about Nancy and some of his homeboys here in Harlem, but he seemed to shy away from the topics. Yes, I believed Nancy was a real person, but I felt that he liked to separate me from Nancy, and Nancy from his homeboys, and all of us from his family. To be honest, this was not a serious issue for me, because if Nancy, his family, and his homeboys were around, we wouldn't have had so many good times alone together. What weighed on my mind, however, was my decision to open up to Carlos about my feelings for him.

CHAPTER 13

Trouble in the Rain

Saturday morning's weather was wet and windy, the kind of weather that makes you want to just stay home. The sun came out shortly after ten, making for an unseasonably warm December day. But by the time I reached the steps of the museum it had started to drizzle intermittently. I was nervous about the conversation about to take place. Some practical jokes I like, others I just can't get into. Carlos now and then likes to sneak up from behind, pulling me backward and saying "Boo!" And of course this is what he did while I was on the steps waiting for him. Wearing a plastic green poncho to protect himself from the rain, I hardly recognized him. In fact, he had the hood pulled down so far over his head that I at first thought this was some crazy person who'd grabbed me. We wrestled around until I managed to pull his hood off and see his face. He laughed and said, "Man, that was fucking funny. You should have seen your face." Embarrassed in front of the onlookers, I walked off toward Central Park with him following me. "Hey, man, you have to admit it. I got you good," he jokingly said twice.

Finding the nearest bench, I asked him to sit, and then I began the conversation. "I'd like you to wait until I'm finished saying all I have to say, because if I'm interrupted I may forget some things that I need to say."

Immediately he groaned. "Aaahhhh, man, this sounds like it's going to be heavy."

But he gave me his full attention and moved closer to me. He also pulled the poncho off his head.

I put my slightly shaking nervous hands into the pockets of my coat. I could feel his eyes looking at me. I broke my rule about looking at people when speaking to them. I knew I would not stay focused if I looked directly at him. I started with the basics, that I value his friendship and the good times we have hanging out. I then got to the near-kiss in the outreach office. "Carlos," I said, looking down at the rain as it fell to the ground, "what almost happened between us must never happen again." His body language totally changed. He moved forward to the edge of the bench. "My vocation," I reminded him, "is to the church as a celibate monk." I was about to continue when he stopped me by raising his right hand. But he reconsidered, apologized, and let me continue to speak. "Carlos, no sex can come of our times together." Seeing his awkwardness, I remembered that he uses the word "encounters" rather than "sex" when he talked about dating other men. When I said, "We can no longer see each other if not being physical is a problem," he couldn't restrain himself any longer.

Nothing could have prepared me for what came out of his mouth next. He stood up and walked maybe five steps in front of me. He then turned back to me and said nastily, "Luis, you're a fucking cocktease." My mind went blank after that comment. He then walked back to me and asked me to be quiet until he'd finished speaking. Angry and pointing at his chest he stated, "Let's keep it real, man. You wanted me. And I wanted you. We both knew that from the beginning. But because we do and like the same things, we kept seeing each other. Why not, right? I understand who and what you are. But I have a hard time understanding the celibacy part. It's not normal, man. People our age should be out dating, clubbing, having fun. Remember what I told you that first night we were eating in the dining room when I told you to look at Father Doug? I can see why someone like him, someone his age, who has lived most of his life—I can see people like him in the role of a priest or monk. But not you, man. When what almost happened in that office … I could tell you wanted it as much as me. And no fucking?! Why, man, am I going to torture myself any further being together if it's gonna be look but don't touch? What's really fucked up, *what's really fucked up!* is that fat fucking priest you work with, who is not totally true to what he is supposed to be. But just my fucking luck, the one I want is not only around my age with things in common, he's also true to a way of life that's totally inhuman to me."

The drizzle of rain turned into a heavy downpour. He was so angry he didn't even pull the poncho over his head. Backing up, Carlos slapped his hands together and said, "I'm outta here."

As he started to walk away, I stood to walk behind him, saying, "Come on. Stay. Let's talk this out here and now. Just don't walk away on a bad note."

He turned to meet me face-to-face. "Look, man, you're the one who said we can no longer see each other if not being physical is a problem. Well, Luis, it *is* a problem." He moved closer and then baffled me with a theological question. "Luis, let me ask you. If two people were together and one shocked the other by committing what the church would see as a sin, is it a sin if the one didn't know the intentions of the other but was involved in the sin?"

I made eye contact and said, "No. If the one didn't have any intention of committing the sin, then I think they stand free from any type of guilt at all."

Now comes the second incredible part of my conversation with Carlos in the middle of Central Park in the midst of heavy rain. I didn't see it coming. Carlos grabbed both sides of my head and planted a kiss on my lips. I was honestly shocked at myself for not being quick to back away since I'd never had anything like this happen to me in any way, shape, or form. Here he was, the perfect guy whom I wished I'd met before I thought of entering the monastery. Here he was, in front of me, making that bold move and kissing me. Again my mind went blank. I didn't know what to say. Looking back on it, I think silence was the best thing at that time.

Carlos let go of me and said, "See, now you have no sin to confess." He backed away, turned, and walked away. I made my way back to the bench and watched him disappear down a path. For some time I was unable to move. A great feeling of loss came over me, as did more doubts about my vocation as a monk.

For three weeks I submerged myself in work, trying to forget Carlos. Some days it worked; other days I just wanted to be by myself on the roof, high above everyone and everything.

CHAPTER 14

Miracle Gift for Christmas

After morning prayers Father Doug introduced an elderly visitor at our morning meeting as Mr. Kevin Mitchell. Using a cane, Mr. Mitchell rose to address the community after we completed the team reports. Father Doug was smiling from ear to ear, so I guessed whatever this man had to say was going to be good. Mr. Mitchell, I must say, had the gift of gab. He talked on and on about growing up in Harlem on 118th and Lexington Avenue and owning a successful realty business in the city for over forty years, but eventually he got to the reason why he was here visiting us. Mr. Mitchell explained that God has been good to him and he wanted to donate three brownstone buildings to our newly developing AIDS project. The room roared with excitement as we all stood from our seats to thank him. Calming the room down, Father Doug gave us complete details on where the brownstones were located. One is on 122nd Street and Lexington Avenue and the other two are on 123rd Street between Lexington and Park avenues. Like Austin House, all three brownstones are four-story buildings that were formerly used as rooming houses. We had prayed so long for this project to finally take off, and now it was a reality. Money that we'd raised from past mailings to buy buildings could now be used to renovate the properties.

At the close of the meeting Father Doug requested all department heads to meet in the outreach office at eleven. He wanted us to think of how we might use our outside contacts to help in renovating the new buildings. The buildings already met the city codes, so that was a big load off our minds. Father Doug went around the room to get ideas from every department head. Robert and I said we would ask all volunteers who wished to work on this project to help in getting donated beds and furniture. Securing manpower will be key to preparing the buildings, so as volunteer director I will also check into international volunteer programs and organizations that might help us get people who want to visit New York and also do volunteer work for four to six hours a day in return for food and shelter.

Sally brought up a point none of us had thought of. It was winter and there were very few international volunteers visiting the city at this time of year. Since the warmer weather attracts more people, we revamped our strategy for finding workers and meeting the technical needs of our future homes for homeless people with AIDS. By the end of the two-hour meeting we'd made the following plans:

- The maintenance team and security will ensure on a daily basis that the buildings are secure from theft.
- Robert and I will ask thrift stores around Manhattan to donate furniture.
- I will wait about two months and then seek volunteers to paint the exteriors of the buildings and do yard work when the weather is warmer. For now we will use the present volunteers to paint and prepare the interiors of the buildings.
- Father Doug and volunteer social workers will work with the interfaith organization of Harlem to seek out nurses or doctors who might guide us in setting up a daily system of medical assistance once we start to get people with AIDS living in these buildings.

One of my biggest fears was relieved when Father Doug announced that three nursing nuns and six hospice caregivers had already volunteered to help residents when they get to the final stages and can no longer care for themselves.

Christmas was in the air now. Community members were playing Secret Santa and decorating the building. My birthday is on December 20. I hated it when I was a kid because my Christmas and birthday gifts were all rolled into one on Christmas Day. Some people don't believe me when I say I never had a real birthday party. It seems my friends or family members were always too busy getting ready for Christmas. Now that I'm older, I don't look for people to surprise me with gifts like I did when I was a child. Now I celebrate my birthday by going to dinner and maybe a movie in downtown Manhattan.

After work I took the train to East 51st Street to walk over to see the ice-skaters at Rockefeller Center. The night air was cold and crisp, the crowds were dense, but eventually I found a spot near the railing of the ice rink. For maybe twenty minutes I watched the backflips and spins of some of the talented skaters. An older woman with two small girls around seven or nine years old had worked their way toward the railing and were standing just behind me. One of the girls started to cry because she couldn't get close enough to see the skaters. Since I'd had my fun watching the skaters, I motioned for the woman and her girls to take my spot. I've heard it said many times that there is something about Christmas that makes people go out of their way to do good things. While walking away from the crowds of Rockefeller Center I saw people opening doors for one another, picking up bags that fell to the ground from the hands of strangers, or just saying hi or merry Christmas.

Walking past the large lighted figure of Prometheus at Rockefeller Center, I could hear the loud bells ringing from St. Patrick's Cathedral. I've never been inside St. Patrick's and this was my perfect opportunity to do so. Walking up the steps on the right side of the cathedral I could heard loud organ music. Next to the violin, it's one of my favorite instruments. I found a seat near the front and sat for a while, enjoying the organ music until my stomach told me it was time to eat. My luck was good. I found the only diner on 51st Street near the cathedral. It was a bit expensive but worth it. The spaghetti and meatballs and the chocolate cake I had for dessert were so good that I made it a point to return soon.

Christmas Eve chapel services were beautiful: the singing, the flowers, and even Father Doug's sermon on the miracle of Christ's birth and the miracles that surround us in our daily lives. It was a thought-provoking sermon, prompting me to reflect on when I first came to Austin House. The community was struggling and living off donated funds and food; the stipends were small. The city contract was our first miracle. Now we had the funds we need to keep the community afloat and are able to have salaried positions, which will play a big part in helping people in our program save and get back on their feet. Our second miracle at Austin House was the gift of the three brownstone buildings that will be used to serve homeless people suffering with AIDS. Without grants or large donations, it would have taken years for us to raise enough money for this project.

Our doors were open from 11:00 AM to 3:00 PM on Christmas Day for the homeless to have a meal of turkey, gravy, ham, yams, and stuffing, all cooked by volunteers. Chris, a student from Fordham University who had volunteered at Thanksgiving and played music on his guitar, surprised us by rallying three of his friends from his band to come and play instrumental jazz while people were eating. The dining room didn't look like a soup kitchen at all. With live music and beautiful decorations on the tables and walls, it looked more like a downtown restaurant. Our reward was the appreciation of the street people. Father Doug and I personally thanked all of the visiting volunteers for a job well done, especially Chris and his friends.

CHAPTER 15

The Unthinkable

Christmas evening, after we'd cleaning up the kitchen, William asked me if I'd gotten my note four days ago. "No," I said, somewhat surprised. I'd like to think I hide my temper well when someone has done me wrong, but the test of fire, so to speak, came when I heard William say, "Yeah, man. Carlos came by around about quarter to nine in the evening, chatted with the fellas, then left you a note." Unable to find the note when he searched the security desk, William casually mentioned, "Father Doug was at the desk getting his messages while he talked on the phone." I couldn't ask William, but I wondered whether Father Doug had seen Carlos leave the note under my name. Luckily William volunteered the answer. "And Carlos borrowed Father Doug's pen because someone had taken the one from the security log."

I asked William to let me know if he found the note and then walked to Father Doug's office. I hid my true intention for being there by talking about how great everything in the soup kitchen went and how far our little program had come in the last four months. "Excuse me, Father, I'm going to call my family on Long Island." I stopped at the office door and turned to face him sitting at his desk. "By the way, William said I got a note at the security desk four days ago. It must have gotten mixed in with your messages or someone else's by mistake." I didn't mention Carlos at all. Just as calm as could be, Father Doug started opening Christmas cards on his desk, shaking his head no and saying, "Nope, Brother, sorry." I still had a strong feeling that Father Doug had taken the note and that nothing else had happened to it. When a message is left for one of us, security puts it under our name using a pushpin. There are no slots or shelves, just the large board with our names on it. William and the rest of the security team are very good about tacking up notes as soon as they get them. My theory was that Father Doug saw Carlos leave the note for me as he stood talking on the phone, and then, just out of nosiness, discreetly untacked the message and put it in his pocket.

Father Doug puts his personal garbage outside his bedroom door, including stuff like letters or messages. The cleaning team then brings it from his bedroom door and leaves it on the second floor next to the bag of garbage from his office. The cleaning team then collects the garbage on the second floor and takes everything out to the street. But Father Doug is habitually late in putting his garbage outside his bedroom and office, so presently he had two small bags of garbage sitting outside his office. After I closed Father Doug's office door behind me, I did the unthinkable, though I felt a little foolish when I did it. Without thinking twice, I quickly scooped up the two small bags and made my way to the bathroom around the corner from his office, making sure no one saw me. I placed the bags on the bathroom floor and started rooting through them for any signs of Carlos' note. But I discovered something so incredible that I would have to report it to the archdiocese.

I'm no expert when it comes to the technical details of bank records, but when I arranged some of the papers side by side according to date, I could tell that the city of New York had been a little too trusting of Father Doug. I don't know what the hell he was thinking, but judging by what I saw, Father Doug had moved a total of at least thirty-five thousand dollars out of the city's contract fund and into his personal checking and savings accounts at Citibank by having Robert, who is a check signatory, and himself sign checks. I also saw a letter to the bank from Father Doug making arrangements for Peter Mills to be a fourth signatory. Astonished by this new development, I moved backward so fast while sitting on the floor that I bumped my head on the sink behind me.

I knew for a fact that the city is paying Father Doug to be the administrator of Austin House. Once when Sally and I went to his office to sign for our checks, I saw his signature on the record sheet and his paycheck sitting on the desk. And even if for some reason the city was giving him an advance, I found it hard to believe that the city would tell him to take it out of the contract fund for the program. As I sat on the edge of the tub, I considered all that I'd heard and seen. I realized I wasn't dealing with a priest but with a man of deception, a man who doesn't live with other priests and only reports to the Manhattan archdiocese when he has to—in short, a man who answers to no one but himself.

I thought about all the past mailings to solicit funds for the works of the community over the years and wondered if Father Doug had a habit of dipping into funds reserved for community use. All this blew my mind, but I managed to keep these discarded documents by folding them and putting them in my pocket. I would decide later what I was going to do with this information.

I continued to look for signs of a note from Carlos. There was some small part of me that wished I was wrong in thinking this man would stoop so low as to take personal notes from people. But as I dug into the second small bag of garbage, I came across a sheet of pink paper from our in-house message pad, torn in half and sticky from orange juice. It was the note from Carlos to me, dated four days ago. I placed it in my pocket next to the bank documents. Despite my anger I was quick thinking. I closed the small bags of garbage and discreetly put them near the other bigger bags of garbage at the end of the hallway, for Father Doug would think it odd if he'd seen his garbage was gone and then it reappeared outside his door.

In my room I separated all the bank records and placed them in the small trunk that I used to hold Carlos' money. Then I sat at my desk and tried to make out what was written in Carlos' note. The ketchup stains made it hard to read, but I managed to get his phone number. As usual, Carlos was direct and in his tough-guy mode.

"Luis, it was really...." The letter *f* had been crossed out and two words put in its place. "... messed up. What happened in the park? You really f—[illegible] made me mad at you man, but you are really cool people, man. Me and my boys do not or have not done the things you and I have done. I can't see the fellas going to a museum or laying on the lawn of Central Park listening to a jazz concert. Or even taking a boat ride just for the hell of it. I thought about what you said. If you are cool with me, hit me up on the phone. Carlos M."

It was still early evening, so I decided to call Carlos to wish him and his family a merry Christmas before I headed to an evening service at St. Patrick's Cathedral. An older-sounding man picked up the phone, saying "Hola." I introduced myself and asked for Carlos; he introduced himself as his uncle Max.

An upbeat Carlos picked up the phone and said, "Yo, man, what's up? How you been?" Carlos wouldn't let me get a word in. "Since I didn't hear from you, I thought our friendship was truly over."

Playing a little with him I reminded him, "Well, Carlos, you did walk away from me."

I suddenly heard "Ppssshhhh," which meant I'd gotten him. He couldn't say anything further about what happened in Central Park. He knew he was the one who walked away and didn't want to resolve our problem. I lied when he asked about his note to me and said it was lost in my papers and I recently discovered it when cleaning my room. We talked as if nothing had happened. We talked about basketball, his mother's health, and his job. He was so attuned and sincerely wanted to know what was going on with me and my world, everything from the city-funded positions to the donated brownstones. I hated to cut him short, but I excused myself for evening prayers at St. Patrick's. We agreed to hook up the next weekend on Saturday morning at eleven at Astor Place.

Changing out of my religious robes into black slacks and a dark navy blue button-down shirt, I felt uplifted from reconnecting with Carlos. I was so glad he'd rethought what I had said and wanted to continue our friendship. Before the commencement of the blessed sacrament in St. Patrick's, I prayed for continued strength in my vocation. I also prayed about the issues surrounding Father Doug, asking God for a way to get help for Father Doug. One thing was very clear to me, I dare not approach Father Doug in any way. This was a man who hated being confronted by people on issues he's made judgments on. I can't go on what other people tell me happened when they confronted Father Doug on serious issues. I can only learn from what I personally saw in the outcome and learn from it. Father Doug has the power to remove me at any given time. My job, my love of Harlem and Manhattan, could be wiped away in the blink of an eye.

While I prayed I came up with a way to make known to church officials in Manhattan what was going on up in Harlem. I would write a detailed letter and mail it anonymously to the archdiocesan office and send a copy to the cardinal. My mind raced with thoughts of what to put in the letter. Keep the letter simple and to the point, I thought, with sufficient evidence to prompt an investigation. I could stretch the truth a little and portray myself as an older religious brother from Manhattan who came across information that could become a scandal if immediate steps were not taken to correct the situation. The letter will contain the following: photocopies of the bank statements with notes showing the transfer of funds into Father Doug's personal accounts; a suggestion that the archdiocese look over past bank records of Austin House; a recommendation to look into allegations of sexual harassment and the flyers left outside Harlem churches; and also the names of the two priests who visited Austin House that morning to see Father Doug in his office. I will also ask that they look into why Peter Mills has three paid salary positions and is a check signatory and why he received all these opportunities while other qualified people who had lived in the building longer than him were overlooked. I wasn't afraid to mention this because I knew others had talked with Father Doug about it.

Father Doug has done great work in Harlem, but he is an older man who has been left alone by the church and needs some type of help and counseling. One final reason attention must be given to Father Doug's actions is the fact more and more people who used to come to chapel services are now declining to do so because of his hurtful actions. If any nun, monk, priest, or deacon is pushing people away from God, then we need to examine our actions; and if others sit by and do nothing, then they are also a part of the problem.

With the sound of the organ slowly playing "O Holy Night," I glanced at the artwork of the statues and the gothic architecture of the ceiling. Moments before the service started I received a slap on the shoulder. I was speechless. It was Carlos. "Hey, am I late?"

"Why aren't you with your family in the Bronx?"

Being cute, he asked, "Why aren't you with your family on Long Island?"

During the service he looked around the cathedral. At one point his inquisitive mind got the better of him and he whispered, "What are those red circles at the top of the ceiling over the altar?"

Trying to keep my voice down, I explained, "When a cardinal who is stationed here in Manhattan dies, his red cap is raised to the top of the cathedral."

"I'm impressed," said Carlos, "that they'd go to all that trouble to hang a dead man's cap up at the high ceiling."

An older woman wearing too much makeup turned to face us and stated sternly, "I'd like to hear the service, please."

Carlos snapped at the woman and raised his voice a little. "So, Luis, what was I saying?" I'm so glad the woman didn't turn around a second time. Given his history, Carlos wasn't likely to back down if confronted. It wasn't nice, but both of us silenced our laughter.

After the service we ended up at Rockefeller Center watching the skaters. Carlos placed his cup of hot chocolate on the ground, reached into his backpack, and pulled out a pair of new sneakers. "Look, man, if you don't like them I can exchange them," he said.

"No, they're perfect. I like them. Thanks." I suddenly felt awkward. Carlos seemed to stop himself from hugging me. He must be afraid, I thought, to hug me after our talk about no physical contact. But I'd meant sex, not friendly hugs between friends. So I moved in to hug him in appreciation. He continued to watch the skaters as I put the sneakers in my backpack. Like a little kid, his eyes gleamed as he pointed to various skaters doing their tricks on the ice.

I've heard it said many times over, always know when to leave the party. After Carlos and I walked around Rockefeller Center, my body wanted sleep after a full day of serving in the soup kitchen and attending prayer services. On the train ride back uptown Carlos answered my question. His family had exchanged presents in the morning and Nancy had joined them for an afternoon dinner. But he had to get out of the Bronx, he said. He hadn't been downtown since we last saw each other in Central Park. And since I mentioned I was going to be at the cathedral tonight over the phone, he decided not to wait until next Saturday. Hearing him say that confirmed my romantic feelings for him. On this cold Christmas night I didn't expect the two of us to reconnect our friendship so fast. I only wished I had a gift for him. So I gave him the small metal angel from my wallet. It was something I'd purchased ten years ago. It was special to me, but I had no problem passing it on to a friend. "I need an angel in my life," he said, as he slapped and firmly shook my hand in appreciation. Before I got out at 116th Street Carlos tossed me a green apple from his backpack, and I said, "Saturday at eleven, Astor Place." Without saying a word, we waved and I left the subway car.

I bumped into Eric on the way to my room. My disdain and anger came rushing back. As I tried to find my room key Eric stood to my left. "Hey, Father Doug invited me to stay a week until things cool down between me and my girlfriend." Once I found the key and opened my door, Eric leaned forward and rubbed his lower stomach, whispering, "Feel free to come and look at ties in my room when you can." I was sure that Eric, like any other masculine bisexual man, did not want his girlfriend or straight friends to know his private desires, so I threatened to expose him if he continued to bother me. I said I'd go to Father Doug and whoever else to keep him from me. Eric almost raised his voice but managed to keep it to a whisper and said, with a closed fist in my face, "I'm not fucking gay! And who's to say people would believe you over me?"

Twice I said, "I don't know. Just please leave me alone."

Eric didn't want me to have the last word. He came even closer to me and with a sinister voice he continued to speak in a whisper. "You truly liked what happened in my room. But I was not the one you really wanted on top of you."

I immediately closed my bedroom door and didn't respond to him. He was right. My thoughts had drifted in this direction with Carlos in my mind. And Eric knew. He'd seen me and Carlos hanging out in the building.

Early Saturday morning while I was cleaning my bedroom before going to meet Carlos, there were two strong knocks on my bedroom door. Wondering what was wrong, I looked through the peephole before opening the door. To my unpleasant surprise it was Peter Mills. He was rude and direct. "Hey, man, Father Doug is giving me an advance on my paycheck. Since Father Doug and Robert are away, you and me are the only two signatories in the building." I looked down at the check. Since I didn't have my contact lenses in or my glasses on, I figured I must be reading the amount wrong. I retrieved my glasses and looked again. The check was for five thousand dollars. Peter shoved a pen at me to sign it. When I refused to sign before checking with Father Doug, he tried to solicit sympathy by telling me he needed it to settle some bills. When I refused a second time, Peter grabbed the check out of my hands and said, "You're fucked up." I closed my bedroom door with him on the other side screaming, "I'm going to call Father Doug." I was more convinced than ever that Father Doug's judgment on money matters was not good.

This was most likely going to provoke an argument. If Father Doug thinks I'm going to help a man who is getting over a thousand dollars a week from three paid positions and now wants an advance of five thousand dollars, *hell no!* He will have to save up all that money he is making. I decided I had to mail the letters to the cardinal and bishop. William stopped me as I was about to leave the building. It was a phone call from Father Doug, who was visiting friends in New Jersey. The reason for the call came as no surprise. Before I could get "Hello, Father Doug" out of my mouth, he jumped on me to sign the check for Peter. But I insisted I would not do so and explained why. Father Doug rudely hung up without saying a word. On my way to the subway with the two letters in my pocket, it dawned on me that if the archdiocese investigates Father Doug and Austin House, Father Doug will now probably think I was the one who called for him to be investigated because of this latest episode with Peter. But I was so damn angry. I didn't care if he were to ask me to leave. I would just have to find a live-in position with Catholic Charities or some other program doing the same type of work.

We met at the Starbucks on the corner of Astor Place. We each ordered a large cup of hot chocolate and found seats near the large glass windows, giving us the perfect place to watch people and have a good conversation. I know that friends should be able to share what's on their minds, but I felt uncomfortable when he nonchalantly pointed out that Nancy was a good piece of ass. I got the feeling she was his sex buddy and nothing more. Obviously this was his way of answering my question about him and Nancy dating and what they mean to one another.

Dropping the subject of Nancy, Carlos said his mother was not doing well and so he would have to go back to Philadelphia. The new medicines were not working and she had taken a turn for the worse. He handed me his parents' home phone number in Philadelphia. Feeling a sense of loss again, like the time he walked away from me in Central Park, I tried to keep my composure and maintain eye contact. My mind is flooded with thoughts I didn't want to deal with just now. He went on speaking about working in construction and odd jobs when he gets back to Philadelphia, while I faced the fact that he may get settled there and never come back to live in New York. Philadelphia is his birthplace, and his mother, father, sister, and relatives live there.

Knowing why he left Philadelphia in the first place, I feared him going back to his gang brothers and whatever trouble he left behind. His boss said he could come back and work in the store if there was an open position. He was to leave on the 3:15 Greyhound bus that afternoon. I wanted to kick myself for almost suggesting to him he wait a while before going to see his mother. How messed up was that? I'm only thinking of myself, not his ill mother. I almost jumped at the chance to see him off, but I declined when he told me Nancy and his cousins Maria and Roberto would be there. I've wanted to meet his family, but not this way. It will have to be at a better time for me. We didn't have much time left, since he had to get back to the Bronx to get his bags and then come back downtown to the Port Authority Bus Terminal. Given how little time he had, I was pleased he took the time to meet me and not just call to give me the news over the phone. Our departure hug was good, but this time I took my time backing away.

There was an official letter from the head council of the monastery waiting for me when I returned to Austin House. I was a little afraid to open it at first, thinking Father Doug was up to something again. But it was just a reminder that new elections were coming up. In most orders in the Catholic church, the superior-general is elected to a four-year term, as are the headmasters of candidates and novices. The role of the father general may be compared to the CEO of a large industrial company. The person elected to this office has the power to open or close any monastery, place people in leadership positions, as well as decide who is good for the order and who is not. Along with his other duties, the father general has to stay on top of the different monasteries within the order around the world. The financial well-being of the order and its future survival plays a big role in the superior's decisions. I've always known our present superior-general simply as Father General, never taking into consideration that he had a real name. The letter referred to him as Father Bill Niles. He and two other candidates, Father Peter Brody (present headmaster of novices) and Father Steven Davis, were seeking election to this position.

The positions of headmaster of candidates to the order and headmaster of novices are also important. But the father general can always have them sitting on the edge of their seats waiting to see what changes or decisions the elected superior will make concerning the community. The constitution of our order states that in order to vote you have to have spent at least ten years in the order after taking the perpetual vows of poverty, chastity, and obedience to the father general and the pope in Rome. Since I had only been in the order for a little under three years, I didn't meet the qualifications to vote.

Monday, Tuesday, Wednesday, and Thursday had passed, and now it was Friday afternoon. Father Doug did not approach me in the matter dealing with Peter and the check. And I sure as hell wasn't going to talk to him, knowing it would bring a serious argument. Our three buildings were coming along quickly, now that furniture had been donated for all the bedrooms and common areas. In about a month, after a city inspector gives the okay, we will accept our first intakes into the new program for homeless people with AIDS.

Carlos called to say his mother was doing much better and had returned home from the hospital. He found a job working with a friend doing construction work for extra cash to help out his family. He saw himself staying there about another month, maybe even until the beginning of March.

"What are you doing for New Year's Eve to welcome the new year in?" I asked.

Then he wowed me. "Can you be by the phone at five minutes before midnight? I'd like to call as a kind of good-luck wish for us and our friendship in the upcoming year. Yeah, I know I'll be with family and friends, but I thought it would be a cool thing to do."

New Year's Eve came. The silence in the building was different from normal. This was one of the rare nights, like Thanksgiving and Christmas, when members of Austin House could stay out late if their counselor approved. Around 11:20 I made my way to the outreach office to receive the call from Carlos. A feeling of great happiness came over me as I passed the bedrooms of the few members in Austin House who didn't have invitations or families to welcome in the New Year. There would soon be a small party in the library furnished with the best of food and decorations I and my fellow volunteers could find. The women were helping each other with makeup tips, and the men were putting on their best clothing. They had worked hard to get to this point in their lives, getting off drugs, working in a job program, slowly regaining their dignity. For some this will be the first time in years they have had a good reason to celebrate anything.

Talking on the phone with Carlos was not going to be a long pleasant conversation. The loud salsa music and the voices of his family members made it hard for us to hear one another, and in the midst of everything, the countdown occurred. Trying to shout over the loud cheers from his family members, we wished the best for each other in the new year. I was about to hang up when I heard him call to his mother in Spanish. Carlos put his mother on the phone. Her voice was weak, but she knew who I was. I don't know why, but I instantly became nervous and stupid. She was so nice and thanked me and our program for helping her son when he needed a place to stay. Carlos made me out to be a saint to this woman. She is obviously Catholic, as she requested I pray for her and her family. We were cut off a couple of times, and when it happened the third time, Carlos and I realized the phone connection was not going to get any better. I returned to my room, listening to the sounds of cheering and firecrackers in the streets below.

CHAPTER 16

❦

The Shit Hits the Fan

It didn't take long. Three priests arrived at our front security desk, announcing that they came from the cardinal and archbishop's office downtown. They requested to see Father Doug. I passed the three priests as I headed to the library for our department meeting. I was almost shaking with nervousness. They have to be here in response to my letters, I thought. Father Doug and the three priests came in on the tail end of our meeting to introduce themselves to the whole community—Father Jim, Father Mike, and Father Anthony—and to say they would be living with us until further notice. No words could describe how Father Doug's face looked in the meeting. With considerable tact, the priests tell us they are here basically to help Father Doug administer the business of the community, working in the business office, auditing past and present files, and improving the system. Only I knew the real reason.

Since I was the only other vowed religious person besides Father Doug living in Austin House, the three priests met with me in confidence to reveal the real reason they were there. I'm no actor, but I tried my best to seem surprised to hear about the information that was recently mailed to the cardinal and archbishop's office. I'm so glad that when I reluctantly became a check signatory I'd made it my personal business to really look at what I was signing the checks for. To clear myself of any wrongdoing, I mentioned the paper trail would show that the checks I signed were mainly for carpentry supplies and paint for our new brownstones, all things for which there were receipts. Once I had briefly stated what order I was from and what work I did in Austin House, their interest in me disappeared. It was very apparent that their goal was to find out if the documents I mailed were true and to report back to the cardinal and archbishop's office.

During the first week after the priests arrived, there were very few sightings of Father Doug. I'd only seen him at prayer services and morning meetings. He must have taken all his meals in his room. These visiting priests hadn't lost touch with their vocation in the church. Every day I saw them not only going over bank records and business stuff but also taking the time to really get to know God's people. I'd even seen them playing basketball with community members in our back lot, listening to those who were distressed, and helping in the soup kitchen. There was a sincere spirit about them that affected the community. The fact that they were young priests may have had a role in this, since they were from the same generation as most of our in-house members. Even our chapel services welcomed back people who had drifted away because of Father Doug. They took turns giving the daily sermon during mass. I appreciated that they could speak from the heart and not stand at a podium constantly looking down and reading from books or papers. Their gift of preaching with eye contact during mass is what I think drew people in.

Another official letter arrived from the monastery. Father Steven Davis had been elected father general. The letter is long but good, describing his background and his joy at being elected. He asked us to pray for him. Three days later I received another letter from the new father general. This one was not to my liking at all. He wanted all non-priests of the order to be geared toward teaching or administrative work. He was honest in saying our order like many in the Catholic church had seen the departure of many members. And few men and women were entering convents or monasteries these days. Our order has had to close monasteries and some overseas mission houses due to the lack of members to run them. Without members generating funds to keep these houses open, it becomes a financial burden on the order. He knew that all brothers of the order presently work for stipends or at low-paying jobs. This new directive meant we would have to go back to school and receive higher education degrees so we can ask to be paid higher salaries to keep our order afloat.

I'm all for education, but this new idea, that all brothers in the order had to be geared toward work we may not be happy doing, was not for me. The vow of obedience came into play here. If I or anyone refused to do as he asked, we would be going against our vows, the holy rule, and the constitution of the order. It's a given fact: the order has changed over the years as the world has changed. I will not be happy in an administrative office job or teaching all day long in a classroom. My vocation is to serve the poorest of the poor. This type of work does not bring in a lot of money, but it's my vocation. I'm not even sorry to say that if I had to give up Harlem and the work I do here for a higher-paying job just to keep the community's assets afloat, then I would choose to stay with the poor. Constant, true happiness is not of this world, and if I were superior-general I would not sacrifice the happy works of my brother monks to save our large assets. I would start from scratch all over again like our original founder. I was to travel the following weekend to Washington DC to meet with Father General. I prayed the outcome would be a good one concerning my vocation in the order and my staying in Harlem.

Father Jim requested that I attend a meeting with Father Doug in his office the next morning at nine. Father Jim, Father Mike, and Father Anthony all had serious looks on their faces. As sure as the sky is blue, I knew their findings were not good. The first meeting did not include me; it was just the three of them and Father Doug. I stood outside his office waiting to be called in. The occasional sound of raised voices indicated that their findings and the rulings from the cardinal and archbishop's office were not pleasing to Father Doug. Father Doug opened his office door and rushed out and passed me in the hall, not saying a word.

Father Anthony motioned for me to enter. Father Mike, Father Anthony, and Father Jim were seated in a circle. I took the seat that must have been used by Father Doug. All three had stern, businesslike attitudes. Father Mike spoke first, informing me of the outcome of the investigation. Father Doug had been found guilty of misappropriation of both donated and city funds. It was the ruling of the cardinal and archbishop's office that Father Doug be relieved of his title of administrator of Austin House. Father Doug will remain at Austin House, but will have nothing to do with funds or financial matters. More importantly, Father Jim and Father Mike will stay on at Austin House until the archdiocese can find a new administrator. They tactfully informed me that Father Doug will receive counseling from the archdiocese on other pressing issues. The real mess, Father Anthony said, will be trying to explain to city officials what happened when they conduct the annual audit. To me, it sounded as if the cardinal and archbishop's office saw it as partly their fault for not looking over Father Doug's shoulder, because Father Anthony casually mentioned the archdiocese will pay back stolen funds to the city. I got the strong impression as I walked out of that meeting that the cardinal and archbishop's office will use their influence with city officials to keep all this hush-hush as long as the money is repaid by the archdiocese.

The three priests continued to rock our program to the core, so to speak, correcting wrongs by making them totally right. As I left the building to get a soda from the corner bodega, I could hear Peter Mills cursing up a storm outside the front door. Father Anthony and Father Mike, who are temporarily in charge of Austin House, looked over the list of paid employees. Obviously they saw what positions Peter held and how much money he was making. They were good to him in that they gave him two options. He could either keep one position and let the other two go to qualified in-house members, or he could lose all three and have no job at all. As he got out of a taxi and walked to the front door, Father Anthony got wind of what Peter was cursing about. Father Anthony silenced Peter by telling him he had checked with city officials; the funds must be used to pay three different people. He was wasting his time trying to get all three back. Having had the last say, Father Anthony turned and entered the building with me behind him. Given the violent history of some of our members, I thought for a couple of seconds that Peter was going to punch Father Anthony in the face.

After watching the Saturday morning news I packed my bags for the 11:35 AM Amtrak train to Washington DC. This meeting will help me decide if I have a future with the order. My plan was to let Father General tell me his plans for members of my rank in the order. If I saw that his mind cannot be changed on this new structure for all brother monks, then the order's new direction is not for me. There has to be some compromise here to allow non-priests who are happy in their current works to continue doing them. I was in the middle of packing when Father Peter called to request I make my visit four days later. It would be very helpful to Father General, he said, if there were as many brother monks in the mother house as possible, so that he could personally discuss his ideas for all non-priests. After changing my Amtrak ticket I immediately informed Father Anthony, Father Jim, and Father Doug about the proposed changes in our order and that I would have to leave in four days for the big meeting in the mother house.

Four days later I was in the mother house waiting for the meeting to start. I saw maybe thirty-six of my fellow brother monks waiting to take on the new father general. He entered by himself and quickly moved toward his appointed seat. He didn't smile or wave at us. He just cut to the chase, maybe to intimidate us. I think my fellow brothers picked up on his attitude; I almost laughed at the sight of some brothers rolling their eyes. After opening the meeting with a prayer, Father General recounted what he wrote in his letter to all of us. His leverage for changing the work structure of the brother monks was the past history of the order, when if superior-generals saw a need, they changed with the times and went toward it in full force.

Judging by their body language, some of the brothers looked as uneasy as I. Some tapped fingers on their knees; others fidgeted, perhaps wanting to stand instead of sit. Most of us were under the age of thirty-eight. Brother Ray, who is almost seventy-three, stood to inquire why the monastery council had not come up with other alternatives to improve the financial status of the order. All eyes were on Brother Ray as he moved toward Father General. He stopped maybe twenty-five feet in front of where Father General sat. Father Ray also wanted to know why the idea of selling off property had not come up. (Everyone knew the order held three million dollars in property assets.)

Father Ray continued in his respectful way to remind Father General that in the beginning our order did not have large properties or the wealth needed to maintain them. He concluded as follows: "The Catholic church has many orders set aside for teaching, nursing, social work, and so on. In keeping with the founding of our order, our constitution states that all non-priests of the order, the monks in other words, are to be educated in sound religious study and then choose a form of humble work, be it caretaking at a church, preaching the gospel overseas as a missionary, working in programs that feed and house the poor, or, if they so choose, teaching. It might even be working side by side with priests in clerical or manual labor. This is why most of us joined the order. It offered what we wanted outside our religious vocation. Most of all, these jobs kept us in line with the vow of poverty we took when we joined the order, a vow to reject the riches of money and power and live simply by the works of our hands."

Folding his hands together Brother Ray returned to his seat while the whole room remained silent. With mixed emotions I stood to give my point of view, which was similar to Brother Ray's. But I also wanted to talk about the future education of brother monks in the order. "Nothing is wrong with education," I said, "but if a brother of the order does not want to get a master's degree in teaching or a doctorate in some field, he should not be forced to do so. If this is done, then I think the other orders in the church that do not require such education of their members will take vocations away from our order, causing us to shrink even more in size as members pass away or leave the order for secular life. Brothers should be allowed to choose the work they want to do; it should not be a mandate set in stone." The nodding heads of my brothers confirmed my statements.

Father General then looked around the room and asked, "Does anyone else wish to speak?" But no one else spoke. My guess is that Brother Ray and I had already laid out the main issues. Father General then stood from his seat. "I remind you, my brothers, that you vowed obedience to the superior-general and the church, a promise you made when you entered the Order of Saint Matthew. I must tend to the future of the finances and the needs of elderly members of the order. Asking all brother monks to move into higher education will bring more income into the mother house. The elder brothers, however, are exempt from this ruling because of their age."

We were proud of Brother Ray for standing a second time to ask Father General why we could not sell some of our assets in order to continue living the vow of poverty by doing humble works for money to sustain us.

Father General made many enemies by chastising us for not accepting what he called his authority. He was so upset, in fact, that he blurted out, "I don't care if no brother monks remain in the order. Obedience must be kept. We are not a cloistered order. We mix and work with the outside world. This way of living may have been more popular many years ago, but not now. If the world changes, then we must change with it. My brothers, this new way will be hard at first, but the council and I agree, this new structure for brother monks is the way to go in order to improve the order's finances in the future. The order will sell some assets to pay for the further education of brother monks." And with this last comment he left the meeting hall, with all of us standing around wondering what to do.

Brother Ray pointed out that the constitution of the order provides no recourse, so there was no action for us to take as a group to overturn his decision. This was a powerful blow to us all, serving as a reminder that even behind the walls of a monastery there can be anger, frustration, and dissent. Basically we must choose either to be trained in areas of work we dislike or to make that dreaded decision to leave the order. Yet this didn't make sense, because many orders in the Catholic church are not getting a lot of new members these days.

I met Phillip outside near one of the pillars of the meeting hall. We hugged and spent time in the gardens of the inner cloister catching up with one another. He filled me in on the latest gossip buzzing around Father General's ruling. It turns out Father General has many priests of the order backing his decision. Phillip and I had never before had a real argument. But now we argued back and forth over the meaning of poverty for a monk living in today's modern world. He raised his voice and said, "What you and the other brother monks are doing is not moving forward in the order. You want to live religious life the way it was lived way before the 1960s. It's a thing of the past. The duty of non-cloistered brothers in today's world is to work as schoolteachers, nurses, or administrators, not in some job with a low-paying salary or stipend. He has to advance for the good of the order."

I couldn't stand it anymore. I walked away from him in the garden. I just could not hear any more of what sounded to me like accusations that I and my brother monks were slacking in the order. For the first time, being in the mother house gave me the feeling that my future was insecure. Whoever became superior-general would have the power to change my job, to put an end to something that I may be happy doing. But according to the obedience rule, we had to comply. These priests wanted us to live a new type of holy poverty by making more money to support the large assets we own. Not even appealing to the statements of our founder and the constitutions could change their minds.

After the Grand Silence, Phillip and I sat next to each other for dinner and made our peace with one another. It would take more than disagreements over monastery politics for us not to be cool with one another. As I rode back to Manhattan on the Amtrak train, it scared me to think of living in the world, paying bills and taxes, holding a job. I have confidence in myself, but outside of living with my family on Long Island, the monastery and Austin House are the only world I've known.

CHAPTER 17

An Envelope for Me

Returning to Harlem eased my ill feelings toward Father General. The Austin House members don't know how much happiness they bring me. When I am gone for any amount of time, they and the people who enter our outreach program give me a strong sense of belonging, sometimes saving *New York Times* articles dealing with art or new movies they think I may be interested in.

After dinner the next day I gave Father Mike and Father Anthony the whole scoop on what was going on in our order. They got me to thinking. If we three along with Phillip in the mother house were all living together, we'd all do really well at working together. Many things added up. We're all around the same age and into sports, we love working with the poor, and we have diverse tastes in music but similar personalities. I've said it before: they brought a good spirit to our Harlem community. Many of us felt their sincere spirituality in work and conversation, which is why I felt comfortable discussing my possible exit from the monastery with them.

Father Anthony inquired in detail about the big meeting in the mother house. Father Mike commented, "In all honesty, what you are now going through is something I avoided by becoming a priest of the archdiocese. As priests we don't live in groups under monastery rules that are subject to change."

"I feel I'm at a crossroads and I don't know what to do," I said.

Father Anthony replied, "I want you to give it some more time in prayer. Only then can you make the right choice and know where God is calling you to be in this world."

Father Mike then handed me an envelope from Father Doug's desk. I opened it hesitantly, unsure of what I might find inside. I was speechless. I thought it must be a mistake or a joke of some kind. It was a round-trip ticket to Rome and a letter from Father Jim.

"Brother Luis, please accept this round-trip TWA airplane ticket to Italy. I cannot go now because my father has been ill with cancer. Father Mike and Father Bradley, whom you don't know, will be going with you. The arrangements were made last year and cannot be changed. I hope you can go. As you can see from the dates on the tickets, you leave in a week's time. This was a gift the bishop's office gave me for my work in Manhattan, but since I cannot go, I give it to you. Sincerely, Father Jim."

My joy couldn't be contained. I jumped up and down, yelling and waving my arms in the air. They both clapped in delight over my happiness. I couldn't sit back down, not even for a moment, to look at the details of the trip. The date of departure, flight number, and where I would be staying could wait. Father Mike and Father Anthony stood to shake my hand, giving me yet another perfect gift. Father Anthony called the mother house to obtain permission from Father General for me to go to Italy. In all cases, the superior of any order has to give permission for members to travel outside the country. Considering all that had happened the last couple of days, I was glad I didn't have to ask his permission.

It feels good when someone is really looking out for your best interests, as I found out when Father Anthony said, "Brother Luis, you've worked many long hours at Austin House building up its programs. And these new developments in the monastery are stressing you out. We both feel, as does Father Jim, that you could use a good getaway." Separating myself from work and the monastery, I thought, might also clear my head in making my next move. I was so glad I'd gotten a passport three years ago when I thought of becoming a missionary.

On my way to my room Debbie stopped me on the stairwell to tell me security was looking for me. I had a phone call. First, the trip to Italy, and now to top it all off, a phone call from Carlos. My enthusiasm about Rome dominated the conversation until at one point I stopped to realize what I was doing and apologized for not thinking of his mother and him working hard to help his family. "You're just happy," he said with a giggle. "Go on, man. I really want to hear what's new with you." When I got all I had to say out of the way about Rome, the Vatican, museums, and hiking around Rome, he told me he would be staying an extra three weeks in Philadelphia. His mother is exceptionally well, but he wanted to help complete a construction job before coming back to New York. Before hanging up, Carlos gave me his parents' address to go along with the phone number I had. He wanted me to mail him a postcard from Rome.

On the evening of my departure, I was to take the train to West 42nd Street and transfer to a shuttle bus that would take me to JFK airport. Father Mike and Father Bradley would meet me at the airport. As I left the building, two volunteers from Germany, Martin and Jane, and in-house members Debbie, Sally, and Matt surprised me by taking my backpack and suitcase and asking me to get in the Austin House van so they could take me to the airport. The unexpected ride became a little going-away party. We stopped at the corner bodega on 125th Street to pick up snacks and sodas before riding over the Triborough Bridge. We all got a little crazy when we heard LL Cool J's song "Mama Said Knock You Out" playing on the radio. We turned it up, singing every word as people in cars next to us stared. Even our German volunteers knew a couple of words, probably from hearing it played around Harlem.

Traffic around the airport was very dense. You would have thought all of New York and Long Island was there. Consequently I didn't have much time when I got out of the van to walk to the terminal. Everyone quickly gave me their best wishes. I thought I was going to be killed by cars cutting each other off. Once in the terminal I found Father Mike and Father Bradley standing by a vending machine sipping sodas. Father Bradley is another cool priest. I guessed he was in his midthirties, with a laid-back attitude. As we got acquainted with one another, we talked about social issues, Muddy Waters' music, and working with the poor of Manhattan. All three of us looked somewhat the same in our short jackets, T-shirts, faded jeans, and sneakers. We looked more like college students going backpacking across Europe than two priests and a monk.

Father Mike gladly gave me his window seat. I had the impression he hated flying but was playing it cool in front of us by telling us he wasn't into looking at the sights down below while in flight. According to my travel guide, we were traveling to Europe during the off-season, so there wouldn't be a lot of tourists crowding to get into or see the sights. Although this was the second week of February, the Manhattan weather hadn't been bad. We were hoping the weather in Italy was equally as nice as Manhattan's.

The plane ride gave Father Bradley a chance to talk about his upcoming work in Alphabet City, Manhattan. Apparently his grandmother had died and left him enough money to buy a fixer-upper on East 7th Street. Once the building construction was finished, he hoped to start several programs for the poor.

He asked Father Mike and me if we would volunteer to live part-time in the building a month from now. Father Bradley wanted people who could help formulate future programs as well as help in the construction. We said we would have to think about it. With the AIDS project taking off and with our continued responsibility for the daily work of the outreach services, taking on a new project just now would leave me being totally burned out. But Father Mike and I agreed that we would see what our workload will be in a month.

Each of us had worked a full day, so we fell asleep quickly. Almost eight hours later I was awakened by the sunlight coming in my passenger window. I overheard the flight attendant tell a family sitting two seats up from us that we were now flying over Spain. Spain's countryside was indescribably beautiful to behold. But only I and Father Bradley enjoyed it. Father Mike was not too pleased at us trying to have him look out or talking about it.

The directions for taking the bus from the airport to the monastery that the archdiocese had given Father Anthony were not totally accurate. We got a little lost and were very fortunate that an older American couple living in Rome saw we were having trouble and managed to put us on the right track. Rome was alive with excitement; there were people from all over the world. In every public area we saw a lot of nuns, priests, and monks wearing their religious garments. Most orders in the States did away with religious garments after Vatican II. We also caught glimpses of many scenic sights, from Renaissance architecture to the Coliseum and Saint Peter's Square.

The New York archdiocese had arranged for us to stay at a Carmelite monastery near the Vatican. This arrangement saved the expense of a hotel and also gave us a community to have daily mass and prayers with. We were met by a senior member of the Carmelites who opened the monastery gate to allow us to enter. He didn't speak any English but knew who we were and led us to the monastery superior, Father John Mariano, who spoke English but with a very strong Italian accent. After welcoming us, Father John showed us to our rooms. Because of the monastery's location, each of our rooms probably offered more scenic views than any hotel.

Feeling somewhat jet-lagged, we decided to rest for several hours before exploring Rome. I was awakened shortly after one by Father Bradley and Father Mike. While I grabbed my backpack for some sightseeing, Father Bradley suggested we needn't be so formal in addressing one another as father or brother. Mike and I shook our heads in agreement. Mike then struck a bad boy pose, putting his hand on his chest and deepening his voice. "Yo! Yo, Bradley man. Let's go out, man, and get something to eat. You down for that?" He had the thug attitude down perfectly. He didn't even crack a smile when Bradley and I laughed.

Before going out to see the sights, a novice of the monastery introduced himself as Brother Peter and handed us keys to the front door of the monastery. Maybe I was a little paranoid, but I got the impression from looks or stares in the monastery that our style of clothing may not be what they were used to seeing on monks and priests. As I said, it was very apparent that most orders in Rome wore religious garments everywhere they went. But we were here to sightsee. Wearing a habit just to fit in and show we were religious just didn't cut it with us. Given all the walking we planned to do, robes would have been bothersome and uncomfortable.

We managed to travel around Rome without paying a lot of money on taxis. On our first stroll near the Vatican, I noticed a bike shop that rented bikes by the hour. Armed with a road map and detailed directions on how to get to different historical sights, we set out. The weather resembled New York's, a little chilly but not uncomfortable. I could see remnants of a snowstorm, but the streets were clear and the sun was beating down on us. Our first stop was the Castel Sant'Angelo, a fortress built by Roman Emperor Hadrian in the second century AD as a mausoleum. Its circular design was unique. I'd never actually seen a round building before. The bridge leading up to the structure, lined with statues of angels, gave it more artistic appeal. The Pantheon was our last stop of the day. The temple structure was very well preserved, considering it dated back to AD 125. As an artist, I was interested to learn that Raphael and other painters were entombed beneath the dome of the temple, along with Italian kings such as Vittorio Emanuele II and Umberto I.

We returned to the monastery in time for evening prayers and dinner. We hadn't foreseen that the chapel services would be conducted in Italian. None of us was fluent in the language, but we managed to follow along. The books of Christian prayer are the same the world over, and all monasteries and convents follow the same schedule of daily readings. So while they read in Italian, Bradley, Mike, and I followed along in English in our personal prayer books. We didn't stay too long to mingle with the monastery brothers in their recreation room after dinner, as we were tired and still somewhat jet-lagged. We also wanted to rest up for a full day of sightseeing the following day.

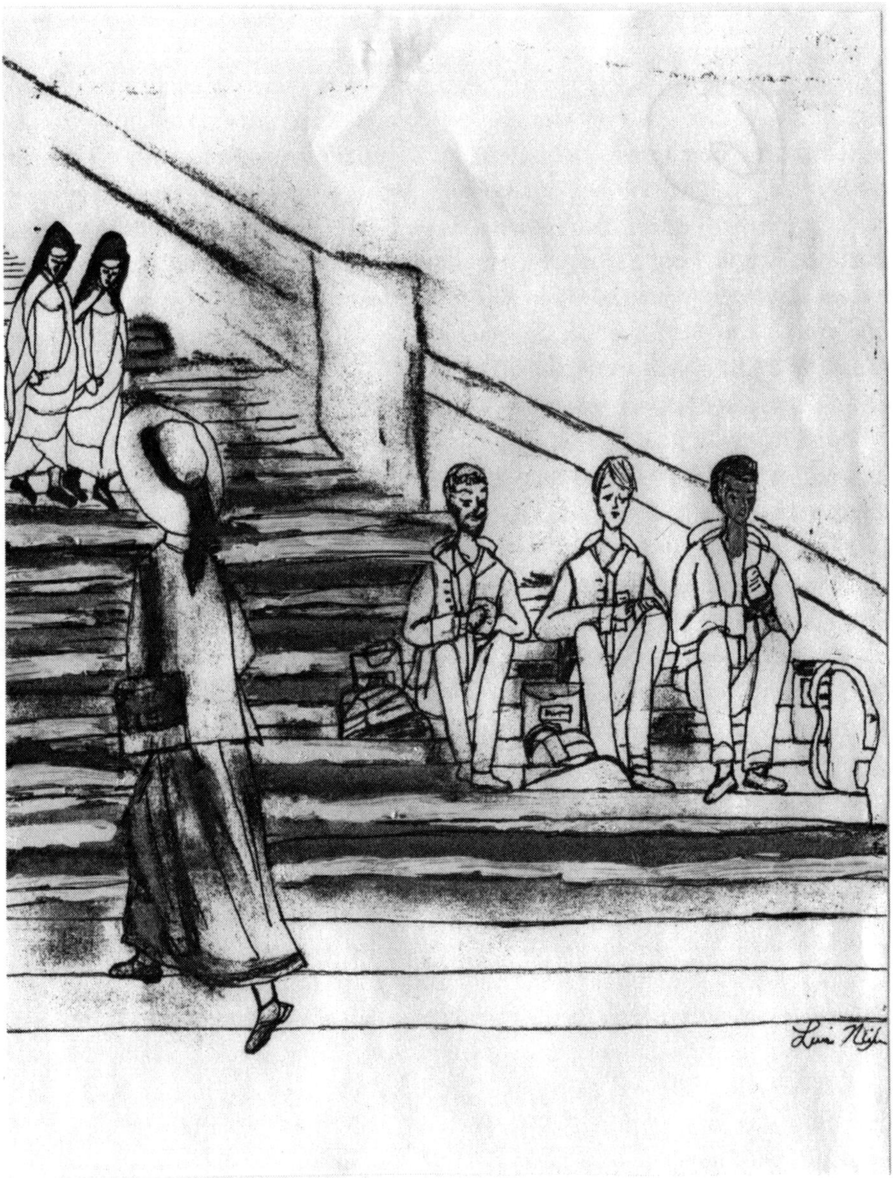

We were awakened by the sound of bells coming from the monastery, the Vatican, and various churches and convents around Rome announcing prayers and mass. I got up out of bed to open the large shutters on my bedroom window. The burst of morning sunlight was blinding at first. If you like to sleep in late with lots of peace and quiet, then lodging near the Vatican may be a problem. But I've never minded it; the ringing of the bells helps me keep track of the time.

Our Rome adventure continued after our personal prayer time in the monastery chapel. We first bicycled to the famous Trevi Fountain, completed in 1762. It has been said that if you throw a coin into the fountain you will return to Rome one day. And if you throw a second coin in, you can also make a second wish. The fountain, designed by Nicola Salvi, is dominated by Pietro Bracci's large sculpture of Neptune.

Strolling with our bikes we came to the Piazza di Spagna. I caught something huge out of the corner of my right eye, but hunger was on our minds. Mike spotted a coffee shop that looked as if it might sell sandwiches. After purchasing our Genoa salami and Swiss cheese sandwiches with orange Fanta sodas, we turned back in the direction we'd just come from. Our mouths dropped open. There was a vast flight of steps about fifty feet in front of us. It reminded me of the biblical story of Jacob's ladder, with angels going up and down a huge ladder of steps. Bradley handed me his sandwich so he could look up our location in his guidebook. It was the Spanish Steps, built with funds donated by the French ambassador in the early eighteenth century and designed by Francesco di Sanctis. We sat on the steps with the locals and ate our lunch in the unseasonably warm mid-February weather. Unanimously we decided to conquer the steps and began heading to the top to work off lunch. Mike urged us not to stop, saying it would make us lazy and waste time. However, I surmised from the tone of his voice that he was trying to hide his fear of heights. When we reached the top of the steps, Mike hurried us into the church of Trinità dei Monti. The view at the top of the Spanish Steps revealed the beauty of Italy. In every direction there was something to behold and point out.

After dinner that evening, Father John passed an official letter to Bradley. It was addressed to all three of us and came from the papal nuncio to the United States. The papal nuncio is normally a bishop who is a permanent diplomatic representative of the Holy See, normally having the rank of an ambassador. The papal nuncios help the pope stay on top of world issues as well as the activities in dioceses around the world. Mike rudely snatched the letter out of

Bradley's hand and opened it, but then apologized for his rudeness as he took out what appeared to be three tickets. Raising his voice a little and stepping back from us a couple of feet, Mike held up the tickets in his right hand and exclaimed, "Here they are, tickets to see the pope." Indeed, there were three invitations to visit the Vatican the next night at seven for rosary prayers with the pope.

Mike explained that three months ago he'd written a letter to the nuncio introducing himself, Father Jim, and Father Bradley and describing the work we do in Manhattan. He told the nuncio it would be a blessing if we could have the occasion while in Rome to pray with the pope at the Vatican. I contained my joy so as to not embarrass myself in front of a monastery filled with strangers. Father John noted that tickets like these are hard to come by, even for those who live in Rome year round, unless of course you know someone who knows someone and so on.

Later that evening two of the novices, with the permission of their superior, offered to take us on an evening walk around Rome. There were snow flurries, and the winter chill was returning. They took us into areas I'm sure we would never have seen or thought of on our own. They showed us piazzas and statues, views of the city along the Tiber River, the dome of Saint Peter's, and more. As we walked along the Tiber I was reminded of those times with Carlos when we enjoyed the moment, taking in what was around us without having to talk about it then and there. It was the same with my spiritual brothers during our sightseeing around Rome. We never questioned or rushed each other if someone wanted to spend more time looking at a work of art.

Night had fallen by the time we approached Saint Peter's Square. We came across what looked like a thousand or more people holding candles. Some American students studying in Rome overheard Mike ask Bradley what was going on. A girl who looked about twenty said it was a vigil for life and against abortion. An Italian cardinal led the ceremony in the square and Pope John Paul gave a short homily. When the pope stood at his window and spoke, Bradley, Mike, and I smiled at one another in silence. We had never seen the pope in person before, so this event was not only a surprise but also preparation for tomorrow night's event. The crowd cheered from time to time during his homily. He quoted scripture and reminded us that life comes from God alone and must be held sacred. I can honestly say I like this pope for trying to bring nations together in peace. It's just his views on homosexuality that I have a problem with. Jesus never mentioned homosexuality but did condemn divorce and other things. Yet the church administers the sacraments to people who have confessed to crimes, who are guilty of lust, priests who have been found having sexual relations with women, people who have committed murder, and even child molesters. But the church is unwilling to receive good Christian gays living good lives. I'm not in a physical relationship with a guy, but if I were, I believe in my heart that God the Father, who knew me before I was born, would not bring me into this life only to suffer in hell for all eternity. Hopefully I've shown my friends like Ryan, Phillip, and others that I'm no different than they are in serving God. I hope this will help them and others form a positive opinion about gays in the church.

The next day Bradley, Mike, and I did things in Rome by ourselves. With road map in hand, I set out for the basilica of Santa Maria sopra Minerva, which was erected on the site of a temple to Minerva built by Pompey around 50 BC. I'd read in a library book back in New York that this basilica is a wonder to see if you love art and architecture. My eyes found it very satisfying. The marble floors and high Corinthian columns and the blue and gold light filtering through the stained glass gave it a special beauty and added to the experience of being there. To really see all the magnificent works of art in the museums of Rome or the Vatican would take years. You meet history everywhere you turn.

Before returning to the monastery for noon prayers and lunch, I purchased some postcards to mail to Carlos and Austin House, something I should have done the first day I was here. Writing the postcards out over a cup of coffee in the Piazza della Minerva, I realized it might be a week before anyone got them. But it didn't matter. This place was so beautiful, and I was eager to show on the postcards where I'd been. Rome got a thin blanket of snow that afternoon. After dinner Bradley, Mike, and I unpacked the garments we would wear to the Vatican, with me in the habit of my order and Mike and Bradley in their black clergy suits. The monastery brothers who hadn't approved of our clothing when we arrived started to warm up to us now that we were dressed in our religious attire.

CHAPTER 18

❀

Praying with the Pope

The line for this Vatican affair must have had a little over a hundred people waiting to get in. We'd arrived about half an hour early and were near the front of the line, which gave us a clear view of harsh reality. According to our tickets, the doors would open at 7:00 PM and we would be seated according to our place in line. But the doors to the chapel hall did not open at 7:00. Minutes passed, then half an hour. The Swiss guards gave no satisfactory answers when asked why we were being delayed. We were standing under the outside columns of Saint Peter's Square to the right of the basilica. At about 7:42 we saw the bright lights of four luxurious transport vans making their way across the square. It was now very apparent that we had been made to stand in the cold until this selective group arrived. They exited their vans under police escort. The tuxedos, long gowns, white furs, and diamonds made it clear these people had money. Those of us at the front of the line had to watch this parade of the rich entering the event before us. Naturally this upset us. The tickets did not have assigned seats on them, so I guessed that if these people couldn't be up front, their unhappiness would get back to the pope. For obvious reasons, all church denominations cater in some way to their rich benefactors. None of us said a word, but the looks we gave each other spoke volumes.

Vatican Affair

When the Swiss guards finally let us in, it was a crazy mad dash to get to a good seat. These nice nuns, monks, and priests, whether living in Rome or visiting like us, suddenly became aggressive and fast. Lifting my robe to climb the long staircase leading to the chapel was a challenge. And once I was there I had to stop myself from constantly looking around at the works of art, since I knew that would disturb the people around me. Mike and I managed to get seats next to each other; Bradley was fortunate to get a seat five rows up from us. As the organ started to play a low sweet melody, the people whispering in their native languages fell silent.

Our folding chairs faced a huge door with two Swiss guards posted on each side. The pope's large white chair was on a raised platform to the left of the door. We all assumed the huge doors would open and he would make his entrance. But to our surprise, he came in the back entrance, and as he proceeded to the front he shook the hands of the crowd on the right side of the chapel. Later, after prayers, he greeted people sitting on the left side of the chapel. I could feel the high spirits of the crowd, which seemed to go along with my own. I detached my rosary from the belt of my robe and followed the pope as he led us in the joyful mysteries of the rosary in Latin, English, Italian, and Spanish. During the Hail Mary I felt as if my soul opened up. It was as if I was in a spiritual trance, leading me not only to pray the rosary but also to confirm my faith in God in personal prayer. After the ceremony the crowd of people trying to shake the pope's hand was so dense that some of us stood on folding chairs just to see him pass.

The next morning in my room at the monastery I sat in a chair near the window listening to the bells. This was another of my "truth being real moments." I came to the conclusion in self-examination, which was painful and disturbing to go through, that I no longer wanted to be a part of the monkhood. I'd drifted so far away from the church that I no longer felt a part of it, especially the church's views on gays. I simply could not be a part of an organization that, were I not a celibate monk, would deny me basic human rights because I am homosexual. As the organ from the monastery chapel started to play, I purposely stayed in my room, missing morning prayers. As I continued my self-examination I acknowledged the fact that a celibate life was not for me any more. Whether it was with Carlos or someone else down the road, I wanted physical love in addition to prayer and God. Up to this point I'd avoided conscious realization of my true desires. Maybe there was a part of me that hated to give up the monastic life. When I get back to the States, I decided,

I would meet with Father General and tell him of my final decision to leave the order. Rising from my chair I turned my thoughts to the present.

This was our last day in Rome. We visited the Sistine Chapel in late morning and shopped with the brothers of the monastery for bread near the Tiber River. Toward evening we had time to pray privately, see the sights, and mingle with the brothers in the monastery. Father John caught up with us while we were walking in the cloister. We'd hardly spoken with him, since either we were too busy sightseeing or he was too busy with monastery business. This was the perfect time for him to talk to all of us at once. Father John has a good spirit about him. I must I confess, I wished I'd had a monastery superior like him. "My brothers," he said, "are you all from the same area in America?"

"Yes," we said, "we're all from New York City."

"What are your apostolates? What do you do in Manhattan?" he asked. We then explained our ministry in detail.

Father John became excited in describing the work of his order in Rome. I quickly realized that his order is what my order used to be. "Each brother," he said, "must have sound theology classes and then later consider his talents and decide upon an area of work in the order. We must put everyone's talents to the best use possible. As a superior I find the best way to keep members happy is to let them do works that they are drawn to in the order and the church." Our conversation was interrupted by the sound of bells ringing for evening prayers. Father John announced, "My brothers, tomorrow Brother Jordan, one of the novices, will give you a ride in the monastery car to the airport, thus saving you money and the risk of getting lost on the bus."

On the plane I made the decision to help Bradley in his new project in downtown Manhattan. But I wouldn't tell him or anyone else until I spoke with Father General. All my meditations and prayers have again led me to feel clearly that the confines of monastic life and rules are not for me any more. As a celibate Christian male, I see it as a great sin that the church is pushing gay people away from God by not accepting them and helping them be the best they can be, with good humanistic values in their lives. I am embarrassed when I see some other Christian groups doing this.

The church has always asked straight couples not to have premarital sex or sex outside of marriage. But gays are asked to abstain from sex their whole lives, which is more than upsetting. Gays have the right to good, loving, physical, monogamous relationships like anyone else. Anyone who thinks being gay is a choice needs to be slapped in the face until they realize the pain that gays often face, the hatred, and sometimes the loss of family and friends, in order to grow into the persons they were meant to become. No one of sound mind wants to experience this type of pain. So choosing to be gay is not like choosing a pair of shoes. No matter what, I will always be a Christian and a servant to the poor and dying. That's my vocation. I have to belong to an organization or group that is going to lift me up, not drag me down, in my journey through life. So I decided: once I get settled back in Austin House, I will give the superior-general a call and request a meeting with him, and I will inform Father Doug, Father Anthony, and Mike of my decision to leave the monastery.

Father Anthony arranged for two German volunteers, Mitch and Dennis, to pick us up. Mike and I managed to convince Bradley to stay at Austin House overnight. To have asked Mitch to drive from the airport to West 90th Street, where Bradley was living with some Jesuit priests, and then drive back over to East 116th Street would have involved too much driving. It was already well after midnight and we were all tired. When we pulled up in front of Austin House, the night owls of the community gave us a lively welcome back with hugs and the latest gossip. As we introduced Bradley, we learned that Father Doug had been reassigned to a parish in Darien, Connecticut, as an associate priest. I stopped in my tracks for a moment, thinking the archdiocese moved quickly in removing him. Mike and I of course knew the situation surrounding Father Doug, but Bradley didn't. Sally, William, and Robert joined the conversation and started talking about Father Doug's wrongdoings, but Mike and I shifted the conversation by asking about different Austin House members.

CHAPTER 19

❦

Celebrations and Meetings

On Monday at 11:00 AM sharp, I phoned the monastery and got Father Peter on the line. He made an appointment for me to see Father General on the following Monday at 9:00 AM. According to Father Peter, the brothers in the mother house are interested in how my trip to Rome to see the pope went off.

It took me no time at all to get back into the swing of working at Austin House. Julia and her son who used to hang out with me in the outreach office came in just before noon. She introduced me to her new boyfriend, Julio. He seemed to have a good head on his shoulders as well as a good job working for the city's sanitation department. He boosted my ego by telling me Julia and her son really admired me and had only good things to say.

After lunch I arranged a meeting with Father Mike and Father Anthony, whom I no longer address with titles since we became friends. I was going to tell them that I was leaving the monastery, but I didn't want to put a damper on all the excitement about Bishop Donald Bray coming from Long Island to bless the opening of the three brownstones. So instead I inquired if all things were set in the brownstones, from the electric to anything else that needed to be done. Later, about 4:30 PM, Carlos called from Philadelphia. It was a call I wish I hadn't taken. I played it cool the whole time I talked with him so as not to reveal how love-struck I really was. I hated that he pushed his return date back another month. And when I inquired about the woman's voice in the background, who kept talking to him while he was on the phone trying to talk with me, he hesitated a moment and said, "Uhh, it's Nancy. She moved temporarily to Philadelphia to be with me." He went on about work and money and told me his mother was now doing well. Finally I couldn't stand it any more. I had to get off the phone. It was breaking me up inside. At that moment I was so jealous of Nancy for living and being with Carlos. I made up an excuse and got off the phone.

Austin House has always welcomed volunteers from sister communities in Europe, but the groups who were here from Germany and France created an upswing in communal life. Most people in Harlem were either black or Puerto Rican and had never been exposed to people from foreign countries. It was wonderful to learn about the languages and cultures of France and Germany. And we appreciated how they wanted to learn about African American history and foods. Some people in Austin House were surprised to see the Germans eat what we considered only African American soul foods like collard greens, ham hocks, and cornbread.

After great preparation, the day arrived for the blessing and opening of our Austin House AIDS project. Bishop Gray presided over mass and then we made a procession to each of the brownstones, where the bishop said prayers and blessed the building with holy water. Our celebration was far more than what we expected it to be. As I stood on the steps of the building at 122nd Street holding the small pail of holy water for Bishop Gray, I turned to see what looked like an impromptu block party of neighborhood people and invited members of the New York interfaith association—Jews, Muslims, and Christians—who had come to lend their support. Mother Teresa's order of nuns in their white and blue habits came bearing donations of canned goods and blankets. Many neighborhood people, including some I didn't know, donated canned goods and deposited their loose change in our donation box, which Sister Ruth watched like a hawk. Out of all the buildings we now owned, only the building at 116th Street was large enough to accommodate the social that followed the blessings. It all became too much for me. After about three hours of music, food, and large crowds, I retreated and made my way to the roof. But I wasn't the only that had this idea. Debbie, Sally, Mitch, Robert, and William had all beaten me to my favorite area of the building. We hung out for maybe twenty minutes and eventually made our way back to the visitors. We were stunned to see Father Doug sitting in the community room on the second floor. I don't know what I was feeling for sure, but to see him again just seemed weird. I guess it was only fitting and right that the man who helped start all this be present.

As soon as Father Doug and I made eye contact, he stood from his seat and walked over to me, requesting we speak in private. We ended up in the chapel standing at the back entrance near the organ. He quickly got to the point. "I know it was you who reported me."

I said, "Excuse me?"

"I know it was you, Brother. And I have nothing but bitter feelings toward you."

His body language bespoke anger. He stepped closer. Immediately I took two steps backward. I didn't wanting to drag this conversation out. "Look," I said, raising my voice, "all the evidence pointed to you."

He then tried to insult me. "You think you're some sort of prince around Harlem, mingling and having late-night fun with Carlos."

I stopped him from speaking and asked, "Are you upset because you were caught? Or are you upset from the embarrassment of it all?"

His face turned red, and as he tried to think of something else to say, I turned to make my exit. This was a man who did not come here today to say sorry to me or the community. He just wanted me to know that he knew I had reported him. But he didn't explain how he knew this; he simply stated the fact. One thing was sure, however; this man was not going to ruin a spectacular day of celebration for me.

Two days later I finally met with Anthony and Mike in Father Doug's old office to break the news of my leaving the order. They were sincerely shocked and also disappointed that I was not only leaving the order but also leaving Harlem to go work with Bradley downtown. Silence fell upon the room as I stood to look out the office window. Anthony motioned for me to sit back in the chair, all the while reminding me of all the important work I'd done in Austin House and the community, from the outreach office, volunteer director, and soup kitchen, to helping get our new project for AIDS victims off the ground. Together they managed to break me down, and I agreed to stay on the payroll as a part-time worker while living and working with Bradley. I also agreed to devote sixteen hours a week to Austin House while spending the rest of my time living and working on East 7th Street in Alphabet City downtown.

I purposely arrived in the mother house on Sunday night to announce to Phillip and Brother Andrew that I was leaving the monastery. In the recreation room I answered the many questions the brothers had about my trip to Rome. I spoke to Phillip and Brother Andrew separately about my situation. They each gave me different reasons to stick it out.

"Most vocations go through difficult times," said Phillip.

"But I gave it two months of contemplation before coming to this conclusion. And with the new education rules for brother monks, I no longer desire to be involved with the order."

Brother Andrew tried to be profound. "Brother Luis, everything in life has its limitations."

"Yes," I said, "but I have to have some happiness, especially in the choices I make. It's up to me to grow from the bad ones."

Shaking my hand and giving me a hug afterward, Phillip reflected, "Damn, man, I am the last one left of us who entered together."

I had to make a point of seeing Brother Andrew and Phillip before I had my appointment with Father General. I remembered another rule of the order. If a brother is leaving, he must have no contact with the other members. Preparations for his departure are set in place by Father General. Phillip and I knew this all too well.

I repeated what Ryan did with me and Phillip, writing my name and address down on paper for Phillip so that if the rule about members keeping in contact with past members changed, he could contact me in Manhattan. This, too, was against the rules of the order, so as when Ryan left, we didn't mention a thing to each other for fear of Father General making us toss the notes into the garbage.

Early Monday morning, the day of my big meeting in Father General's office, I spent time in the chapel meditating before prayers and mass. This left me with a feeling that everything was going to be okay.

I knocked on the door. Father General answered in a low tone of voice, "Enter, Brother." Some of my anxiety was taken away by the sweet sound of the organ playing distantly in the chapel. Music always has a calming effect on me. Father General blessed my head with a small sign of the cross and welcomed me back to the mother house. Then he motioned for me to sit in the guest chair near his desk as he sat behind his desk.

I tried to break the ice by reporting on the new works of Austin House. But Father General slapped his desk and said, "Come now, Brother, you did not come all this way to talk about Austin House. I get most of what you're telling me from our monthly phone calls and newsletters." Leaning back in his chair with his hands folded over his stomach, he said sternly, "Come now, Brother, get to the point of your visit." His abruptness shocked me momentarily, but I managed to bounce back. I laid all my cards on the table, everything from my disappointment with the order's new direction to my final decision to leaving the order. Father General struck me as a man who is very old school. If I had made known my feelings about the church's views on gays, which is another reason for my leaving, I really felt he would have shut the whole conversation down and dismissed me. His stiff body language and his coldness gave me the impression this was best. I wanted to make a clean break without any problems at all.

For several minutes I seriously contemplated his suggestion that I get a master's degree in social work. I was already involved in it anyway at Austin House, he pointed out. He almost had me until he said, "You, Brother Luis, would do well working in the office of any diocesan headquarters. I see you as a head director of social work activities, leading a staff of people." I immediately retreated to my original reasons for leaving the monastery. Sitting in some office high above the city, pushing papers is not going to make me happy in the long run. Total everyday contact with the poor is what I desire. And any of the positions this new father general wants for our brothers is totally not for me, and I know for sure others feel the same way. I cut him off when he suggested, "You know, Brother, you could volunteer a couple of hours a week in a soup kitchen or outreach program, if need be."

For twenty minutes he tried to convince me to stay in the order, using the examples of a consecrated life like Saint Francis and Saint Clare. What really made me want to fall off my seat was him using the example of our founder, who wanted our brothers and priests of the order to be totally mindful of the poor. And here he was changing the rules in order for brother monks to have better-paying jobs working as schoolteachers or administrators. These can be good jobs, but you have to be called to them. Anyone forced into it would be unhappy, I think, if it meant doing a job he had no desire in doing. I put myself in this category. It's simple. You have to have some level of desire in your life's vocation and shouldn't just go where the money is. This rule of mine I feel can be broken if you have dependents or are working toward a goal to get somewhere else.

Looking eye to eye with me, Father General suggested, "Brother, what you need is a spiritual renewal retreat. You need to spend a week in the mother house and receive counseling from Father Ray, who's a trained therapist."

His cold manner of expression led me to feel for him. Did he really think I needed serious psychological help because I wanted to leave the order? He became silent and appeared disappointed when I stood up and paced in front of his desk. Stopping about six feet from his desk I said, "Please take my case to the monastery council and inform them of my departure from the order. And please have my papers ready to sign tomorrow." The papers I asked for are formal papers releasing me from my vows and connection to the order. They are then entered into the order's records and a copy is given to me.

I thought it ludicrous when he said, "Brother, you are making a big mistake. Rest today and tonight, and tomorrow morning you will see your serious mistake in leaving the monastery."

"Father, as I said, I spent two months in contemplation."

He moved a couple of feet back from me. Shaking his head from side to side and looking at the floor, he said, "We're losing brothers like you, brothers who just cannot obey and respect their superior, who was elected by the Holy Spirit."

I had to bite my lip. I wanted to say *"You fucking idiot!* Brothers would not be leaving if you and your infallible rules were not taking them away from jobs they've performed for years in the service of God."

He looked up at me and said, "Come back tomorrow morning around ten. I will assemble council members to witness your signing of papers. Before you leave, Brother, remember that you are not to tell anyone you are leaving."

I lied. "Of course," I said, nodding my head.

I quickly went to find Phillip to arrange a final secret meeting. We would have little time for good-byes because of his class schedule at Catholic University. I left a note under his door telling him to meet me around 11:30 PM in the bell tower. Phillip is so cool, sometimes I think he's too cool and worldly to be a priest in the monastery. He made me laugh when he came toward me in the bell tower and whispered, *"What the fuck, man!* You of all people should be staying here. So this is final?"

"Yep," was all I could say. We sat on the floor of the bell tower. I hadn't said anything about having a party like we did when Ryan left, but Phillip had brought a small bottle of wine and chips, all packed securely under the scapular of his habit. I promised Phillip I would get in contact with Ryan as soon as I could. We both wanted to know how he and the girl were doing. It's hard to believe that Phillip, the one who I thought would never become a priest because of his need to have fun and break rules, was the one to stand firm. I could see the strength of his convictions in the way he passionately talked about his studies and the kind of parish he hoped to work in after ordination. After an hour of being silly, drinking wine, mimicking Father General and Brother Stanley, and talking about American politics and the music world, we both stood and hugged one another. Phillip said he hoped I would find what I was looking for in the world.

At mass the next morning, the members of the order approached the altar one by one to receive communion from Father General. Phillip and I made eye contact knowing this was maybe the last we would see of each other. He and other candidates for the priesthood left right after mass for their classes at Catholic University. As we passed one another after he received communion, Phillip nodded at me once and put his right hand over his heart as a gesture of friendship.

Later that morning, Father General, Father Peter, and Brother Andrew were present for my signing of the documents. I approached Father General's desk while the others stood nearby. Father General and I did not make eye contact. This was a divorce, and like many divorces in the world, it was an emotional procedure. Two basic traditional questions were asked of me by Father General before I signed.

"Are you making this choice of your own free will, Brother?"

"Yes," I responded.

"Are you final in your decision?"

Again I responded, "Yes."

Father General pointed out where I was supposed to sign my name. Holding the pen in my right hand, I said to myself, "This is it. Luis." After I signed the documents, Father Peter and Brother Andrew signed as witnesses. Father General handed me an envelope and said, "Luis, here is some money to help you get started in the world." When all was said and done, Father Peter shook my hand and left to attend noonday prayers. I could tell Father General was annoyed when Brother Andrew shook my hand and asked, "What are you going to do next?" He broke in on our conversation just as I began to tell Brother Andrew of my plans to work in Manhattan. Father General pointed to Brother Stanley, and said, "Luis, Brother Stanley will instruct you on what to do from here."

When the door had closed behind us, Brother Stanley coldly said, "I want you to return to your bedroom in the cloister. Disrobe and place your habit on the bed. When you are finished putting on secular clothing and packing your things, your are to leave by way of the back stairwell, in keeping with the order's rule that no one is to see you leave or have contact with you. A taxi will meet you at the end of the walkway in about thirty minutes to bring you to the Amtrak station to board the train for New York at 1:30 PM." Brother Stanley is known for his coldness and rough edges, so I was stunned when, after explaining everything, he moved close to me and put his right hand compassionately on my right shoulder, as if to say "Everything will be just fine. Good luck."

Standing in the dim light of the cloister with the signed papers in my pocket gave me a weird feeling. I thought to myself, I am no longer a member of this group and this is no longer my home. I walked to my room in the cloister for the last time.

With my robes now placed neatly on the bed, I could hear the sound of the organ playing in chapel and the brothers chanting. I knew it was time to exit by the back staircase. I stopped midway down the stairs. Hearing the brothers chanting gave me strength and banished any doubts I had of making it on my own outside of the monastery.

CHAPTER 20

❀

Moving Ahead

As the train neared Manhattan, my anticipation grew greater to begin my new life. On a whim I decided to head over to Alphabet City in hopes of finding the building Bradley is living in and renovating with volunteers. I remembered it was on East 7th Street, so I took my chances and went looking for it. Alphabet City gets its name from having the only single letter streets in Manhattan, avenues A, B, C, and D. Although Harlem gave me experiences rich with my own culture, a mix of African- and Puerto Rican American, the trendy East Village would do the same. It bustled with graffiti artists, musicians, writers, poets, rappers, and painters hanging out in the cafes or in Tompkins Square Park.

Manhattan, like other cities, has problems with illegal drug activity. Walking toward East 7th Street, my eyes captured a group of five characters making quick drug deals. They didn't scare me, but I got the strong impression I should just pass quickly and get to where I was going. On East 7th Street I spotted a run-down building that looked in need of total repair. But it wasn't Bradley's building. A group of squatters had taken over the building. They were laid back and friendly. I noticed some of them were wearing cool hippy-style clothing. This was also the first time I'd seen a white guy wearing dreadlocks, which reminded me of the ones I used to have before I became a novice in the monastery. I asked about a priest who was renovating a building on the block with live-in volunteers. It appeared that Bradley had made some good friends among the squatters. In return for helping him gut and renovate the building, they received canned goods and referrals to Catholic charities for social services to help meet their other needs, especially those who had children.

I was pointed in the right direction by a squatter named Paula, who sat smoking and holding a guitar. In the distance I spotted Bradley dumping some old beat-up furniture into a Dumpster. His surprise at seeing me made me even more pleased with myself for taking a chance and venturing over to the area without knowing the address. After meeting all the live-in volunteers—Mary, John, Dana, Roger, and his wife Pat—Bradley gave me a tour of the four-story building. This was by no means an easy project. Only the first floor and basement had electricity, and only the small bathroom in the basement worked. It had no sink, so you had to wash and brush your teeth in a little room in the basement that had what looked like a tiny fountain of cold water coming out of the wall. Water had to be heated on the stove to get hot water to bathe with. What an eye-opener. I noticed a small kitchen area in the basement which seemed to be in better shape than the bathroom. Everyone slept in one room on the first floor, dormitory style, waiting until the bedrooms upstairs were finished with Sheetrock. The bathroom situation set me back a bit, but I still wanted to help Bradley.

After the tour we both sat on crates in what will be the future community room on the third floor. Before Bradley started to go into the details of the money and supplies needed to complete the building, I surprised him in an unpleasant way with the news that I was leaving the order. Bradley, like Mike and Anthony, somberly expressed his sincere concern. I asked if the offer still stood for me to lend a hand in his new project. This excited him and he jumped up to shake my hand. Bradley accepted the plan I worked out with Anthony and Mike to live and work at both places. But instead of my original sixteen hours, I would be at Austin House from Sunday night to Wednesday evening. And from Thursday to Sunday afternoon I would live and work down on East 7th Street.

I returned to Austin House that afternoon. Back up in Harlem rumors of my leaving the order spread like a wild forest fire. I never knew who spread the news, but one of the few people I confided in had apparently revealed my secret. Actually it was no big deal. It saved me from having to speak to the Austin House community at morning meeting. I've never been comfortable talking in front of a crowd of people. Some people wanted to know what was next for me. Some actually thought my leaving the monastery meant I was no longer a Christian. I assured them that I was still a Christian and that I could do good works without being a monk. My exhausted body was pleased to finally get to my room to lay down on my bed before dinner.

After dinner I collected my messages at the security desk. There was a message from Carlos, asking me to call him because he was returning to Manhattan earlier than planned. He said he'd be back living with his uncle in the Bronx four days from now. For all of six seconds I wanted to toss his message in the garbage. In another of my "truth being real moment," I said to myself, "*Yo! Hey, man,* this guy is a bisexual. You cannot have anything real with him, just maybe sex, that's all. He has a girlfriend. He has a need to be with women and maybe want children. Wake up, Luis. You can never totally have his complete heart. The word bisexual is what it is: *bisexual.* And think about what he stated on the roof that time, that he has had encounters with men but loves women. That should tell you he's not in a confused layover state on his way to being totally gay like you."

During the next five days, my circle of friends became enriched with the few gays in Austin House. It was obvious to me they knew I was gay, or at least suspected it. Dan stated, "Now you can truly live. You don't have to wear that long ugly robe. You can show your legs, maybe even in heels if you're into it." Before, when I was a monk, they'd kept their distance and only discussed work issues. Now that all changed. Justin and Dan in a way became my mentors, teaching me everything about gay culture, clubs, bars, and what style of clothing to wear. Dan is hard to take at times, with his light makeup and feminine ways talking about which hot guy fucked him or which one would be with him tonight down on Christopher Street. His honesty can be brutal, but he is totally real at being who he is. He did make me want to punch his face when he talked about a hot guy like Carlos being with someone like me, referring to my clothing and not meeting his standards of physical looks. I'd forgotten Dan and Justin were among the gays in the building who, along with the girls, wanted Carlos. Knowing Carlos as I do, if he was telling me the truth about not liking guys that were feminine, then I knew for a fact he'd have a problem with Dan's in-your-face personality. From time to time I played the bitch game with Dan if he made a negative comment about me and Carlos, especially in front of Justin. I'd say things like "Oh yeah? He left a message. I've got to call him back" or I'd mention or show off a gift from Carlos.

Justin was more my speed. He's laid back and is not an in-your-face type of guy, though he does constantly wave his hands to get attention. All the stories of the people that come to Austin House have touched me, and Justin's story was no different. Justin joined me on the roof one evening after my personal time of prayer. We laughed at how Dan almost fell during soup kitchen trying to show off in front of some male volunteers. After a good laugh I said, "So, Justin, how did you get to Austin House?"

Justin puffed on a cigarette and then opened up. "Well, I'm thirty-three. I came to New York at the age of twenty-two after leaving Richmond, Virginia." He paused and took another puff of his cigarette. "My parents found out I was gay. Before you ask, Luis, I'm not telling you how they found out. Maybe at some later date, but not now, okay?"

I nodded and said, "Yeah, okay, no problem."

"Being strict religious Baptists, they kicked me out of the house in shame, telling me not to return until I'd left my demonic lifestyle forever. So I made a new life for myself and came to New York. Manhattan was hard on me. With no education beyond high school, I had to work in dead-end jobs, from messenger to washing dishes in restaurants. The little bit of money I made went to feed a cocaine habit. Being evicted from my apartment, homeless, and needing money, I was convinced by a film director in Times Square to appear in gay porn films. I made sixteen films and earned enough to put myself through administrative assistant classes. But I lost everything again to my addiction, which got me in 1985 to Austin House seeking help. And now, six years later, here I am. I've been in Austin House all this time working for the program."

Part of me felt he hadn't moved out of Austin House for fear of losing his support group here. In time I hope he gets his strength from himself, not others.

In such a short time all us down on East 7th Street had bonded. We shared the view that the government should give more money to building affordable housing for the poor and put more money into public schools for new books and repair work. All of our construction work in the building was divided equally between us and trained professionals. Since there was no real privacy, it's a good thing we all get along sleeping in one big room. Traveling back between Harlem and Alphabet City did make me wonder in the beginning if it was going to be rough, but it wasn't. The change of scenery every week gave me the energy I needed not to burn out in my work.

Coming down the steps from the third floor after helping Roger put up some Sheetrock, Bradley yelled, "Luis, come in the front room." Looking up after I dusted off the Sheetrock dust, I saw Carlos standing near the front entrance. All at once my disturbed feelings about him disappeared. It scared me how much love I had for him. One good look or stare from him always broke me down, leaving me wanting to be with him and forgetting any problems that may have stood between us. After my initial surprise wore off, I became embarrassed for him to see me looking so dirty. Carlos, being Carlos, turned the charm on right away with a half smile, offering me some soda from a can he was holding. That led to a hug and a slap on the shoulder. "Yo. It's been awhile!"

Curiously looking around the room, he asked why I'd left Harlem. After I explained my new work situation, he stuck his hands in his jeans pockets and said, "Man, you know how long it takes to get to East 7th Street from the Bronx?" I was afraid he was going to say it was way too far for him to visit me. But he redeemed himself. "Well, if it has to be done, then so be it." It was the way he said it that made me hold back and not show any signs of blushing.

I showed him how we were living temporarily until the building was finished. Judging by the look on his face I could tell he wanted to say something. And I didn't feel it was positive, especially after he saw the bathroom situation. But he said nothing, not one criticism, only words of encouragement. We ended up in our little enclosed backyard. He glanced at a cross on the wall, slapped his hands together, and said, "You guys are doing God's work." I was curious how he found me here. Before I could ask the question, Carlos answered it. He'd gone to Austin House to visit me and had to bribe William with a pack of cigarettes to get him to tell where to find me. Obviously our strict rule against giving out personal information could be broken for the price of a pack of cigarettes and God knows what else.

While Carlos sat on a small bench in the backyard, I excused myself to change out of my filthy clothing. I figured no one up in Harlem had told him that I'd left the monastery. He must have arrived at Austin House at the end of soup kitchen and outreach hours when people are busy cleaning up and in a hurry to get to their personal time. This was good. I wanted to tell him myself. After a splash of water from the basement and fresh clothing, we walked all the way over to Saint Mark's Place and then back to Alphabet City. As we talked about normal stuff—basketball, movies, music groups—the sun started to go down. We ended up sitting on a bench in Tompkins Square Park. It was time, I felt, before the evening went any further, to tell him about my departure from the monastery. His reaction was a little insulting to me at first. He smacked his hands together, stood from the bench, and paced joyfully in front of me, proclaiming, "Luis, people our age are not cut out for that kind of life." I tried to express how happy I was when I entered the monastery, but he waved me off and suggested we celebrate by having a drink over in the Saint Mark's area.

CHAPTER 21

❈

So, You Wanna Date?

Walking around New York University after our drink, I stopped at a vending machine to get a free copy of the *Village Voice*. It doesn't matter who the hell you are, you can always find some type of entertainment in that paper. When I took a copy, the entertainment section dropped to the ground. Carlos picked it up and started reading to himself. We walked into Washington Square Park and sat on a bench; Carlos continued to flip through the paper. The park was alive with the sound of Jamaican performers singing near the pond. Carlos became anxious, starting sentences but then stopping after two or three words. Finally, he took his eyes off the performers and looked back at me. "So, Luis, you wanna go on a date with me?" It was as if the blood and oxygen suddenly left my brain. I couldn't respond. Carlos showed me an ad for one of New York's hottest gay clubs on the West Side. As I read the ad, he leaned back on the bench and gazed at me. "So, you wanna date or what?" My voice cracked at first as I strained to say "Sure." I felt as if I was going to pee on myself, especially when he gave me a handshake and said "Bet" to seal the date. We arranged to meet at Astor Place Friday night at ten. Since I had to be back up to Harlem early the next morning for work, our time together had to end. I expected him to walk me halfway back to East 7th Street, but he walked me the whole way.

I sought Justin's help with buying some new clothing for my date. Jason proclaimed himself the patron saint of gays who needed help being fashionable. After work around four we headed over to some outlet stores on 125th Street. Justin picked out a pair of oversized baggy jeans. When I modeled them for Justin, they fell to my ankles, showing my boxer shorts. I clearly didn't know how to wear them. The second pair I tried on were so long that they caught on the bottom of the boots and I fell flat on my face. The whole situation was pretty laughable. My final outfit was a pair of dark blue slacks, a light gray short-sleeve shirt, and black slip-on shoes.

When I got back to Austin House, Anthony and Mike pulled me into Father Doug's old office. "Luis, we've noticed that since you left the order, your chapel attendance has fallen off. Chapel attendance is of course optional here in Austin House, no matter who you are. But we're concerned about you. Where are you at spiritually with God and the Catholic church?"

This question made me realize that I hadn't fully expressed how I felt spiritually to some people. So I tried to address their concerns. "I am a Christian, but I don't consider myself only geared toward Catholicism. I'm now geared up for studying other Christian and non-Christian groups. I see myself as taking teachings from Eastern and Western religions and applying them to my own life. I've always been open-minded, and if the occasion arises for me to go to a Protestant service or a Buddhist service, I'll go. I believe strongly that God loves us all no matter what place of worship we enter."

When I arrived on East 7th Street Thursday morning, Bradley called an organizational meeting to assess work on the building. The last item on the agenda was Bradley's proposal to have a Sunday night bread run. Waving his hands about, he said, "We can borrow the van from Saint Paul's Church and bring donated cakes, soup, and rolls to the homeless, circling Manhattan and going into areas under the Brooklyn Bridge, Central Park, 42nd Street, the Port Authority, and parts of Harlem." The idea of using a van to bring food to the homeless was not a new idea. We knew that homeless people who are sick cannot always make it to a soup kitchen. We all jumped on the idea. We drew up a round-robin schedule so that no one would get burnt out from doing it every week. On Monday I planned to ask Anthony and Mike if the Austin House volunteers could help, if they wanted to. It'd be good, I thought to myself, if both groups of volunteers could help each other.

Friday finally came, the night of my first date ever. Naturally I was nervous and excited. Roger and Mary boosted my ego. "Luis, you look really sharp." Some people were attuned to my being gay and others were not. Roger was not. I mean, I don't wear a sign stating it for all to read. As I was leaving, Roger said, "Some lucky lady is going to have a good man on her arms." I chuckled as I closed the door behind me.

With each step I took toward Astor Place, I wondered if this was all a mistake. I was insecure about my physical looks and my new clothing. Neither of us apparently wanted to make the other wait. We both showed up twenty minutes early. Carlos looked like a Latin prince. He wore a black leather coat that I'd never seen before, fancy navy blue pants, a black shirt with a long, thin black tie, and black shoes similar to mine. The moment we hugged I wanted so badly to kiss him on the mouth. But even if most people would accept it, I'd still be afraid of someone or some group bashing us. I have to work on being stronger and more comfortable with who I am. Carlos and I hadn't taken into consideration that it was going to be a hike from Astor Place over to the West Side where the club was located, but it didn't dampen our spirits.

The high I felt the moment we entered the club, with loud house music blaring, was one of the greatest feelings I've ever had. The club was packed, a sea of people everywhere I turned. Carlos and I were briefly separated but found each other near the bar. He pushed my money back into my pocket when I tried to buy us some beers. He insisted on buying as I watched the guys dance and enjoy themselves. My insecurities returned when some pretty boys tried to pick Carlos up, ignoring my presence beside him and busting in on our conversation. I thought, *How fucking rude!* Carlos just brushed them off politely. The real challenge was a brash straightforward drag queen, who also didn't care if I was there talking to Carlos. He handed Carlos a flyer. "What's this?" Carlos asked. The drag queen pushed his long wig back over his shoulders and said, "Well, Papi, it's for a party next Saturday at my house. It's a very selective one. I'd love it if you could come." He glanced past Carlos and looked me. "And come alone," he added. Instantly I wanted to slap the shit out of this unattractive drag queen, who couldn't find a dress loose enough to cover his flabby legs. I felt better when Carlos said, "Well, me and my lover," he pointed to me, "will check our schedules." The guy finally left us alone and disappeared into the sea of guys on the dance floor.

Having admitted to each other that we couldn't dance, we were content to stand at the bar people-watching. One sight almost made me choke on my beer. I thought my eyes were playing tricks on me. It was Dan from Austin House with what I guessed was his date for the evening. Dan's outfit for the evening left me at a loss for words. His suit was a blackish purple color made from some shiny fabric that glimmered whenever one of the spotlights in the club hit it just right. Talk about bringing total attention to yourself in a crowd. I turned away, hoping he hadn't seen us, but oh yes, he picked us out of the crowd. His bitch attitude was in full gear. "Hello, boys. What's up? Enjoying yourselves?" Looking directly into Carlos' face, Dan transfixed him. "So, Papi, how's your job?" Dan was both stupid and drunk and didn't give Carlos time to answer. "How long have you been back in Manhattan?"

Carlos smiled. "Not that long."

Fondling the buttons on the leather coat Carlos was wearing, Dan moved closer and screamed over the music. "Are you dating anyone? If not, I'm available." His silly little laugh made me want to kick his ass, just for the hell of it. What really made me mad was him trying to give the impression he and Carlos once had something going. "Papi, you were so good at hanging the shelving in my room. I miss our talks after soup kitchen was done. We have to hook up one of these days. If I didn't tell you before, Papi, I really appreciate how you were helpful at times bringing up my laundry." Dan's flirting progressed. "Carlos, how about coming out to dance?" But Carlos turned him down. I reminded Dan of his date, who was standing behind him looking none too pleased. Surprising Carlos with a bear hug, Dan said good-bye and disappeared into the crowd on the dance floor.

The club was beginning to bore me. Carlos sensed my feelings and suggested we leave. The night air was perfect for walking around Manhattan. It was nearly two in the morning. We zigzagged over the Lower West Side. We talked about everything from God and criminal law in foreign countries to what was in and what was out in the music world. We ended up at an all-night pizza place just off Christopher Street. Afterward we strolled to the pier at the end of Christopher Street. The light of the full moon reflected perfectly off the Hudson River. It now almost four. I told Carlos we'd better go, since I had to work later at East 7th Street. We headed back up Christopher Street. At one point I noticed Carlos wasn't walking beside me. He'd stopped some fifteen feet back and was just standing there. I walked back to him and stared him in the face. "What's wrong?"

I got no response at first. With his hands in his pockets he moved closer. "Don't go back. Stay with me. Hang out the rest of the night, till morning. There's a hotel in Saint Mark's we've passed from time to time. You know, the one that has their cheap hourly rates posted in the front window." My nervousness was very apparent. "Have you ever been to a hotel with anyone?" I shook my head and a quick no came out of my mouth. It's happening, I said to myself, the fantasy guy of my dreams has now finally asked me to stay with him until dawn at a hotel. With all my heart and soul I wanted to say yes, but sadly I declined. It was almost four in the morning and I had work to do over on

East 7th Street later. Moreover, I didn't have a change of clothing, so I feared the other volunteers might gossip.

The distant side of Carlos came out when I gave my excuses. He took two steps back and said, rudely, "You're not a monk anymore." Loudly sucking air through his teeth, he turned and headed up Christopher Street. At the subway station he wouldn't look at me. He just took my right hand, shook it, and said, "Peace, man. Call ya later." For the first time he didn't see me at least halfway back to East 7th Street. I think my no meant something else to him. It is my theory that men and women like Carlos, who are charming and have beautiful bodies and faces, are rarely turned down. His attitude did stun me a little. I thought he'd at least understand my responsibilities.

As I snuck into the building, Mary, whose bed was near my area in the dormitory, scared me by tossing two tiny pillows. "How was your date?" she whispered. Mary turned over without giving me time to answer and whispered sassily, "It's 4:58 AM. Honey, you obviously had a good date and whatever else." I couldn't make out who it was, but one of my fellow volunteers on the other side of the room was trying his best to stifle a laugh.

During noonday prayers I couldn't focus on God. I kept seeing flashes from last night. I lost my place twice as I read the Gospel readings. The rest of the day was no different. A couple of volunteers asked me where my mind was. At 5:15 PM Carlos called, wanting to hangout that evening. The first thing I noticed was his voice. It was low, soft, and very seductive. It was impossible to misread him: the next time we hang out, sex will be on the agenda. We arranged to meet at 116th Street at 7:00 PM so I could drop off a book for Sally at Austin House on the life of Saint Clare. After dropping the book off, I visited Justin's room. Listening to a Janet Jackson album, he told me about his new love interest, Rolando. Rolando was a Fordham University student who, I have to admit, was one hot cookie, next to Carlos of course. The mood altered when Dan knocked and invited himself in. Immediately he asked me about Carlos and the rest of the evening. I tried my best to talk it up without seeming silly or going overboard.

Dan continued to act bitchy. "Man, don't Carlos have a big cock?"

"Oh," I said, "so you two must have had sex."

Making his way toward the door and acting like some big movie star, he turned to face me. "Well, let's just say the ten dollars I gave Carlos one time for cigarettes really paid off."

Holding a T-shirt of Justin's that I was admiring, I assured Dan, "I've never paid Carlos for his attention, and most of all I didn't have sex with him just in order to point a finger and say 'I had that guy.' The difference between you and me is the fact that you use material things to get the guys. And here I am. I got the guy you want and yet he buys me things." I pointed to the sneakers I'd won in the bet.

Dan tried to speak one last sentence, but Justin spoiled his exit by asking him not to continue the drama in his bedroom. After Dan left Justin filled me in on Dan's history and his delusional idea that most men want him. When they show no signs of wanting him, he tries to make whoever they're interested in look bad by playing silly faggot games of "get the man if you can, by any means possible." Justin and Dan seemed to have had conflicts in the past. I could feel the anger inside him as he reminisced about episodes in which Dan flirted with his dates. But soon we turned silly, making fun of Dan, everything from his sex stories to the way he walks into a room seeking attention. Our attempts to mimic him had us falling down with laughter. Justin had Dan's mannerisms down so perfectly that I felt he'd be a good actor. Calming down a little, Justin suggested we both get back at him for all the shit he had done. He brought over his typewriter and said, "Let's write a note. It'll be a fake love note from Dan to Nathan, you know, the Nathan who lives here at Austin House. Dan's all twisted in love with him, but as far as we know, Nathan is straight."

"No fucking way," I shouted.

Justin started typing. It was as if we were high on drugs; we couldn't stop laughing. We purposely made mistakes to make it seem like Dan was in total distress over Nathan. Our finished product was as follows:

"Nathan, What happened, Papi? If I done something wrong, tell me. I miss you so much, baby. I seen you with that bitch up on East 129th Street. I can't stand seeing you with that open-legs bitch. When we made love and you removed the sweat from my face, you said I was the hottest thing in Harlem to date. You used me for blow jobs and that's fucked up. Iz loves you so much. Pleaze come to my room late like you use to when everyone went to sleep. I remember when we both looked into each others eyes. I could tell we had something so real. Get back to me Papi. You know the room number. Totally yours, Dan."

The note, we agreed, should go up where all can see it—on the large community board on the second floor. But after I calmed down and came to my senses, I realized it was a stupid idea. It not only dealt with Dan but also with Nathan. I feared the straight guys in the building might pick on Nathan. "Shit," I said, "we're not in high school. This was just a way to vent against Dan, nothing else." I tried to convince Justin not to go through with it. It was hard at first, but he finally gave in and tossed the note in the garbage.

I rushed off to meet Carlos, who was standing near the token booth. Hearing the downtown train we wanted coming into the station, we exchanged quick hellos as a woman held the train door open for us to board. When we landed in our seats, Carlos smirked and then looked away. "What's the deal?" I asked.

He turned off his Walkman and faced me. "Because you were late, I went to see if you were still in Austin House." I must not have heard William page me to come down because Justin and I were busy laughing and being silly. "Father Doug was visiting. He was sitting on the bench near the door, making me feel uncomfortable with his constant staring." (I for one am glad I didn't see Father Doug. I would not know what to say to him other than hello.)

I made the mistake of joking with Carlos. "You let an old priest govern your actions? Here you are, a tough guy who doesn't take shit from anyone but turns soft at the sight of an old priest." I stepped in a big hole with that remark and realized it immediately from the look on his face.

He raised his voice and pointed to his chest. "I'm no fucking punk. That fat fucker better stop looking at me or I will embarrass his ass in public."

When the smoke cleared, there was a small period of silence. We ended up on West 42nd Street at Pier 83. I'd kept our destination a surprise. When he discovered we were going on a Manhattan Circle Line Cruise, his face lit up. Our tour took us past seven bridges with a skyline of evening lights that reflected off the river below us as we drank our root beer sodas. The boat cruised up the East River, around the northern tip of Manhattan, then south down the Hudson River, passing parts of New Jersey. For awhile it looked like we were miles away from Manhattan.

At one point while we were enjoying the sights with our Walkmans on, we bumped our fists together. Gestures mean different things to different people. To some, this may be a greeting. But for us it's not only a greeting, it's also a way to say "everything is cool in the moment" without words.

After the cruise we ended up on West 86th Street. We'd intended to look around Lincoln Center, but we missed our stop because we were busy discussing Allan Houston's basketball career before he joined the Knicks. Walking east on 86th Street we ended up back in Central Park. We conversed about work and professions while sharing a green apple. We came across the Great Lawn, vast, desolate, and very dark. He seemed reluctant to follow me. "What? Are you afraid of the dark?" I asked. The night breeze swept away the smog; with no haze over the city, it was possible for us to see stars. On a whim I took my backpack off and started to lie on the grass to look up at the stars.

I could barely make out his face, but I knew he was not amused as he turned his body in a circle and made a bullhorn with his hands, yelling, "Are you fucking crazy, man? This is not the time for this." But I just placed my backpack under my head and pleaded with him to join me. I laughed when he said, "Luis, you have lost your fucking mind."

Turning on my left side to face in his direction, I asked, "Come on, just this once humor me. The stars are cool to look at."

He muttered something in Spanish. I asked him what he said, but he refused to tell me because he said it would hurt my feelings. But he did untuck his shirt and lay down next to me, sharing my backpack as a headrest.

With the sound of distant traffic in the background, I pointed out the different formations of stars. The gentle breezes and clear sky made us both feel comfortable to discuss things we'd never discussed before. Carlos turned his head toward me and said sincerely, "Hey, I'm sorry for that time I got upset when you asked why I was hanging out with known drug dealers." I was about to say "It's okay," but I realized tonight was the night he was going to speak openly about his past, one episode after another. He was about to make a big confession. Turning his head toward mine a second time, he made me swear not to tell what I was about to hear. Bumping our fists together, we each said "Bet" to seal yet another deal between us. Carlos turned away, looked up into the night sky, and began to tell the story of how he got to Harlem.

CHAPTER 22

Central Park Confessions

"Back in Philadelphia I belonged to one of the toughest Puerto Rican gangs, a gang that even the police in South Philly were scared to encounter. Some members like me sold drugs for quick cash and harassed store owners for weekly protection money. Our rivals were the Colombian gangs. The turf wars became so severe between us that there were weekly shootings. Fistfights were common, as were stabbings." Carlos paused briefly, then lowered his voice and continued. "Me and my boys made a fire bomb and threw it into the main hangout of the Colombians. No one was killed, but twelve were injured. The investigations of the police detectives were intense. I felt them getting closer to finding out I was involved. My boy Manny was arrested in connection with the incident, based on the testimony of a credible witness who remembered his car and plate number. We used Manny's car in the getaway that night. I fucking decided the only way to stay low was to enter a drug program out of state. I decided on New Jersey's New Start program. I could have gone to another program in New Jersey, but I wanted to be near enough to see my uncle and cousins in the Bronx. And then I landed in Austin House."

I interrupted because I was curious. "Did the police ever question your family?"

"No, it never happened. And my friends and family kept their mouths shut. True brotherhood," Carlos said, "is part of sworn membership in the gang life. Manny got off because the credible witness suddenly lost his memory, for some odd reason."

Using and selling drugs was the real reason he joined a program to get off them. Joining one out of state not only got him away from the gang life but also away from drugs. After his confession, his body language gave me the impression that he was prepared for me to totally trash him for his crimes. And yes, I did to a point. My main question was this: is he totally and truly repentant for all he has done? My answer came quickly as he turned to face me almost shouting, "Man, I wish with my entire being I could take back that night and not have committed such a stupid act. And oh, by the way, Luis, those men you saw me hanging out with by the alley are not drug dealers. They're some of my AA buddies. That's why I haven't introduced them to you. AA is anonymous and no one is to know who you are."

I really felt his sincerity, but I made the point that nothing can change the present outcome. Carlos then gave me a short litany of how he's changed his life, from a good-paying job to weekly meetings for substance abuse and AA. For me it was a bit much to take in at first. But I reassured him that our friendship hadn't changed. He faced a little more toward me after I said that. A minute went by. Then Carlos asked, "Why don't you visit your family more often? What's the deal with you and them on Long Island? You once said it isn't far if you take the Long Island Rail Road."

My family background had always been painful to talk about. But I realized if Carlos could tell me something that might land him in jail, then I could at least deal with my personal pain and answer his question. I sat upright, looked into the darkness, and began telling my story.

"Early on I knew I was different from my other male friends. I wasn't attracted to girls. However, I did all the things boys are supposed to do by society's standards, like baseball, football, and boxing. I think the real embarrassment started when my family couldn't provide a good answer for friends and neighbors who in my teen years kept wondering why I didn't have a girlfriend. I never wanted to be a girl or had a desire for makeup or a sex change. It was just that I felt sexual attraction for some of the guys around me. It was a painful process, discovering who I am. Every time someone brought up the idea of me being gay to a family member, I was shot down. It was a 'don't ask, don't tell' type of situation. They would rather die than say in public, 'Yes, my brother or son is gay, and we love him no matter what.' My reality as a teenager was made apparent on more than one occasion when neighborhood friends of our family would call me faggot to embarrass me. Sometimes my family members stood there giggling themselves. I quickly realized I didn't have their support. Yes, I could defend myself. But it helps when your family is on your side.

"And so over the years I gradually separated myself from them. I didn't feel support for any work or choices I made. My 'truth being real moment' was realizing I used my religious vocation to escape all the bad things I experienced growing up on Long Island. As a celibate monk, I didn't have to worry about anyone asking me questions about women or sex. I really mean it when I say my vocation was true in wanting to serve God. I strongly believe that those who used the word faggot toward me were trying to shame me into living up to their image of what a man is supposed to be."

There was much more to tell Carlos, but I edited it out, not wanting to make the rest of the evening a total downer. And I made a special point of telling Carlos some positive things. "God put very good people in my path. My classmates from high school, Susan, Robert, and John, all knew I was gay, but it didn't matter to them. We all went everywhere together. In school I had no problems. I was popular. I had my artwork, and my grades were good. And many, I suppose, thought I was some straight guy anyway, since girls played around holding my hand and most of us hung out behind the school. If it hadn't been for their friendships, I fear I would have gone crazy dealing with my family."

When I finished speaking, the only comment Carlos made was, "Totally fucked up, man. It seems they cared more about what other people thought of you, as if it reflected on them."

I laid my head back down next to his on my backpack. We were silent for awhile, digesting all that had been said.

The peaceful moment came to a sudden halt. A blaring spotlight swept in different directions across the Great Lawn. The light stopped on us. We were told to stand up by a voice coming over a loudspeaker. We stood and shielded our eyes; we could now make out the police squad car. We stood still as the squad car raced toward us, stopping maybe ten feet in front of us. A heavyset officer got out of his car and spoke to us in a perverse tone. "Well, what you boys up to tonight?" He placed our IDs on the hood of his squad car, and we moved back as he requested. "The city never sleeps," he said, "but this area of the park is off limits after dusk, mainly to cut down on crime and people having sex or dealing drugs in the park." Apologizing to the officer was not enough to get him to say "Okay, don't do it again." Instead he insisted on giving us a ticket, making us pay a fine for violating a law we didn't know about. Carlos nearly exploded when the officer asked, "Do you boys have any warrants?" The officer took our IDs off the hood of the squad car and proceeded to call his dispatcher.

Carlos whispered, "Luis, follow what I do, okay?"

I pleaded with him. "Don't do anything stupid. Just be calm. It will be over as soon as the officer hears we have no warrants."

Just one look at his facial expression, however, led me to believe Carlos might have a warrant out for his arrest. He assured me, "Nothing bad is going to happen if you just do as I do." We both noticed the officer place our IDs on the roof of the squad car as he stood at the driver's side adjusting the belt of his uniform. He got back into the squad car, forgetting our IDs on the roof. Carlos counted to three. My heart was racing as if it was going to jump out of my chest. I picked up my backpack without the officer noticing. Then I braced myself for whatever Carlos had in mind. We then ran fast as we could toward the squad car. Carlos grabbed our IDs off the roof of the car, taking the officer by complete surprise.

We ran toward the eastern side of the park. The cop was screaming for us to come back, as if we actually would. Catching our breath behind what looked to be a large oak tree, we both laughed at the situation. But I soon became serious, realizing that if this cop was really crazy, he could have shot at us. Both of us looked around. We were in no way clear of the police. We noticed a second squad car coming in our direction with its sirens on. Leaving the oak tree we dashed behind the Metropolitan Museum in order to escape the spotlights. The first officer we met had obviously radioed his fellow officers to be on the lookout for us. My fears of going to jail were swept away when Carlos reminded me that the officer didn't have a chance to call into his dispatcher with our ID information, leaving the police with no way of contacting us.

Even though my heart was beating fast, it almost stopped when Carlos pushed me to the ground behind the bushes and jumped on top of me, hiding us from the spotlight that continued to scan the area. Carlos was calm and cool, but I was a little beside myself, wondering how the hell were we going to get out of the park with police scanning spotlights everywhere. Despite all this craziness, Carlos noticed the pebbles under my head were uncomfortable and placed his hand under my head for temporary relief. The sound of the loud sirens little by little disappeared as the police moved to another area of the park. Not a word was spoken between Carlos and me. I felt his heavy breath on my neck. Even when we were sure the police had gone, we stayed on the ground. Our bodies responded to the moment. It was embarrassing at first, but soon became very relaxing and arousing. His soft lips kissed my neck, sending my mind into a fast spin. As I moved my pelvis slowly, he followed my movements. We acted like two kids discovering sex for the first time, humping and kissing one another. The intense rush eventually came to a close. It wasn't over for Carlos, though. He wanted us to do this right.

We brushed the dirt off our clothing and silently made our way to the hotel in Saint Mark's. Without missing a beat, Carlos took care of getting the room while I stood outside. Just my lousy luck. I bumped into Debbie and Roberto from Austin House. They were on their way to meet friends at an all-night diner. As they inquired if I would be in Austin House next Monday, I looked over Debbie's left shoulder and spotted Carlos hiding near the hotel, looking in our direction. It was hard for me to get away from them at first; they tried to get me to go with them. It's not like I could forget my manners and say "Sorry, but I am on my way to have sex." So I made up a story about feeling bad and needing to go out for a walk before I went back to East 7th Street.

Still, I wasn't able to get away from them. Debbie and Roberto could not help but mention the latest gossip up in Harlem. "It's a bad soap opera," said Debbie.

Roberto interrupted Debbie. "Yesterday before morning meeting some of the community members were standing around the second floor, reading a note left on the bulletin board by someone who may or may not have found it in the garbage." Right away I knew it was the letter Justin and I had written to get back at Dan.

Debbie now interrupted Roberto and finished the story. "It was a love note Dan wrote to Nathan."

I remembered that we tossed it into Justin's trash can. He must have taken it out and gone through with putting it on the bulletin board. Thought it was a stupid act to help Justin write the note, I was pleased to hear Roberto say, "Nathan finds it all very humorous. He's been acting conceited, making statements to people, like 'See, all the ladies like me, and so do the men. I'm just that fucking hot.'" I'd originally feared Nathan, being straight as far as I knew, would be ridiculed by the other straight guys in Austin House.

CHAPTER 23

❀

All That and More

When I finally managed to break away from them, I hurried to the hotel, where I met Carlos inside holding the number five key. The room was modestly furnished, with a single bed near the window. Taking off our jackets, we sat across from one another, Carlos in a chair and I on the edge of the bed. I broke the ice by trying to be funny. "Is this where you bring all your whores?" I stupidly realized I was possibly stating I was one of his whores too. His retort, however, did break the ice. "Yeah, you're my hundredth. I got a discount on the room."

We both stood up at the same time and moved toward one another until we were standing face to face. But neither of us touched the other. "Since we both know what the deal is," I said, "who is going to make the first move?" Carlos walked to the door to make sure it was locked, dimming the lights before he came back to face me. "I'm going to make the first move," he said. And with that he pushed me onto the bed and laid on top of me. We had a kissing session that would put straight couples to shame. In the rush of things I accidentally tore a button off his shirt. I also poked him in his left eye. The sharp pain made him sit upright. I went to the bathroom and soaked a towel in cool water. Then I made my third blunder. When I turned around to put cold water on the towel, my elbow smacked him hard on his head.

Carlos sat there with a blank look on his face, his left hand over his eye, and right hand on his head. I wondered if he was thinking "What the fuck have I gotten myself into?" But Carlos just asked me to stand still and relax. He took the towel from my hand and placed it on the chair. Then he started to undress. "You too," he said, "because I'm not going to be the only one naked in the room." His body was as perfect as can be: a six-pack stomach, muscular legs, beautiful olive skin, and a small cross tattooed on the left side of his chest. There was no damn way I was going to get totally naked in front of him. It was cute how he moved behind me and guided me toward the bed, no doubt making sure he was out of the way of any sudden moves on my part. Once beneath the sheet and blanket, I removed my T-shirt and underwear. Any second thoughts about my untoned body were immediately dispelled by his strong hands and gift for knowing what to do and when to do it.

Lying next to Carlos in bed the next morning, I didn't want this high feeling to end. When Carlos awoke, he looked at his wristwatch. It was 7:38 AM. Not much was said that morning, though we often caught ourselves staring at one another. The great experience of the previous night said it all for the both of us. After turning in the room key Carlos met me at the bottom of the hotel steps outside. I assumed he would leave me outside the hotel and catch the subway back to the Bronx in order to be at work by nine. When he motioned with his right hand for me to walk in the direction of Tompkins Square Park, I said nothing. Normally I would have, since I don't let my own feelings get in the way of someone else's responsibilities. But this time I said nothing. Sex had changed things. But what were we? Boyfriends, companions, or just friends with benefits? I'd like us to be boyfriends, but he once stated that women are his first love and that his few encounters with guys never amounted to an ongoing relationship. I cannot be mad at him for that. It's not like I don't know how he feels about relationships with men and women. This whole situation is going to kick my ass, I thought. I've fallen in love with a true bisexual who shows no sign of thinking he might be totally gay.

It had rained overnight and the first rays of morning sun gave the streets of the East Village a golden hue. Surprisingly few people were on the streets. I was always the one to back away first from one of Carlos' bear hugs, but this morning was different. I thanked my lucky stars that no one was around, probably out of fear of being called a faggot or ridiculed for being gay. We bumped our fists together, as we often do when things are really cool with us. Carlos said he planned to call me around six, after he finished work. As we walked away from each other, we played a silly game that I thought was cute at the time. We kept turning back to look at each other, and whoever turned later than the other person was playfully shot.

I returned to the East 7th Street in time for breakfast. I must admit I was a little embarrassed walking to the downstairs kitchen. Everyone knew I had had an overnight date with Carlos. They lowered their heads and smiled as I entered the kitchen, but I played it cool and acted as if nothing was going on. I'm an adult, and Bradley didn't say we couldn't stay out all night.

Bradley rushed into the kitchen and screamed, "I've got it! I've got it! The name of the building will be Shepherds House." Bradley eagerly explained how the building could play the role of a shepherd, bringing in and sheltering people that need help getting off drugs and helping them find the social services they need. The idea was unanimously approved.

The conversation turned to our first bread run that night and the final preparations. Looking at the round-robin schedule Bradley put together for tonight, I noticed my name.

After breakfast Bradley took me aside and asked me to sit with him on the bench in our small backyard. What he had to say reaffirmed for me that he's not only a cool priest but also a good friend. "I feel the need," he said, "to play big brother. I noticed that you didn't sleep here last night. I figured you had a liking for Carlos. I want you to be safe, whatever you do. I'm not just talking about sex. I want you to guard your personal feelings, take it slow." I liked this feeling of having someone look out for me. I thanked him for taking the time to speak to me.

During dinner Carlos called like he said he would. All eyes were on me as a answered the phone, especially Mary's, who sat there with her arms folded and glared at me with a sinister smile. With only one phone line, privacy is difficult to come by in Shepherds House. Carlos and I had work schedules that didn't allow us to meet until Wednesday. We decided to have dinner and made the Brooklyn Bridge our destination. He paused a couple of times. I could tell he was making sure no one was around. He lowered his voice and began to say that last night was really nice, but he suddenly cut himself short. And then I heard his uncle in the background. I couldn't say anything either, for lack of privacy.

Back up in Harlem my first task was to receive Marie, Jon, and Alex, three volunteers from France who would be staying with us for two months. They also volunteered to help with Bradley's first bread run that night.

The van we borrowed from Saint Paul's was cramped. Bradley drove and Pat sat in the only passenger seat. Roger, the volunteers from France, and I had to sit on the floor, along with the large pot of vegetable soup, bread rolls, juice, and sandwiches. The van radio provided good background music for our assorted conversations. All stops were heartbreaking, from Penn Station and Times Square to the Port Authority. Seeing people living in boxes underneath the Brooklyn Bridge was the hardest. Bradley, Marie, and I spent time with a woman named Joan and her nine-year-old daughter Gail, listening to their story of being evicted and living in a shelter that had abusive characters who stole their belongings and what little money they had. Bradley and I noticed the marks on the mother's arms and legs, possibly from a beating. Fearing for her daughter's safety, they left the shelter earlier that day hoping to find something better, but all the shelters in the area were filled for the night. We all agreed we had to do more for this woman and her daughter. Bradley borrowed change from the volunteers to make a phone call uptown to the Sisters of Charity, who run a women's shelter over on West 125th Street. There were no open beds, but Bradley used his status as a priest in the archdiocese and managed to convince the nuns to let Joan and Gail sleep on cots. We dropped Roger and Pat off at Shepherds House and made the long drive uptown to leave Joan and Gail with the nuns. I spent the night at Austin House since I was scheduled to work there the next morning.

CHAPTER 24

The International Meeting

By the time we returned to Austin House, it was early in the morning. My bed wasn't just calling me, it was screaming. It was no surprise to find Justin and the other night owls still up. Looking at one another, Justin and I broke out laughing over the note he put up. According to him, the effects rippled though the building. In one of the morning team meetings, Anthony and Mike asked everyone to be more adult and not be deceitful or vindictive toward people they don't like. Justin gloated over how Dan got teased and ridiculed by people who really thought he wrote the note. Justin led me into the second-floor library to tell me the bigger news. The Austin House international organization holds an annual five-day summit on the workings of each house. Every four years, the main headquarters in London votes on where to hold the meetings. Justin was excited because, according to him, he and I had a chance to be delegates to this year's meeting in Florence, Italy. I perked up, despite my fatigue, when I heard I may be visiting Europe again.

Justin, who had spent more years than I at Austin House, explained in detail what had to happen for both of us to be delegates to the international meeting. We were sitting on the edge of the library sofa. "We have five department heads eligible for election to attend the meetings: Stanley in maintenance, Michael in the kitchen, Robert in the outreach office, you as volunteer director, and me in the business office. Each department head votes on who he or she thinks would be a good representative. In order to actually win the election you have to have two or more votes, and you can't vote for yourself. Justin and I agreed to vote for one another, hoping several other department heads would also vote for us.

Our little strategy meeting was interrupted by Rolando, a volunteer and Justin's love interest. I excused myself, giving them some time together to talk. I had the feeling they'd planned to meet in the library to read up on the international meetings.

In the morning meeting after team reports, Anthony brought up the international meeting. After he explained the focus of the meetings and what it meant to be a delegate, he read off the names of all the department heads in the building. The election would take place upstairs in the fourth-floor community room at three that afternoon.

After lunch I made a spur-of-the-moment decision to visit one of our new buildings for homeless people with AIDS. I must admit, even though I'd scheduled volunteers to work in the buildings, I'd stayed away myself. It breaks my heart to see other human beings suffering and dying from a disease like AIDS, which has plagued the world and taken so many lives, both young and old. I was met by two African American nuns, Sister Ann and Sister Patricia, who greeted me at the door and took me to a small office on the first floor. They filled me in on how many residents they'd had to date and the daily schedule of what's done for each resident. Their long navy blue veils were pinned back and they had on gray aprons. They gave me a guided tour, introducing me to residents who were listening to music and chatting in the community room and to others who were helping with the everyday running of the building. Most of the residents I met showed no physical signs of being terminally ill. And those who were in the end stages had a peace about themselves. "God is here," I thought. I felt a spirit of grace in the building, especially when the sisters led me to the small chapel area in a back room on the first floor. Near the altar I noticed a short list of residents who had died in the program, even though it was such a short time since it started. When I left I thanked God again for seeing our project come to fruition.

I held my regular weekly meeting with all volunteers in the library of Austin House to discuss any issues or problems. This day I saw a familiar scene unfold before my eyes as I sat in my chair. It felt like I was at the United Nations here in Manhattan. I glanced around the room as the volunteers assembled. Many were speaking in English, but some were speaking in their native language. Here we were, people from many nations—France, England, Germany, Canada, Italy, and the United States—all coming together, trying to make the world a little better by using our talents, be it carpentry, cooking, clerical work, computer work, or physical labor. I've been very fortunate as volunteer director in having no real problems with volunteers who are lazy or too homesick.

Everyone here is strongly motivated to be here and to work for the length of time they agreed to be here. Knowing that there is always work to do, I kept our meetings short and to the point. I was particularly glad of this today, since I was anxious to get to the voting taking place upstairs.

I tried not to rush to the fourth-floor community room. Justin and I didn't speak or look at each other, lest we bring attention to ourselves or our plan. Mike presided over the voting process and began by reviewing the rules. Anthony and Ed, a longtime volunteer, handed out small pieces of paper. After writing down our votes, we placed them in a small basket. Ed, Anthony, and Mike took them out into the hallway to count and determine the winners. The administrator of the house automatically goes, so Mike and Anthony had to decide which one of them would go. With the new city contract and the mess Father Doug left behind, one of them would have to stay behind and attend to the regular business of the program. The three returned to the community room with blank stares on their faces. Anthony sat and took a piece of paper from his shirt pocket. It was a fax from the international headquarters in England informing us that our voting process should have been conducted a month ago. Father Doug had apparently misplaced all the information and forgotten to tell anyone. There were loud groans and someone said, "You gotta be kidding us."

After apologizing, Anthony threw another wrench into the meeting. Anyone nominated must already have a passport, since it takes at least a month or so to get one and the international meeting was less than five weeks away. Nothing was said for a couple of seconds as Ed prepared to read off the names of the two nominees. When I heard my name I jumped from my seat, clapped my hands, and announced, "Yes, I have a passport." I sat back down to the sound of their applause. Justin's name was the second one called. But our brief happy moment was crushed—he didn't have a passport. Angered, Justin nevertheless stopped himself from calling Father Doug a fat fucker. All of us agreed this would not have happened if Father Doug had planned it out properly. There was nothing we could do at this point but have a show of hands to find out who has a passport. Roberto was the only one in the room besides Mike who had a passport. So it would have to be Roberto and me going to Europe with Anthony or Mike. We all admired Justin's persistence. He really wanted to go to Europe and was determined to go downtown to apply for a passport. We let Justin have his way: if his passport didn't come in time, Roberto would go in his place.

The topic of conversation switched to a community situation that needed attending to. Stanley, Justin, and I brought up the nasty attitude of Peter Mills, which was affecting every team he works with. The consensus of the department heads was that it was time he moved on and out of Austin House. He hadn't gotten over the fact that all but one of the jobs Father Doug had gotten for him were taken away by Mike and Anthony. He calls Anthony and Mike harsh names no one wanted to repeat. Anthony and Mike agreed that he was doing nothing to move forward in his life. And everyone agreed with me that we should have our volunteer social worker Martin Kean sit down with Peter to help him make out a plan of action for himself.

Returning to the outreach office after the meeting, I faced an unpleasant embarrassment. Four Italian volunteers from the University of Rome had just shown up for six weeks of work. I had totally confused the dates and was expecting them two months later. At the moment, Austin House was filled to capacity with volunteers and residents. But I said nothing to them and calmly asked Debbie to show them to the library until I figured something out. I paced the outreach office, telling Roberto, Sally, and William about my mistake. Sally saved me by suggesting I ask Father Bradley if they could stay down at Shepherds House. That way they could work there some days and also work here in Harlem.

Bradley willingly accepted all four volunteers. Shepherds House is nearly finished, he said. In my absence they'd finished hanging Sheetrock in the bedrooms on the upper floors. I sighed an inner sigh of relief; now I had a bedroom to go to when I stayed there. When I told him my news about traveling to Florence, he said, "You lucky dog. You're always receiving great trips." The new volunteers were very understanding. I think they didn't care where they stayed, as long as it was in Manhattan. Like me when I visit a place I really want to see, they didn't care where they stayed as long as it was clean and safe. The word free made it even better.

During dinner I sat at the same table as Dan and Justin. I zoned out when Dan overly dramatized his travels in the United States. I think he was just trying to compete with me because I was telling Justin about where I'd been in Italy and places we both could visit if his passport arrived in time. Justin's overconfidence about getting his passport had me feeling a little sketchy about him, especially when he refused to give Dan or me insight into how this could be done in such a short amount of time. But Dan and I gave it a rest when we saw our questions were agitating him.

When I woke up Tuesday morning I lay in bed thinking about Carlos and our date the next night. I tend to lose focus when I think about him, wanting and wishing we had more time together. On the flip side, I also think being apart a couple of days or more makes it all the more special when we do come together. After walking Justin to the subway on his way to apply for a passport downtown, I proceeded walking up to West 124th Street to the library across from Mount Morris Park. I repeated what I did for my first trip to Europe. I checked out what looked to be five good books on Florence. I enjoy reading, but it's the illustrated books that give me a good idea where I want to go and what I want to see. The weather was nice, so I walked as far as West 125th Street, past the Apollo Theater. The merchandise of the African vendors intrigued me; there was everything from paintings, statues, and masks to jewelry and books.

When I stopped at the corner of 125th and Lenox Avenue to adjust my backpack, another one of my "truth being real moments" slapped me hard in the face. I did a double take. It was Carlos and what looked to be the girl he's been dating, Nancy. They looked very involved in one another, holding hands and playfully laughing as they crossed 125th Street going north on Lenox. My inner voice told me, "Luis, you can't be jealous. You know the reality; he is not totally yours and can never be, given what he's told you." But I was in shock. When I went back to Austin House, I didn't accept any invitations from the volunteers to go see the movie *Circle of Friends*. Instead I went straight to my bedroom, put on a jazz tape, and laid on my bed. My only recourse was to speak with Justin about all this. Besides being gay like me, he was older and had to know what I was going though with Carlos. And I felt I could lay my cards on the table with him; it wouldn't be like going to confession and trying to be tactful in what I say to the priest, fearing he would say I was going to hell or try to make me feel guilty for loving another man. With Justin I felt I could get some honest feedback on what to do or not do.

Peter Mills disliked the idea of moving out of Austin House into his own apartment. On my way to visit Justin in the business office, I saw Peter telling Anthony and Martin, the volunteer social worker, that he doesn't want to make a plan to move out of Austin House and doesn't need any advice or help. I slowed my pace, trying to hear everything that was said. I heard bits and pieces of the argument. Anthony raised his voice, which was a side of him I'd never seen before, and told Peter he had better change his ways in community life and become more positive, otherwise his job will be given to someone else who not only appreciates it but needs it more than him. I picked up my pace when I heard silence, taking it to mean Peter had backed down.

Justin was flirting with the UPS delivery guy in the business office. I waited as long as I could before I said, "Excuse me, Justin, could I talk to you?" You would have thought I'd slapped Justin in the face. Seeing the look of anger on his face, I had to hold back my laughter. I knew I'd walked in on him trying to see if he could get this guy's phone number and possibly make a date. James (that's what his name tag said) excused himself, smiling as he returned Justin's pen. Justin stood with his palms flat on his desk. "In the future, Luis, do not disturb me when I'm talking to a man, especially a hot man. I know you haven't been out of the convent long, but there are some rules gay friends always follow."

"What did I do?" I asked.

Justin yelled, "You cock blocked, Luis. True friends go away and come back. Unless the building is on fire or it's a medical emergency, you are to never intrude or ask any questions."

I corrected him when he used the word convent instead of monastery. "I didn't make a mistake, Luis. I'm gonna call you Sister Intruder."

Laughing, I promised never to break the rule again. I asked to meet with him after work to seek advice. We planned to meet at seven in the community room on the fourth floor. People go out in the evening, so it's normally empty at that hour.

When Justin walked in I was closing the large windows in the community room in order to drown out the loud salsa music coming from a car on the street below us. Justin spoke first. "I know what the deal is, Luis. It's that boy." I sat down next to him on the sofa. "I know it's about that boy. I know you're in love with Carlos and that Carlos loves to swing both ways. I've seen him with women and I've seen him with you. And I know from Dan that you and Carlos have been to a gay club. I've seen you two talking, and twice I saw you meet up in the subway."

Turning more toward me he continued. "Look, I've been where you are now, and let me tell you, honestly, bisexual men should stay with each other because they understand one another. You, Luis, are totally gay. He is not and he is comfortable with that. Having you on one side and a girl on the other is perfect for him. He can play house with her and come to you in private. He can get from you what she can't do sexually, and go back to her for what she can do that you can't. It's all perfectly clear. If you really like this guy, you have to accept his sexuality, or else move on."

I felt his sincere compassion. He was trying not to hurt my feelings. I could tell he was asking me not to get so wrapped up in the fantasy of thinking I could change Carlos into what I want him to be. Out of curiosity I asked, "Say, Justin, could you elaborate on what you said in the beginning of the conversation, about the fact that you know what I'm going through?"

His eyes widened and he broke into a big smile. My ears were even more attentive; I could tell this was going to be good. He was finally about to open up about why he left Richmond, Virginia. "This is going to sound like a story of forbidden gay love. In 1981 I had a secret love affair with a married man, which was exposed when my parents, who were supposed to be away in California, returned home early and found me and this guy Dylan in the middle of a sexual act. My parents asked me to leave the family home the same day. I see Carlos and Dylan as having the same mentality when it comes to sexuality, in that they're truly bisexual and show no signs of ever crossing over to being totally gay. A woman will always be the object of their desires. I remember those days. I found it hard to deal with loving Dylan, but I wasn't willing to give him up so fast because of the deep feelings that were there. Eventually Dylan didn't want to see me anymore and moved on, finding someone else."

This older gay man I now call my best friend looked me straight in the eye. "Luis, I want you to always be realistic when dealing with any man. If it's good, then it's good. But always remember, a heart can change at any time. Live in the moment, and if it lasts for years, then fine. If not, then you can at least say you had fun sex and all. Never have regrets for venturing into something further if it was good at the time."

After having some personal prayer time in the chapel, I headed upstairs. Cheers coming from the library reminded me that it was game night. When I walked into the library, all the volunteers were either playing board games, singing at the piano, or engaged in conversation. Mixing and talking with everyone gave my mind a break from thinking too much about Carlos. Roberto came in to tell me I had a phone call at the security desk. It was Carlos, calling to confirm our getting together the next night. I almost cancelled, thinking about him and Nancy being together. But then I remembered what Justin said, "Live in the moment and see where it goes." My mood lifted when Carlos reminded me that we were going to the Brooklyn Bridge after dinner. Picture-perfect views of the bridge at night have never disappointed me. Given our work schedules, we decided seven was the best time to meet at the Brooklyn Bridge-City Hall subway station.

I had a great surprise later that evening. Patrick, a volunteer, handed me a letter from Ryan. It was an uplifting letter. "Dear Luis, When I called the monastery to make sure my donation of money had reached the monastery, Brother Max, a younger member of the monastery, informed me that you had left the order but stayed in Manhattan instead of returning to Long Island in order to continue the work you were involved with." Next to this sentence Ryan had drawn a frown face that said, "Oh my God, the holy rule is broken yet again!" This was a reference to the monastery's rule against giving out personal information on past or present monastery members. "I took my chances in thinking that you would be still living in Austin House and got the address from a directory of Catholic ministries in Manhattan. My girlfriend and I are both involved in social work here in Corpus Christi, Texas. We are both getting our master's degree in the field and are very happy with one another. We're going to New York City in about a month for a vacation. We expect you to show us around Manhattan. I'm sure you'll be better than any tour guide."

I wrote him back the same night. I described our works in progress in Harlem and in Alphabet City. I also mentioned my upcoming trip to Florence. I wrote a little about Carlos in response to the last sentence of his letter, "So how's your love life?" And I repeated some stuff I'd already told him that night when he and Phillip and I were in the monastery station wagon making confessions about what was going on in our lives.

CHAPTER 25

❀

Dinner, the Brooklyn Bridge, and More

I caught my first glimpse of the bridge while waiting for Carlos. A stream of cars stretched across the bridge from Manhattan to Brooklyn. I moved out farther from the subway station to get a better view. The bridge's lights reflected off a thin layer of fog that hung over the bridge, lighting up the night sky like some old Hollywood murder mystery. Before I knew it, Carlos was coming toward me. He produced a small brown paper bag from behind his back and waved it in my face. I was pleased to see four green apples, something we both have frequent cravings for. We ate at a seafood restaurant near South Street Seaport. We both had the shrimp scampi, which was so filling that I found myself getting lazy after polishing it off.

Over dinner we talked about his promotion at work to manager, his uncle drinking too much, current events, and my upcoming trip to Italy. I don't know why, but I was taken aback by one of his questions: "Do you see yourself living in the city a year from now?" I answered yes. "The city life," he said, "sometimes bothers me. The crowds, the noise, the rude people—it makes me wonder about the country life."

Putting down my glass of merlot, I looked up and said, "My love affair with Manhattan will go on for years to come, I hope."

Sitting near our table were two older white ladies who looked to be in their late fifties or early sixties. At first I didn't notice one of the women staring at us, not until Carlos dropped a spoon and bent over to retrieve it. I must admit, I was looking at his form in his blue jeans. I thought I was being discreet, until I noticed that one of the ladies across from me was observing me as I looked admiringly at Carlos. Just before he sat up, I saw her whisper something to her companion, and then they boldly looked at us and chuckled. It didn't faze me one bit. I was just glad Carlos was sitting with his back to them. I feared a scene like this would cause him to go over to them and say something so nasty that it would get us thrown out of the restaurant.

These ladies continued to glance occasionally in our direction. Their looks were designed to make me feel like an ant that needed to be squashed. No one makes me feel less than them because of my race, religious beliefs, or sexuality. So I played with the situation at hand. When Carlos wasn't looking at me, I caught the eye of the woman facing me, then pursed my lips in a seductive kiss. I could tell it shocked her from seeing her tell her companion about it. I did this twice when Carlos and the woman's companion weren't looking at me. But whenever Carlos looked at me in conversation over dinner or the woman's companion looked back at me, I acted as if nothing was going on, looking out the window or at the dessert menu on the table. By chance we happened to leave at the same time. Carlos and I were right behind them as they put on their coats. I politely said, "Have a nice night, ladies." The lady that had stared me down rolled her eyes. Carlos caught her reaction but stopped himself from saying "What the fuck was that about?" Chuckling, I moved quickly toward the door with Carlos behind me. I didn't want these women to get angry enough to have the pleasure of having the manager toss us out.

Anyone who has stood at the foot of the Brooklyn Bridge has probably felt, like me, that in terms of creativity and style, it is one of the world's most impressive bridges. There was no mistake. Our legs were in for a good workout, but the walk would help us digest all that delicious seafood. The fog had disappeared, and now we could clearly see the lights of the Brooklyn skyline. We rested at the first arch to take in the view. Looking straight out into the darkness, we pointed out different things to one another. The Staten Island Bridge was far out to our left. The twin towers of the World Trade Center looked like two mountains hovering over the city, yet the Statue of Liberty was so small I could hardly make out its outline. Looking north, Carlos pointed out the Empire State Building and, not far away, the Manhattan Bridge.

Anyone visiting or living in Manhattan should walk over the Brooklyn Bridge if possible. The views, especially at night, are captivating. I find it puts me in a calm meditative state, an effect I noticed not only in myself and Carlos but also in others on the bridge. We amused ourselves by taking in every view possible, looking down and looking up, looking out from one borough to another, and noticing the different types of boats floating under us, the speeding police boats, the Circle Line, and even private party cruises with loud party music. Carlos wandered on a little when he saw me talking to two young Buddhist monks who were visiting Manhattan from Chicago for a two-day conference on Eastern spirituality and philosophy. He seemed to shy away from them, which reminded me of his opinion that young men and women should not adopt such a lifestyle. He can't be moved from this type of thinking, so I never bring religion up out of respect for his views of the religious world.

We took a second break on the second arch of the bridge. I already knew a look from someone can speak volumes, like the ladies in the restaurant who tried to make me feel small with their stares. Now Carlos began giving me flirtatious looks. Eventually he grabbed the left shoulder of my jacket and drew me closer to the arch of the bridge. Even without an explanation, I immediately caught on to what he wanted to do in this very public place. Carlos could see if someone was coming behind me, and I could see if someone was coming behind him. After a quick jog around the arch to make sure no one was on the other side, he recalled our conversation in the hotel room. I had said, "Well, we both now know we like each other, so who's going to make the first move?" And just like that night, he stepped face to face with me and announced he was going to make the first move.

We kissed, but it was only half a minute before I noticed joggers coming in our direction. We skipped having dessert at TCBY and made straight for the hotel in Saint Mark's. Incredible. That was all I could say after the rush of satisfying our desires. We lay in the semidarkness on the floor, reminiscing about things like funny points in Godzilla films, who has the highest jump in basketball, and hip-hop music. Carlos has never been out of the country, but he listened attentively, which I liked, when I talked about Europe's art and artists, and my participation in the upcoming international meetings in Florence. It didn't go over too well when I tried to leave. He wanted me to hang out all night. He just couldn't understand where my thinking was coming from. I said it was cool being like this, but I couldn't make a habit of staying out all night. I don't want to deal with or create any gossip at Austin House or have people at Shepherds House ask me where I've been all night. Carlos even went so far as to actually think up a lie about situations like this. He said if I am scheduled to be at Austin House and we are together for the night, the next morning I should just say I spent the night at Shepherds House, and vice versa. The perfect evening soured. We irritated one another, each trying to convince the other about what's a good idea and what's not. My whole thing is not to go overboard with staying out all night. It's not like I live alone and there's no one to question me when I come in the next morning. As I dressed, Carlos acted like a child who wasn't getting his way, greeting anything I said or asked with stony silence. I left him lying naked on the floor with only a sheet from the bed covering his lower body.

I called him the next evening. I had a gut feeling Carlos was there, but his uncle said he was out. It could have been a bad phone connection, but I thought I heard whispers in the background. Or perhaps his uncle is just not good at telling lies, because I got an uncomfortable feeling as he spoke. Whatever the case, I certainly got to see more of Carlos' childish side. He waited two full days before calling me back. But I played it cool and showed no sign of anger when he finally called. I was more irritated than angry. I wanted to show him I do have a life outside of our running around Manhattan. He finally admitted he was still upset about that night. My feelings went from irritation to impatience. I snapped at him. "Carlos, you gotta realize other people have feelings. Stop playing mind games like choosing not to call me back because we had a disagreement. Stop acting like a little bitch." I bit my bottom lip after I said that. It was not premeditated at all. I couldn't believe I'd actually said it.

Carlos was angry. "No one speaks to me that way. I'd fuck anyone up for saying that to me."

Strangely enough, I patted myself on the back for successfully breaking him down. The mood of the phone call changed very quickly. "You'll have to use another word," I said, "because 'fuck' has already been done."

I was about to whisper things we intimately did in the hotel room, but he stopped me. "Luis, just don't get me so fucking worked up. Look, I have to work tonight and I don't want to go to work thinking about such things."

We agreed this friendship shouldn't be overshadowed by sex, as if that were our main thing to do or talk about when we were together. "Sorry, but I can't see you this coming weekend either. My uncle and cousins and I are going to Atlantic City to gamble. We're gonna stay in a cheap hotel four blocks from the boardwalk." I felt jealous, knowing it was very possible that Nancy was going as well. Of course, as usual, he didn't mention her, and I was at the point of not bringing her up at all.

The next day at Austin House we received a visit from Rosalind Hamlin. She stopped by to see how the program was doing and chatted with Anthony and Mike in Father Doug's old office. Roz, as she's known to her closest friends, is one of Manhattan's richest residents. Her father was a British diplomat and her mother had distant ties to England's royal family. I've become so fond of this woman; she's one of the few people, besides Justin, who I want to have as a friend. She's in her mid-seventies and looks very good, judging by what you read in New York's society papers. Some might think because she is a woman of means, she shouldn't go into certain areas of the city or mix with the lower class, but she breaks the mold. She is her own person. And I might add, she loves gay men. Justin, Dan, and I go crazy when she is here. Her wit and charm have us doubling over with laughter. It's no secret that if she stops by, there's a check for our program in her purse. Some may simply see dollar signs when she's here, but I see a lovable woman who stuck by us through all the Father Doug garbage. Unlike some other benefactors, she didn't choose to take her money elsewhere. (Apparently trying to keep secret what Father Doug had done did not work. I tried to put it out of my mind, but in some religious circles this was the hot topic of the year, besides allowing gay marriage in America.)

Less than a week before I was to fly off to Florence, Justin came rushing into the dining room to show his passport. We were rather surprised. Anthony and I looked at each other. I could tell we were both wondering if the passport was real or if it was a forgery made at one of those shady places downtown. I had some idea of what to look for on a real passport since I had one of my own. If this was a fake, then it was the best fake passport ever made. The government envelope it arrived in proved it was genuine. Anthony took this opportunity to announce that he and Mike had flipped a coin. Anthony won and would be taking the trip with me and Justin. Roberto was shocked. Like the rest of us, he thought there was no way Justin could get a passport in less than five weeks. After he'd been congratulated by all the department heads, I pulled Justin aside. "So tell me, Justin, what's the deal? How did you get a passport so fast?" Well, I was sorry I asked. It seems Justin knew a guy named Sam who worked as a supervisor in the passport office. Justin had known him for years from the clubs and bars near Christopher Street. Sam's been wanting, let's say, to be with Justin for a long time, which Justin found disgusting, because Sam is very unattractive, older, balding, and his belly hangs out over his belt. To make a long story short, he did the deed with this man, in exchange for which his passport papers were expedited. My face must have expressed my shock. As he explained while holding up his passport, this was business and now we both are going to Italy.

Later in the evening while lying on my bed listening to a Nina Simone cassette, Anthony knocked on my door with a faxed copy of the itinerary for the international meeting. One thing is for sure from looking at it, this trip would not be like my first trip to Italy. The first trip was for pleasure; this one is more business. It looked like it would be difficult to squeeze in any sightseeing, mainly because we would be there for only five days and there were meetings scheduled throughout the day. And on several evenings there would be socials where people from various countries could get to know each other. Anthony said we would meet the next morning to determine how to present to the international conference the work we do here in Harlem for the poor.

Unable to sleep, I left my room to get a breath of fresh air on the roof. The night owls—Debbie, Sally, Ed, and Roberto—were up there reminiscing about unforgettable characters who'd lived in Austin House. They were drinking sodas, eating potato chips, and smoking cigarettes. Sally's small radio was placed on the edge of the roof playing jazz. I raised my arms to overdramatize my dismay at finding a party had been planned and I'd not been invited. Sally handed me a root beer and gave me a quick kiss on my left cheek. Ed let out a big sigh of relief: Peter Mills will be moving out that coming weekend. He will still have his job here as security supervisor during the week, but he won't live here. Roberto and Debbie clapped their hands and, taking the cigarettes from their mouths, shouted "Thank you, God."

I had another "truth being real moment" while observing them laughing and joking with one another and showing affection with hugs. It hit me: this is my family. The people at Austin House and Shepherds House accept me just as I accept them. Many gays live in a society where they feel alienated because of who they are. I thanked God for being surrounded here in Manhattan by supportive friends.

After morning prayers I met Justin and Anthony in the office for our planning meeting. I was thankful I had such great people to live and work with. Our meeting went smoothly, and in no time we knew who was going to do what and when. Anthony would cover our history in Harlem and tell how we adjusted over the years to the needs of the people by having not just a soup kitchen and pantry but also GED and job training programs for ex-convicts and homeless people who were looking for a better life. He would also talk about how they live in a community within the building and how we provide structure to help them help themselves.

Justin will follow Anthony in talking about the business end of Austin House, giving a detailed report on monetary donations and where the money goes and how it is used in the community. He and Anthony will also shed light on the city funds we now receive, emphasizing that we pay community members a salary for the work they perform and give them a chance to save money before leaving the Austin House program. This segment on funding worried me. The Austin House organization has a rule against receiving government funds, as doing so can destroy our community life if the government tells us what to do and when to do it. Hopefully, when people in Florence hear that nothing major has changed other than the fact that we cannot advertise religious services, it will put their minds at rest and allay their fear that the main goals of the organization in Harlem were not compromised by Father Doug's contract with the city.

I will speak on the international volunteer program of workers, our three brownstone buildings for homeless people with AIDS, and our Sunday night bread runs that bring food to homeless people. I will of course give credit to Bradley for starting this Sunday project with the help of volunteers from Shepherd House and Austin House. I also had a good idea, which went over well with Anthony and Justin, that we should create something visual. I volunteered to spend the next three days assembling pictures from our files to display the works we do here on a daily basis.

Justin beat me to mentioning concerns about the busy schedule of our trip. All three of us felt the same, that it would be a shame to travel to Florence and not see the beauty of the city. Anthony suggested we get to Florence two days before the first meeting is scheduled and also stay one day after the conference ended. This would give us time for sightseeing and anything else we wanted to do. Justin and I went along with the idea. Anthony knew more about airline travel offers and would try to make new arrangements to leave New York in four days. I would contact our sister community in Florence to ask if coming to Italy two days early presented a problem.

I returned to the outreach office to work with William and Roberto. They were trying to separate two prostitutes who were having a fistfight over some belts in the clothing room. Once the situation was under control I sat at my desk and prepared for a shipment of canned goods. This was one of the rare times when our pantry was overflowing, but as a rule we never turned down a gift of canned goods. If we had a space problem, we just donated them somewhere else. We didn't want to give donors the idea that we didn't need canned goods, otherwise we might never get stock for the pantry.

Because of the time difference I had to wait to call Florence in order not to wake anyone up when I called. The administrator in Florence gave us the okay to arrive early. I immediately informed Anthony so that he could revise our travel arrangements.

CHAPTER 26

To Bless and Sanctify

Today's afternoon mass in Austin House was celebrated by Father John, a Haitian priest. Local priests had invited Father John to visit Manhattan to see our programs for the poor and the other work we do in the archdiocese. His sermon on work as prayer in action moved and uplifted all who were present. When he knelt before the altar, summoning all holy spirits, I felt his sincerity and spirituality. He lighted the incense, and while the old chapel organ played softly, we approached the altar to receive communion from his hands. I truly felt God in our midst.

After the service Sally, Ben, Eric, and I volunteered to accompany the body of a homeless man to be buried in a city plot for unknown persons. Father John overheard us talking about meeting with city morgue personnel and decided to join us in our ride over to Brooklyn for the actual burial. We all knew the homeless man from his daily visits to our soup kitchen, pantry, and chapel services. He was a quiet man who didn't speak much and never gave us his real name or said where he was from. We got wind of his death from police investigators who came to us showing a photo of him. They were trying to find out information on him and his next of kin. He died of a heart attack while sleeping in Mount Morris Park. Sally called the city morgue and arranged to bury him in a city cemetery. We went to the cemetery to have prayers and a period of silence at the grave site in Brooklyn.

We were met at the cemetery by two young men from the city morgue, Jim and Danny. They were both surprised. They had taken bodies of unknown persons to be buried by the city in the past, but had never had people who really knew the deceased come and pay their respects. As Jim and Danny carried the plain pine coffin to the grave site, we were disconcerted by what we saw only six feet in front of us. There were about ten coffins stacked on top of each other already in the grave; the coffin of the man who used our services at Austin House was placed atop them. Though it stunned us at first, Father John offered us comforting words. "Everyone in the grave may be unknown to us and the city," he said, "but God knows each of them and in his grace and by our faith has given them rest. Whatever their worldly problems may have been, they have now been released into a higher state of being and are now truly with our Lord, resting in grace and peace." After observing a few minutes of silence, we looked toward the skyline of Manhattan, and as the sun set over the city, we departed in silence for Austin House.

CHAPTER 27

Before I Go

Two days went by. Carlos and I were too busy to see each other. In fact, Carlos was so busy in his new position as manager that if I called him or he called me, we couldn't talk long.

The next night Justin, Anthony, and I would fly off to Florence. Our plane was scheduled to depart at 9:35 PM from JFK airport. Carlos and I made arrangements to see each other that afternoon for a movie and coffee near Astor Place. We saw a matinee showing of *Boys on the Side*. We knew nothing about the film other than that my favorite actress and comedian, Whoopi Goldberg, was in it. Afterward we walked in the drizzling rain and talked about how good the film was, how it depicted friendship in good times and bad times. Carlos called it "deep"; the film had explored some real issues, issues people have to face in life whether they want to or not.

Our conversation in Starbucks at Astor Place was also deep. We discussed some serious social issues in America. I had to agree with him, the rich get richer and the poor get poorer. What our government needs to do is tax the rich more and raise the minimum wage for workers across the country. Glancing at his wristwatch, I noticed it was 2:34 PM. "I leave in four hours for the airport," I said.

Carlos, being Carlos, didn't miss a beat as he took a sip of his coffee, put the cup down, and then raised his eyebrows up and down quickly. "A lot can be done in just two hours," he said. There was no way to misread what he wanted to do. He looked out the window toward the subway and said, cutely, "Saint

Mark's is only a couple of blocks away." He knew as well as I that our hotel was only a short walk from Astor Place.

All I remember was lying next to one another on the bed after it was all over, me looking up at the ceiling and him smoking a cigarette. We looked at each other at the same moment and began laughing. We both remembered our phone conversation about not having sex every time we meet. I thought maybe our desires would have calmed down a bit, but I guess not. Our time together was as golden as other times had been. We lay there listening to the sounds of the people, traffic, and music of the street below our window. In fact, we were so comfortable lying naked under the sheets that we fell asleep. A loud truck horn woke me. I screamed "Fuck! Fuck!" as I noticed the time. It was 7:25 PM. We dressed quickly. Carlos turned in the room key and I went to the nearest pay phone to call Anthony and Justin. Fortunately, they hadn't left for the airport yet and were waiting for me. I realized I couldn't get back to Austin House in time to go with them to the airport, so I followed Carlos' advice and asked Anthony and Justin to get the passkey to my room, get my passport and three packed bags, and meet me at the airport. We then flagged down an unmarked taxi. We had no way of knowing if the driver was trying to rip us off by asking for fifty-five dollars. Between us we didn't have the money. Seeing my anguish over the possibility of missing the plane, Carlos slapped me on the shoulder and said he could fix the situation in just a couple of minutes. Carlos asked the driver not to leave and hurried into a shop near the hotel. It didn't register at the time why he went into that shop. I was just thinking about how to get to the airport. He came out counting eighty-seven dollars in his hands. He took ten and gave me the rest. While the taxi driver screamed "Are we going?" I was yelling at Carlos, "*No fucking way!*" He'd hocked the gold ring from his right hand. Everything happened so fast after he gave me the money and I jumped in the taxi. After I calmed down I felt stupid because in the rush of things I hadn't property thanked him for what he did for me, giving up something of personal value to help me be happy.

CHAPTER 28

❀

Making Our Way to Florence, Italy

JFK was a madhouse. People were going every which way, and I didn't remember my departure gate. A TWA flight attendant directed me where to look for departure schedules. Arriving at gate ten, I found Justin and Anthony waiting for me. The three of us breathed a sigh of relief. It was perfect timing. It was 8:53 PM and our flight was scheduled to leave at 9:35. As we were checking our bags, Justin waited for a moment when Anthony had his attention elsewhere and whispered, "You didn't button your shirt right." Then he taunted me. "Did you even shower before coming to the airport?" He clearly assumed Carlos and I had been together. I chose not to comment. Instead I got Anthony's attention and thanked them both for taking the time to get my passport and bags from my room. As I settled into my seat on the plane, I could smell Carlos' cologne, which had rubbed off on me. It gave me a very pleasant feeling.

I awoke seven hours later. "Beautiful" is all I could think to say when I looked out the window of the plane. It reminded me of my first trip over the Atlantic. Looking down I could see fast-moving clouds under the plane and ships in the distance on the ocean. Keeping in mind all those in Harlem and in lower Manhattan, I prayed my morning prayers while Justin and Anthony slept.

An added bonus was the train ride from Rome to Florence, which would take us through Spoleto, Perugia, Siena, and Figline Valdarno. I was amazed at the old-fashioned trains still used in some European countries. We had to step up onto the train holding onto a railing for balance. Our tickets may have been second class, but to us it felt like first class. We shared a compartment with an elderly couple from Germany. All three of us declined their offer of food, knowing we had enough money to buy our own, but Anthony and I did accept a cup of the beer the couple offered us.

Justin and I were feeling adventurous, so we left Anthony and the German couple and literally walked the length of the train from one end to the other. We encountered some interesting and not-so-interesting people. Two cars down from us we came across a crowd of young Italian soldiers singing. We were surprised to see them drinking wine out in the open and inviting us and other passengers to drink with them. I hesitated at first, but not Justin. He handed me a cup of wine. I could tell from his furtive glances that he wanted to hang out with these good-looking soldiers. And I have to say, I quickly settled into talking and drinking with them. No more than fifteen minutes had passed before I caught Justin and a soldier glancing at one another. I pretended not to notice when the soldier nodded for Justin to follow him. I stayed put, enjoying conversations about American sports and describing New York to a young French couple. Justin returned twenty-five or so minutes later looking flushed and acting giddy. As he began to drink a cup of bottled water, I said, "So, Justin, did you shower before coming back here?" He immediately choked on his water. He whispered, "Is it that obvious?" I said nothing.

The next group, one car over from the soldiers, was not so inviting. Three older Italian men who looked to be in their seventies and a boy maybe seven or eight years old didn't even politely say hello in response to our hello. Our behavior while passing them wasn't out of the ordinary. Justin couldn't keep his thoughts to himself. "Didn't your mothers teach you politeness?" he quipped. They obviously didn't understand English. I was glad of that. Their cold stares gave me the impression there would have been a fight if they knew what Justin had said.

Another train car over, however, we got a surprise that really made our day. Rosalind Hamlin, our friend and benefactor, was standing by one of the large windows in the passageway smoking a cigarette. She screamed our names just as we shouted hers. We explained why we were in Europe, and she told us about her new boyfriend, Mark Hernandez. He walked up behind her, giving her a glass of wine, and she introduced us. He was a handsome friendly man from Barcelona who looked to be in his seventies. They were on their way to his villa outside of Siena for some privacy and rest. They invited us and Anthony to have dinner with them in the dining car. Justin and I jumped at the idea, knowing that an invitation from Roz meant a first-class evening. She separated herself from Mark to hang out with us for a while. Being a woman of means, she had visited every major city in Europe and was able to give Justin and me a little history of each town and city the train stopped at or passed through. This eased my disappointment, for I had wished the train would stay stopped for awhile in some major cities, long enough to give tourists like us a little time for sightseeing. But the train only spent twenty to twenty-five minutes at each stop, giving people just enough time to get on and off before proceeding north on its way to Florence. Roz and Justin talked about the handsome men on the train. I guess I was too quiet and didn't join them in talking about men, because they both advised me to loosen up a bit and to get out there, meet some men, and see what the world has to offer. The conversation shifted to the art schools and museums of Florence.

Roz continued to entertain us at dinner, telling us stories from her childhood and why she chose to live in Manhattan rather than London. Mark also contributed to the conversation, telling us about growing up in Spain and his family's export business. I was pleased to see how interested he was in our backgrounds. Sometimes I've felt rich people are only interested in having people marvel at them. Knowing Roz, and now Mark, I concluded that I shouldn't generalize. All rich people are not the same. Our meal consisted of tortellini soup, pasta with a sauce of heavy cream, shrimp, and mushrooms, and the perfect white wine. The meal was so filling that none of us even looked at the dessert cart. It finally hit me at dinner who Roz sometimes reminded me of. It's one of England's famous actresses, Maggie Smith. She and Roz could be sisters. Her mannerisms, the English accent, and her physical looks—they could have been twins separated at birth. After mentioning this, I was happy to hear that Roz liked Maggie Smith. Roz and Mark got off the train in Siena. As they said their good-byes, they promised to see us next month back in Manhattan for the grand opening of Shepherds House.

By the time we arrived in Florence, it seemed as if we'd spent two full days traveling by train. We were met by Franco Bennetti and his brother Marco. We couldn't miss them; they were holding up a sign in big red letters saying "Austin House Harlem." I didn't even look at Justin. I knew he was thinking the same thing I was. These brothers, who appeared to be in their mid-twenties, looked more like male models than a couple of manual laborers working at an Austin House in Florence. Justin, who was more attracted to Marco, was not happy to learn that the woman driving us to Austin House was Marco's girlfriend.

After we'd put our bags in our rooms and rested a bit, Franco gave us a tour. The setup of this Austin House was not too different from ours in Harlem. The offices were located on the first floor along with the dormitories for the homeless. The single bedrooms of people living in the community program were on the upper floors. Judging by what I saw out of my bedroom window, we were located near the Basilica Santa Maria del Fiore, the cathedral of Florence, whose famous dome helped me get my bearings on my pocket map.

It was no surprise to find that other members of the organization had shown up a day or two before the conference began in order to get in some sightseeing and visits to museums and landmarks. Each delegate received a memo from the international secretary saying that she would type up all the ideas arising in our meetings so that we could use them to guide discussions when we returned to our home programs.

The next morning I awoke to the sound of bells, reminding me of when I was in Rome. I opened the large old shutters to my bedroom window. It felt so good standing there with the sun and warm breezes playing upon my half-naked body. It must have been a good minute before I opened my eyes. Much to my embarrassment, I saw Franco looking up at me. It's not the fact that he saw me naked from the waist up. It was the facial exercises I'd been doing, which must have made me look like I was some deranged crazy person. He nodded and said hello, and I returned the greeting. Then he sped off on a motorcycle wearing a backpack. Judging by the medium-size drawing pad I saw sticking out of his backpack, I guessed he was an artist or an art student.

During breakfast we became acquainted with more members who lived in the Florence community and some local teens from the Basilica di San Lorenzo who volunteered once a week. The students—Daniel, Isabella, Andrew, Joseph, Emma, and Jacob—were very good to us. They showed us on our maps where to shop and eat good food, and where to find the best views of the city. Because Daniel and Isabella were both art students and shared my love of the art world, I was drawn to them. My hopes came true when they volunteered to take me to some museums in the area, suggesting we meet the next morning around 9:30 and head over to the Bargello, a museum located on the other side of the city. Anthony informed us that he would not be going sightseeing with us. His day would be spent catching up with some friends who were priests in a Dominican monastery. Since Father Doug was the founder of Harlem's Austin House and had been its administrator for so many years, many delegates asked us about his sudden exit. Prior to coming we'd come to the consensus that we would only say he had retired and was working part-time in a parish in Connecticut.

Justin and I set out on our own to see the city. As we were leaving we bumped into Franco, who asked us if we'd slept well. Justin, who seemed to be in "man alert" mode, made me uncomfortable. He flirted openly with Franco, commenting on everything from his short leather jacket and cologne to his long curly black hair tied in a ponytail. I guess Justin felt since he couldn't succeed in getting the attentions of Marco, then why not go after his brother Franco, who is equally as handsome and charming. Though I'd known Franco less than forty-eight hours, I felt he was no stranger to having men and women come on to him. I could tell by his relaxed mannerisms, half smile, and his quick thank-yous to Justin's compliments. As Franco took his backpack off, his art pad fell onto the steps, exposing some of his personal drawings. In amazement I commented on his handling of light and shadow and his use of charcoal. He seemed bashful at first but became more at ease when I mentioned some master artists. Even without looking, I knew this scene was not to Justin's liking. As Franco and I briefly discussed which artists and styles most influenced our own drawings, Justin made one last attempt to get Franco's attention by pretending he was a real art lover who often attended openings in Manhattan. Knowing this was a whopper of a lie, I turned my head and tried to make my chuckling seem more like coughing. If Franco hadn't caught on right away, he certainly saw through Justin after he asked him some basic questions about things like impressionism and works by Michelangelo. Justin struggled to answer by replying to each question with a question of his own. I almost stepped in to help him, but I was having too much fun watching him drown in a subject he should have just left alone. To hide his embarrassment Justin left us quickly, saying he suddenly remembered he had to go ask Anthony a question. Justin's so-called rule against disturbing a gay friend when he is talking to a good-looking man was beginning to look as if it was only legitimate when he's the one actually talking to a good-looking man. After conversing more with Franco about art, he too offered to show me what Florence has in the way of art. I was right in guessing he was a student at one of the art schools; he was hoping to become an art teacher or a museum curator. We agreed to meet that afternoon around two and visit the museum of San Marco.

Enjoying the city as any tourist would, Justin and I came to the Ponte Vecchio, Florence's famous bridge. The Ponte Vecchio has shops built on it which sell a variety of goods, including clothing, food, wine, jewelry, and souvenirs. Standing in the middle of the bridge gave us a beautiful view of the city. On this particular day there was a rowing team in the Arno River. I stopped to purchase a green apple from a fruit vendor while Justin purchased some mementos. We then walked all over before coming to the Palazzo Vecchio. We toured parts of the large building, seeing the famous chambers of Eleonora of Toledo and the quarters of Leo X, where the present mayor has his reception rooms. The square in front of the building is a rather large impressive space with many statues, including a reproduction of Michelangelo's *David,* the *Fountain of Neptune* by Ammannati, several statues by Cellini, and *The Rape of the Sabine Women* by Giambologna. The performing artists in the square added to the open-air scene.

After lunch we continued walking around, going in any direction that looked good at the time. Finding a coffee shop near the Arno River, we rested and examined the purchases we'd made. We returned to our sister community shortly after one. Waking up from what was to have been a short nap, I glanced at my bedside clock to see that it was already ten minutes past two. Jumping up from my bed, I gathered my things and looked out my bedroom window. I was relieved to see Franco waiting for me, standing next to his motorcycle and calmly reading some papers. I rushed past Justin in the hall, but playfully he yelled, "Stop a second." When I turned to face him, he whispered, "I'll cover for you if you don't come back until tomorrow morning." As was often the case, I didn't have a good comeback answer. I just smiled and proceeded downstairs.

I apologized for being late. Franco handed me an extra helmet and showed me where to place my feet and how to hold on to him once we were in motion. Thinking it his way was a little too close for comfort, at first I held onto his waist. But I quickly learned there was no other way to hold on without falling to the ground. I felt like a little kid riding a rollercoaster for the first time. It was as exciting as I'd hoped it would be. I definitely put my life in Franco's hands as we went from moderate to fast speed. It did make me nervous when we squeezed in between cars and trucks on the Via della Scala.

While I like to read information pamphlets, I much prefer having an actual person explain what I am looking at in museums. So I was delighted to have Franco as my guide today and Daniel and Isabella tomorrow. Franco began by giving me a verbal history of the San Marco museum. It was built as a convent in the thirteenth century and now holds a large collection of sacred artworks. The museum receives many visitors each year, especially those interested in the works of Fra Angelico. As we walked across the Cloister of St. Antoninus designed by Michelozzo, Franco spoke of the different sections of collections in the museum. Near what is called the Alms House is a rather large fresco by Giovanni Antonio Sogliani as well as works by Mariotto Albertinelli. What I most admired was Fra Angelico's fresco depicting the Crucifixion. I was deeply moved, looking at the fresco and remembering the Gospel accounts of the events in Christ's life leading to this scene on the cross. The cells of the cloister were adorned with frescoes of religious scenes, also painted by Fra Angelico. We completed our tour by visiting the impressive library, where we examined several old hymn texts that were under protective seal. After the museum we stopped at the San Lorenzo Market, which reminded me of the Spanish markets up in Harlem on 116th Street. Franco purchased some ingredients for his mother to use in preparing that evening's meal. I declined his invitation to have dinner with him and his family, feeling that I should get back and reconnect with Anthony and Justin.

Just before going to dinner Justin pulled me into a hallway to give me his exciting news. He was smitten with a French volunteer named Jean-Pierre. Apparently they'd walked around Florence that afternoon and, as he put it, "No fucking museums, Luis." At dinner Justin introduced us to one another. Jean-Pierre was a tall, nice-looking guy with a goatee, probably in his mid-thirties. There was no misreading his sexuality, as he talked openly about founding of a gay dating service, which started in France and then opened branches in countries like Italy and England. Jean-Pierre seemed to have a good sense of humor. He parodied some American commercials, saying, "I'm not just the founder, I'm also a client of the business." Jean-Pierre's work at the Austin House in France is the same as Justin's, working in the business office part-time. Anthony was late joining us for dinner and still wore his clerical collar. The refreshed look on his face told me that the day with his old friends had done him a world of good. Lately it looked as if he was getting a little burnt out from his work in Harlem.

Conversations over dinner with delegates were as upbeat as that morning's had been over breakfast. The conference would open the next afternoon at one with speeches from the leaders of the organization. I happened to overhear the administrator John Fazione of our Florence community tell the international secretary that all delegates had arrived and were accounted for. As we ate our dessert of chocolate cake after a filling meal of veal and buttered noodles, the administrator of the community stood and asked for everyone's attention. "Tonight," he announced, "if anyone is interested, the Basilica di Santa Maria del Fiore is having a free concert at seven featuring the Vienna Boys' Choir accompanied by an orchestra in a performance of both sacred and secular selections." Justin wasn't interested, but Anthony and I decided to attend the concert and also go early to roam around the Gothic cathedral and examine the frescoes and the architecture. Since it would be evening, we would miss the full beauty of seeing the sunlight coming through the stained-glass windows. Perhaps, I thought, we could go back during the day.

Nine of us walked to the cathedral, while eleven others traveled by van. Walking gave us glimpses into everyday life in Florence. We saw markets, retail shops, people interacting with one another, and children playing in the streets. The wide arches and high ceiling of the basilica reminded me of Manhattan's Saint Patrick's Cathedral on Fifth Avenue. In the dim light it was little difficult to make out details in the dome's frescoes by Vasari and Zuccari. But luckily a Dominican priest, Father Andrew, recognized Anthony from his visit to the monastery earlier that day and offered to take us up the bell tower. Lifting the hem of his white robes, Father Andrew led us up the stairs, giving us a brief history of his religious order and the cathedral as we climbed the stairs. The bell tower afforded a view in all directions. Father Andrew pointed out different areas of the city. Anthony and I stood in amazement for twenty minutes or so before heading down for the concert.

As we settled into our seats and waited for the concert to begin, I spotted Franco to my left and what looked to be his date for the evening. The dimly lit cathedral was a perfect setting for the array of beautiful voices in the Vienna Boys' Choir. From beginning to end, the entire audience was absorbed in the great performance of the choir and orchestra. Mixing with the crowd afterward, I had a chance to talk with Franco again. The woman he was sitting with happened to be his sister, Mary, and not a date as I had originally thought. Franco was friends with Daniel and Isabella and consequently had heard of our plans to visit the Bargello. When Anthony joined our conversation, he and Franco asked if they could tag along. Of course my answer was yes. Franco's sister accompanied us halfway back to Austin House. It turned out that their family lived only a couple of blocks away.

Franco and I weren't feeling sleepy, so we met in the library to view some more of his sketches. I was so glad I didn't have my own sketchbook. His work intimidated me. He was definitely far more advanced than I in what he was able to create on paper. It wasn't long before Justin and a couple of volunteers came into the library and disturbed our quiet time together. Whenever I looked up, I could see Justin looking in our direction. I was hoping and praying he would just stay on the other side of the library talking with the volunteers. But of course nothing keeps Justin from doing whatever he intends to do.

I wanted to punch him in the arm when he sauntered over to Franco and me sitting on the sofa. It then hit me, Justin and Dan are definitely one and the same when it comes to men.

Franco withdrew his sketch pad and said, "Excuse me, I will see you tomorrow. I'm going to bed now." My guess is Franco knew as well as I that Justin liked him sexually. Justin's outright flirtations yesterday in front of the building now seemed to make Franco feel uncomfortable. As Justin sat down I glared at him. "Fucking ass!"

He laughed. "What's that for?"

"Look," I responded, "I know what you were doing when you came over."

Justin continued to laugh. When I noticed Jean-Pierre had entered the library to socialize, I decided to play Justin's game of "get the man if you can." Thinking quickly as Jean-Pierre walked over to us, I stood up and asked, "Hi, Jean-Pierre. Say, would you join me for a walk?" Even without looking I could picture Justin's eyes cutting me in half for moving in on his guy. Jean-Pierre accepted my offer and mentioned a bar we could visit for a drink.

For the first time since I'd known him, Justin was at a loss for words. Then he lied, making it seem Anthony and I had to prepare a presentation for the conference the next day. I could see Justin grow more upset as Jean-Pierre showed interest in my having been to Europe before. Justin was really irritated and insisted on inviting himself along on our walk. Before we left the building, Justin abruptly pushed me into an empty room on the first floor. I was quite sure that whatever he had to say was not going to be positive. To my surprise, he apologized for his behavior and begged me not to go out with him and Jean-Pierre. It had been a stupid mind game on my part, but I wanted Justin to know where I stood. "Okay, Justin, but if you try any of this silly shit in the future, you'd better be sure I have no problems moving in on any guy you're interested in. Showing respect and observing boundaries are necessary if we were to be friends." Now that I felt Justin knew where I was coming from, I slipped out before him and told Jean-Pierre I was too tired after all and needed sleep if I was to be ready for tomorrow.

My guest room was on the second floor, but my fascination with high places led me to the fourth-floor balcony. After admiring the view I took advantage of the moment alone to pray my rosary. My quiet meditations were disturbed by the rumbling sound of Franco's motorcycle. Looking over the balcony wall I could see him riding away into the night, with Justin and Jean-Pierre waving to him as he passed.

My new friends met up with me after breakfast in front of the building. As Franco, Daniel, Anthony, and I waited for Isabella, we joined a soccer game in the street with some teenagers from the neighborhood. We became so engrossed in the game that we nearly forgot about our outing to the Bargello, but when Isabella arrived we remembered time was an issue, since the conference was starting that afternoon at one. Daniel drove us in his small two-door car. It really only seated four people. Daniel and Isabella rode up front. It was really uncomfortable for Anthony, Franco, and me in the backseat. By the time we arrived at the museum, all three of us had leg and arm cramps.

It was cute, I thought, how our new friends cut each other off and finished each other's sentences about the artworks of the museum. I could feel their passion in explaining the art to Anthony and me as we walked across the medieval courtyard. After examining the sixteenth-century sculptures of the courtyard, our eyes moved along the walls of the courtyard, which were decorated with the armorial symbol of the Podestà. We then moved to an area on the ground floor that contained works by Cellini and Giambologna, including the latter's excellent *Mercury*. In yet another room we found a host of different types of art: oriental carpets, wooden sculptures, and damascened bronzes. I enjoyed seeing more masterpieces by Michelangelo in the museum. We kept a close watch on the time so that we wouldn't be late returning to Austin House. Franco directed us toward Donatello's *David*. We made a quick tour of the second-floor display of small Renaissance bronzes and rare Italian medals. Daniel pointed out that the museum was originally a palace, completed back in 1256, was later used as a prison in the eighteenth century, and got its present name from having once housed the chief of police.

We ran late and arrived back at Austin House with only enough time to grab a quick bite to eat from the kitchen before the first meeting. To everyone's surprise, Nancy Austin, the founder of the organization, made her entrance by wheelchair. She was greeted with a standing ovation and cheers from every delegate and visitor. Ms. Austin was over ninety years old and her health had been failing for years. It had been whispered that this might be her last international meeting. Despite her age and failing health, she was upbeat and very alert. I could feel everyone's love and admiration for this woman. I am sure everyone couldn't help but reflect upon how she pulled together a small group of people in England, people who had nothing after the Second World War, and helped them rebuild their lives by helping others, and how her mission to help the homeless by living together in a community setting and following a structured set of programs spread to other countries outside of England. The cheers and yells died down, and Ms. Austin was given a microphone. Most delegates, including myself, moved from our seats to get a better look at her while she spoke. Apart from looking thin and frail, she didn't act helpless or needy at all.

Donning her reading glasses and removing a piece of paper from under a blanket on her lap, Ms. Austin addressed us as brothers and sisters and began to reflect on her life and the values she and her cofounders shared. She made four main points in her succinct speech. First, never turn anyone away from our doors who needed help. Second, it does not matter whether the person has a religious affiliation; we must first look upon each person as valuable, regardless of their religion or lack of one. Her voice cracked and she had a little coughing fit, but after pausing a couple of seconds and taking a sip of water, she recomposed herself and continued with the last two points of her speech. Third, the more we look toward good examples, like Jesus, Buddha, Anne Frank, Martin Luther King, and Mother Teresa, the better we become in our lives of service to the poor and dying. Placing her paper and reading glasses down on her lap, Ms. Austin tried to make eye contact with everyone in the room as she got to her fourth point. We are the servants of the poor in our programs, she said, and not the other way around. She ended her speech with the Prayer of Saint Francis, which begins, "Lord, make me an instrument of thy peace." Ms. Austin wished us well with our meetings and continued success in our work. Everyone applauded as she was wheeled to a side table.

The international secretary, Joan Allen, distributed a list of the small groups and a schedule of presentations. She instructed us to look over the list and find which small group would be ours for the next three days. My group would meet in the second-floor community room at the end of the hall. I also noted that the Austin House Harlem presentation was scheduled for 2:00 PM on Wednesday. In between presentations from various Austin House communities, there were guests speaking on topics such as world hunger, homelessness, economics, and the impact of organizations like ours, both those that have been successful and those that have not. If I remember correctly, the members of my group were Peter and Mark from England, Steven from Germany, and Barbara and John, an older married couple from France. After everyone in my group greeted one another over coffee we got down to business. I knew right away this group was going to be a good one when I saw everyone had come prepared with notes and ideas.

For me the time went rather quickly, even though some presentations were rather boring or repetitive. I had to force myself to keep my eyes open at times. Justin and I made a point of sitting near the back row, slipping out for fresh air when needed. I also noticed that within every group of delegates, someone was always missing; I wondered if they might be out sightseeing in the city. My suspicion was confirmed by Franco during a quiet chat we had on one of our breaks. According to him, if your community doesn't have a presentation and you are discreet, then slipping out of the large assembly really is not noticeable unless your group has less than three people. Of course, if everyone left the meetings to go out sightseeing around the city, the top administrators of the organization would have no choice but to chastise everyone for disrespecting the organization and disregarding the main reason we were all here in Florence. Pausing, Franco puffed on his cigarette and nodded his head in the direction of a delegate from France who was slipping in a side door instead of the main entrance in order to not be seen.

Late nights were spent roaming Florence with Franco, Daniel, and Isabella. We were treated to good home-cooked Florentine cuisine from Daniel's parents one night, and then dined with Franco's family the next night. For all of us it was good to get out of the building. It made our minds fresh for listening to different presentations and speeches during the day.

CHAPTER 29

Damn, Boy!

After dinner with his parents, Franco took me upstairs to see some of his older sketches while the others stayed downstairs talking with his parents. I sat on the edge of his bed as he took down some old art pads from a high shelf in his bedroom. I tried to maintain what we would call "custody of the eyes" in the monastery, trying not let my eyes roam where they shouldn't lest it lead to my embarrassment or someone else's. But as he reached for sketches that were hard to get, I couldn't help but notice his flat muscular stomach. His T-shirt kept rising whenever he reached up to look for his art pads. "Damn, boy!" is all I could think.

For the first time, as we talked over what he was trying to capture in his sketches, I found myself lusting for him. I tried to really focus on his sketches but found myself nervous, like when I was with Carlos, especially when Franco moved even closer to me on the bed to point out monuments in his sketches. This was also the first time I really felt Franco was trying to feel the situation out and see if I had any interest in him. There was no mistaking what was transpiring in his bedroom as we continued to look over his artwork. At one point we were actually so close I could feel my right cheek lightly touching his left cheek as his finger followed my finger in pointing out the detail of his sketches. There was no doubt in my mind, if we had turned toward each other our lips would have met. My next thought, however, was a great *"Oh fuck!"* For his mother just then screamed up the staircase for us to come down for dessert.

We both needed a moment to calm down before returning downstairs. When I stood and saw his reflection in the mirror over his dresser, I left quickly. I didn't want him to feel embarrassed because I knew why he was holding his art pad in front of himself. This was one of those times when more than ever I was glad to be a dark-skinned black guy. I'm sure if I were a white guy my face would have been flushed. Franco did not have that luxury, so he went outside for a smoke to calm down, and I returned to the group for dessert. Justin was in his detective mode and was the only one as far as I know who made out that something had happened. His raised eyebrows said it all, "Oh yes, we are going to talk."

Later back in Austin House Justin surprised me from behind and pushed me into my room, closing the door behind us. I played dumb at first, but I finally gave in and related all the details of what had happened in Franco's room. Justin was like a child hearing a good story. I found it humorous to hear him react to what I was saying by making sounds like ah and um. I was glad I had a friend I could share with. Our conversation was going great until he saw that I was hesitant to pursue Franco because of Carlos. Justin moved toward me as I sat in the chair and raised his voice. "What you and Carlos have is just sex and entertainment. You should just stop this shit of thinking he's going to be totally yours. Stop looking for Carlos and date a little. Have some fun." Before leaving my room, he left me with some advice. "Don't end up one day regretting that you should have gone for something and didn't." I leaned back on the chair and digested what he said.

The next day was Wednesday, so the spotlight would be on Anthony, Justin, and me giving our presentation. The three of us had an organizational meeting over breakfast to make sure all the pictures were ready and decide the order in which we would speak. For much of the day Franco and I couldn't speak to one another because of conferences and us preparing for the afternoon presentation. Our presentation rocked the house, so to speak. Anthony, Justin, and I played off each other very well. There were some expected bumps in our presentation when delegates asked about our government funding. Anthony made it clear that nothing in our house had changed. The contract with the city states that we can live the way we always did. We were restricted from announcing religious services, but we reaped the benefit of being able to use a portion of the funds to pay salaries to some people and help them save money. Robert Kearney, one of our guest speakers from England and an expert on world hunger, stood and spoke in our defense. Every country and city in the world, he said, is different when it comes to donating funds to nonprofit organizations. Some governments are inflexible in negotiating contracts for funding and only seek out what's in their own self-interest. Our blessing, as Mr.

Kearney put it, is that in Harlem, New York, we are able to follow the Austin House principles while having a government contract that really is not asking us to change much. Having put the issue of funding to rest, we moved forward. It was my turn to speak. I was so glad I had large photos of our daily work to display as I talked. I've always felt visual tools such as pictures and videos can draw people into the subject you are talking about. The delegates listened attentively as I spoke about volunteers, our AIDS project, and our outreach services. I even went so far as to briefly mention our job training programs and the system we use to help people save up money for when they reenter the world.

The delegates signaled their approval of our presentation by applauding as we left the stage. Ever since I was a child I've been told it's not nice to gloat or have too much pride or think I am better than anyone else. But it was very hard at this moment for me not to have these feelings. France, England, and Germany, for instance, all have two houses located in areas that need them and have money to expand into more areas and programs, but I didn't feel there was motivation in some of these communities to move forward and implement the types of programs we have in Harlem. I really hoped for the sake of the poor in these European communities that their delegates get what these five days were about. Austin House Harlem is the youngest program in the organization, and yet we offer the poor more in the way of programs than our older and richer sister communities.

CHAPTER 30

❦

Let's Go to Venice

Later that afternoon I bumped into Franco coming out of the library as I was going to my bedroom. There were a few seconds of awkwardness because of the previous night. But then I noticed the large book of Venetian art he was holding. As we stood near the library, Franco opened the book and we began to look at Venetian architecture and frescoes. Daniel ran past us and reminded us that dinner was in seven minutes. Franco motioned with his head for me to follow him onto the back patio. He'd come up with the idea that the two us could take a train ride over to Venice and proceeded to lay out the plan as if he'd thought of it long before asking me. It was an excellent idea, but I stood there stunned that he'd asked me on this little adventure. He whispered, "We could leave tomorrow after lunch and arrive in Venice before dinner time. Then we could visit Murano, renowned for its glassmaking, St. Mark's Cathedral and Square, and anywhere else I can think of. My aunt Olivia lives in Venice and has two guest rooms we could stay in overnight. The following morning, which is the last day of the conference, we could take a 10:00 AM or 11:00 AM train back to Florence, making it in time for the closing speeches."

My first reaction was "Yes." But then I added, "It would definitely have to be only a small group of people knowing about it. Trouble is assured if the leaders of the organization got wind of members skipping meetings. On my end, I have to be honest and open about it to Anthony and Justin. I just can't leave from one afternoon to the next and not let them know where I'm going. Tomorrow morning the small groups will present their ideas for improving our programs to the international secretary in the conference hall. That leaves us with socials and guest speakers on group dynamics and meditation. I'm going to have to think about it, but I promise I'll get back to you around seven tonight with my answer."

I pulled Anthony and Justin aside after dinner and presented the situation to them, asking for their help in covering for me. Anthony at first made me nervous. He was, after all, the coadministrator of our Austin House, and so it was his place to chastise me and say, "No, that's not why we're here in Europe." He sat still with eyes lowered, giving me the impression loud and clear that his answer would be no. Justin, on the other hand, was very enthusiastic and happy for me. He turned to Anthony, and said, "Our main job, and the reason we came here, is done, and we're leaving in two days." Anthony stood from his seat, looking at Justin, slapped his own right leg, and said, "You only live once."

They both agreed that if anyone asked where I was, they would say I'd be in soon or I was sick and in my bedroom for the evening. Personally I felt Anthony being a priest showed some hesitation about lying, but he did want me to have this art adventure before returning to the States. Later I got found Franco on the back patio drinking soda with Daniel, Isabella, and Matthew, a close friend of theirs. I said nothing at first about Venice, since I didn't want to let everyone know what our intentions were. But Franco gave me the okay to speak freely in front of them, so I said, "Okay, I'll go." Franco, too, said okay, slapping me on the back and shaking my hand. All five of us raised our cups of soda and toasted the beauty and history of Venice.

Steven from the small group I was assigned to typed up our suggestions for improving our communities. Knowing that each community offered different social services to the poor, we came up with eight basic ideas that, as far as we knew, were not part of any Austin House programs. Our four top ideas were as follows: (1) provide in-house support meetings for families coping with members who are on or are getting off drugs; (2) have family days on the weekend with interactive activities, especially for families with small children; (3) hold group retreats for inner-city Austin Houses to expose community members to the countryside and give them a change of scenery, and find places that will donate rooms; and (4) give weekend passes to those about to graduate from our programs so they can stay with family members.

Anthony surprised me at lunch by handing me an envelope of extra cash for my trip. For someone like me who always lives on a budget, this gift came at the right time. I quietly thanked him and snuck out after lunch. I stuffed a shirt, underwear, and my toothbrush and toothpaste into my backpack along with a Venice map. Franco and I decided the night before we would meet each other at the train station so as to not give anyone reason to wonder where we were going. Lunches didn't start until noon in Austin House, so I had to move quickly to get to the train station in time for our 12:52 PM departure. At the last moment Justin decided to walk me to the train station. As if we were breaking out of jail, we were very careful about not letting anyone see us leave, especially me. Halfway down the block we cracked up with laughter over something that happened in the early hours of that very morning. Anthony and I rose early with a small group of people for Catholic mass and prayers around 6:45 AM. The chapel is located on the second floor, down the hall from the guest rooms. Who did I see peeking out from the door of Jean-Pierre's room but Justin, trying to get my attention. He needed my help in diverting Anthony's attention so he could leave Jean-Pierre's room after their night together. Anthony is our friend and a Catholic priest, so we always give him respect and don't let him see or hear things from our mouths that should not be said in church. At the station, Justin shook my hand and said good-bye, and then, being in a flamboyant silly mood, he snapped his fingers and then rubbed two fingers together, one on top of the other (that's the international sign for two men having sex). "Work the situation as much as you can," he said, also referring to sex.

We both shrieked. Franco had come out of nowhere saying, "Hey guys, what's up?" Justin quickly excused himself. As Franco asked if I'd gotten my ticket yet, I was looking over his shoulder at Justin. I mumbled no. Justin glanced back at me, smiling. I'm sure he was thinking the same thing I was. Did Franco hear anything, and if he did, how much did he hear?

We had a very upbeat conversation on the train. We talked about many things, art, European versus American horror films, his skiing in the Italian and Austrian Alps, and our tastes in music and whether we liked rhythm and blues and rap. Franco stunned me when he talked about the music he loves, mentioning performers like Bob Marley and LL Cool J. It showed me that in some ways I'd put him in a box by thinking he would know nothing of black people's music from the Caribbean islands or the States. And there he was, taking a Bob Marley tape out of his backpack and showing me which songs were his favorites. As the conversation died down, he put on his Walkman and read an Italian newspaper, while I studied my Venice map and looked out the window at the scenery. Slowly we both dozed off. The train conductor eventually woke us up. As we gathered our stuff together, Franco pointed out the window at Venice in the distance.

CHAPTER 31

❀

Beautiful Venice

The crowd getting off the train was crazy. Everyone was pushing in the same direction. I soon discovered it was the ferry station they were pushing toward. My first thought, looking at the boat, was that there was no way in hell we were going to get on that boat. We managed to squeeze onto the second boat that came quickly behind the first one. Sheer madness, I thought, but when it quieted down I enjoyed the views with my tour guide friend. The evening sunlight reflected off the windows above the canal onto the water below, giving it a calm golden effect as the gondolas passed us carrying lovers. I felt like I was stepping back in time as the ferry passed buildings in the Byzantine, Gothic, Renaissance, and Romanesque styles. Because time and daylight were in short supply, Franco suggested we go to his aunt's house later. Our first stop was St. Mark's Square. We disembarked from the ferry and passed through the columns of Saint Mark and Saint Theodore. Ahead of us on the right, said Franco, lay the Doge's palace, home to the chief magistrate of Venice since the ninth century. The facade of the building caught my eye. I'd never seen anything like its pink and white patterned walls or the elaborately carved gothic balconies beneath them. Further ahead on my right was St. Mark's Basilica, with the bell tower on the left; beyond the basilica stood the famous clock tower designed by Mauro Codussi. Before entering the basilica we both stood back and admired its incredibly ornate facade. Within its rounded arches are scenes depicting the removal of Saint Mark's body from Alexandria, Egypt, the arrival of Saint Mark's body in Venice, Venetians worshipping the saint's body, and the carrying of the body into the church. Looking further up over the main entrance, above depictions of the resurrection and ascension of Christ, I noticed the four horses I'd read about once in a history book. The horses date from fourth century BC and were brought to Venice from Constantinople in the early thirteenth century. In the interior, the mosaics in the floor and ceilings were something to behold. As I walked from one area to the next, my eyes tried to capture every detail. Franco went to examine the baptistery, while I rested in prayer near the main altar. We both lit candles for our families before exiting the basilica. My only disappointment was that the balcony over the main entrance was closed.

Walking through the main doors of the basilica, we blended into the sea of sightseers and locals who were either sitting at one of the renowned cafes or feeding the pigeons in the middle of the square. We were hungry ourselves but didn't want to spoil our dinner, so we purchased coffee and a small cake to hold us over. We sat beneath the bell tower enjoying our snack. "In America," I said, "the pigeons fly away when you get close to them, but here in Venice the pigeons walk and it's the people that get out of the way." Suddenly Franco acted a little odd. He looked at his watch and excused himself, saying he'd be back in ten to fifteen minutes. I watched the people while I waited. To my left I noticed the fancy gowns of women tourists from India. Franco returned from the ferry area with another guy at his side. I could tell from the pleased look on his face that something good was going to happen. I also noticed the family resemblance as Franco introduced me to his cousin Michael. Knowing we had such a short time in Venice, Franco had arranged with his cousin, a waiter at one of the cafes nearby, for us to borrow the family's small motorboat. This would make traveling around the city much faster than taking public ferries for transportation. Franco obviously knew how to get around Venice as well as what to see and when to see it. Our second stop was the island of glassmakers, Murano. Riding in the small boat was not easy for me. The wind and choppy waves coming from the open sea made the boat unsteady. But Franco was clearly not afraid of a little bad weather, as he put it. He reminisced about fishing out on the ocean near Venice when he was in his early teens. If there was a violent storm, he said he'd row himself back to shore until the storm died down and then go back out again. If he was trying to impress me, I thought, it wasn't necessary; I was impressed well before this Venice trip.

Franco led us to one of many glass factories where we were met by three older men having a smoke near the entrance. One of the three men, Antonio, showed us around the factory and demonstrated the process of glassmaking, though it was difficult to make out much of what Antonio said because of his thick Italian accent. He first heated the tip of a long blowpipe, then dipped it into molten glass, gradually gathering it onto the pipe. Then he rolled it onto a thick flat steel surface. We watched intensely as he blew air into the pipe to create a bubble. Taking the blowpipe and bubble away from the fire, he sat on a bench, and using smaller handheld tools that looked like tweezers, Antonio formed it into a simple pitcher with an elaborate handle. Afterward he showed us about sixty rejected pieces. I held some of these pieces and, personally, I couldn't find any flaws in them until Antonio pointed them out. They were so small that I was about to say I thought it ridiculous to destroy them, but I changed my mind. Antonio took pride in making sure every piece was perfect before it left the factory.

We headed back to the boat and agreed that going to dinner was next. We docked along the Grand Canal. Over dinner we discussed our sightseeing plans for the next morning. "Tomorrow," Franco explained, "my uncle has agreed to let us borrow a bigger and better boat. Because our time is short, I suggest we make a tour of famous bridges." We dined on pasta salad and chicken parmigiana, along with two glasses apiece of red wine from southern Italy. Full from our dinner and tired from sightseeing, we made our way to his aunt's house. His aunt Olivia, the mother of his cousin Michael, met us at the front door. Her second husband, Christopher, also welcomed us. They took our backpacks and invited us to sit on the balcony overlooking one of the canals. We became further acquainted over yet another glass of wine.

The guest rooms were next to each other overlooking what I took to be the Grand Canal. When Franco showed me to the small but modest room, he corrected me. "No, Luis, that's not the Grand Canal." He hesitated slightly before he left and made eye contact. I moved to sit on the edge of the bed. I now knew what the deal was. It was late. His aunt and uncle had gone to bed, and his cousin was still at work. This was another classic situation, as it had been with me and Carlos in the hotel room. You have two people that like each other, but each is afraid to make the first move. I stood from the bed to move toward him, but at that moment we heard someone coming up the stairs. Instantly, we knew this was not the time or place. It was Michael. He stopped at the open door of my room and asked, "Hey guys, did the boat help you in getting around any faster?" In unison, we said yes, it had. I really wished Michael wasn't with us, and then he invited himself into my room. "Franco," he said, "did you know there's this girl who has a crush on you? Her name is Sara and she's very well built." Michael illustrated the shape of her body with his hands.

"She'd like to see you if you have time tomorrow to drop by her parents' apartment."

I put my backpack and small jacket in the corner as Franco replied, "I will call her some other time, but our time in Venice is very limited." Michael excused himself to go to bed, with Franco following behind him. He gave me a half smile and a wave of his hand before closing the bedroom door behind him. I took off my jeans, keeping only my T-shirt and boxer shorts on for bed. The excitement of the day kept me from being able to fall asleep right away. As I lay on my bed I could hear the whistles of boats out in the distance in the lagoon. The half moon shining in my window led me to get up and walk onto the small balcony. Though I didn't have a bathrobe, I was very comfortable in stepping out onto the balcony. It was very dark and no lights were shining in my direction. I had just leaned over the balcony resting my arms on the cement ledge when I heard Franco appear on the balcony. He couldn't sleep either and had come out for some fresh air, hoping it would help him sleep. I was so glad I didn't yell when he surprised me. The last thing I needed was for his aunt, uncle, and cousin to come find me standing there half naked. I've never been comfortable being naked or even half naked in front of people, even a lover. But this time I felt comfortable because it was dark and Franco and I couldn't fully see one another.

Franco apologized for surprising me. I began to feel nervous as he moved closer. And as the clouds parted, I could see in the moonlight that he was only wearing the bottom half of his pajamas. He rested his arms next to mine on the ledge of the balcony, and we looked out into the stillness of the night.

During breakfast with his family the next morning on one of the balconies of their home, we planned our last few hours of sightseeing. Michael agreed to meet us at the train station to pick up the boat before we boarded the 11:00 AM train back to Florence. His aunt and uncle gave us big bear hugs and invited me to come back when I had more time to visit. Knowing we had so little time, Franco's aunt prepared bag lunches for our train ride. Now in a much larger and better boat, we sped along the canals to the Franchetti gallery, which had closed by the time we made it into Venice the day before. Fighting the morning rush hour of boats and ferries was bothersome at first. As we maneuvered around them, some drivers became heated and leaned on their boat horns. The Franchetti gallery is located in Ca' d'Oro, a palace donated along with its collection to the Italian government by Baron Giorgio Franchetti. The gallery contains a marvelous collection of artworks and furniture from different time periods, but we only had time to view six rooms of oil paintings and antique furniture.

Franco pointed out the famous bridges of Venice, such as the Rialto, Accademia, and the Bridge of Sighs, which prisoners crossed when they were brought to be interrogated about their crimes. Reluctantly we ended our brief tour and headed for the train station. Because Michael was late, we almost missed our train. We tossed him the keys and made a mad dash for the train.

Exhausted from running to catch the train, we flopped down into the first seats we saw. After catching our breath we moved to our assigned seats in the third-class section. Without overdoing it too much, I praised Franco for suggesting we come to Venice. The sack lunch from his aunt Olivia contained two sandwiches of ham and cheese and, to our surprise, two small plastic containers of red wine. I borrowed his Walkman and Bob Marley tape while he read more of the Italian paper from yesterday. Later we had a conversation about friendships in our Austin House communities. He mentioned for the first time that he, Matthew, Isabella, and Daniel had attended school together since they were small children and had known each other for most of their lives, which explained why they all get along so well.

Franco looked at me strangely when I mentioned that Justin is a good friend and that we look out for one another. I laughed when he said shyly, "I thought you and Justin had a thing going on between you."

"No. Not at all. Justin's a true friend. He's not my type, nor am I his type."

Of course our conversation once again drifted to discussing art techniques. He was so cute. When I said I couldn't draw human hands, Franco reached into his backpack, took out some scratch paper, and had me practice drawing hands with him. It helped a little, but much more practice is needed. As the train approached Florence I took out the conference schedule. We wanted to make sure we returned to Austin House at the right time in order to slip back into the building without being seen.

We successfully made it in without anyone seeing us. I went to my bedroom and Franco went to slip into the meeting that was in progress. On the floor of my bedroom near the door was a simple note from Justin dated that morning. Everything was cool, he said, and I should stay in my room until he came for me. Within less than thirty minutes, Justin came to my room. Instead of knocking, he opened the door and entered. And instead of saying "Hello" or "How are you doing?" he burst in and asked, "So, do you have something juicy to tell?" Not wanting to let him down, I shared what had happened the night before without being too explicit. He then shared what he and Jean-Pierre had done on their nightly outings. It went without saying that what we had with these two men was nothing more than a passing thing. Neither of us talked about the possibility of a long-distance relationship. Both Jean-Pierre and Franco knew we were leaving for America the next day, and neither had mentioned keeping in contact through letters or postcards.

Anthony came by my room later to confirm that our plan had come off without a hitch. Of course, what I shared with Justin about Venice was much different from what I shared with Anthony. It was funny to me, because Justin was almost jumping up and down and making little sounds as I told him about my time in Franco's room, and now Anthony was showing the same excitement as I told him about the churches, galleries, and museums we visited.

Before I got dressed for the final ceremony and banquet, I stood at the window of my room, amazed at how fast the days had passed. From beginning to end the evening was charming. The large conference hall used for lectures and presentations was transformed into a nicely decorated banquet hall. Anthony and a Buddhist monk gave the opening remarks and prayers, followed by Nancy Austin, who shared the news that our organization was finally opening a house in India. Everything was perfect, the table flowers, the live band, and the food made by volunteers. What also added to the charm of the night was that everyone dressed so nicely. I'm not a dancer, but I did participate in dances with the larger groups, following others' movements in what I later learned was Italian folk dancing. I left everyone for a little while for some time alone and went to pray in the chapel. When I returned to the crowded banquet hall, Isabella suggested that our little group leave the party. So Daniel, Matthew, Franco, Justin, Jean-Pierre, Isabella, and I left Austin House. Daniel and Isabella found two bottles of wine and led us to an excellent quiet area near the Arno River.

Our little party turned silly from too much wine. All of us climbed on top of a low wall that separated us from the river. And with our eyes closed, we tried walking straight along the top of the wall, with our arms held out for balance. Daniel, who was behind me, lost his footing and fell about twenty feet or more into the river. As we looked on in horror, the current pushed him away from us. We were frantic, to say the least. None of us could find anything for him to grab onto, and there was nothing in the water he could grab onto. The barrier walls were smooth. Eventually he swam against the current to a pole imbedded in the retaining wall. Grasping it tightly, he slowly made his way up out of the river by placing his feet on the large bolts on either side of the pole. Franco and I extended our arms to help pull him up and over the wall. Appalled by the tragedy that nearly resulted from our drinking and silliness, we ended our little party and returned to Austin House.

Though it was well after one in the morning, a good number of delegates and guests were still hanging out, not only in front of the building but also in the library and first-floor areas. In the midst of our friends, Franco said nothing to me and I said nothing to him. I excused myself and went back to my room, hoping he would stop me to chat, but he didn't. As I finished packing and placed my passport and Italian money together, there was a tap on my door. I was thrilled, thinking Franco had snuck up to my room. Instead it was Justin, who wanted to borrow my jean jacket so he could go out with Jean-Pierre. Justin got short with me when I suggested it was late and he should get some sleep. He then waved his hand up and down in front of me. "Luis, you're not going to get any ass, because instead of pursuing Franco on our last night in Florence, you're staying in your room packing what little shit you have into your backpack and suitcases, while everyone else is downstairs having a good time hanging out and enjoying themselves." Like other times when Justin spoke the truth, I kept silent.

Justin left. Within minutes, however, I discovered that he'd set me up, in a good way, by lying to Franco and saying I'd been looking for him. Franco responded to this by coming to my room. I tried to think of something quick to say but couldn't think of anything. Lying myself, I apologized for not remembering why I was seeking him out. I felt as low as an ant, for clearly he'd caught onto this as a ruse to get him up to my room. He smiled after I came clean about what Justin had done. "Justin," he said, "was just being a good friend." It was almost two. Franco invited himself in and sat next to me on the edge of the bed. Our conversation at first was fitful, with a lot of small talk.

"Are you all packed?" he asked.

"Yes," I responded. "Do you have art classes tomorrow?"

"Uh, yeah," he replied. "My motorcycle gets me across the city on time." I looked at his face. He made an expression that seemed to say "I can't believe I said my motorcycle gets me across the city on time."

Looking back, I can honestly say we tried to respect each other by not jumping into it and letting our sexual desires get the best of us. But the waiting and respecting each other didn't last. It was laughable, in retrospect, because after one look we got it on like a drag race. We'd obviously said to ourselves, "Fuck this beating around the bush." Everything was fine until the zipper of his pants refused to come down. I was just seconds away from taking a razor to cut those motherfuckers off. I didn't care and neither did he. Happily, however, it didn't come to that. He just forced them down and peeled them off. In the rush of sexual excitement you can end up doing some crazy shit if you don't check yourself.

It was uncomfortable at first in that single bed, but we soon relaxed, both of us facing the window with his arm around my waist. In our haste, I'd forgotten to close the large shutters, so we were awakened by the bright morning sun. We dressed in silence, and then he handed me a small note from his back pocket. The note definitely made my day. It was his parents' address, where he said I could write him. Franco was in a rush to get a quick breakfast before going to class, so he stopped my hand from writing my address. "Luis, write me first with your return address."

I'd now broken one of the organization's rules on romantic interests by letting Franco sleep in my room. I looked both ways down the hall, and then he left. Timing is everything, they say, and this was one of those times. Not even two minutes went by before Anthony knocked on my door. "Hey, Luis, we have less than an hour before leaving." I showered quickly and went down to say my good-byes to the members of the Florence community and the delegates who were leaving to return to their countries.

While Franco's brother Marco took us in the van to the train station, Anthony expressed concern about Justin and me being so silent. We said, "Everything's okay," but he wasn't convinced.

He looked at us with curiosity and asked, "Did you guys have a disagreement?"

Justin answered while I nodded in agreement. "Father, we're just coming down off the high of our trip. And we didn't get much sleep last night."

Not knowing what to believe, Anthony finally left us alone. Justin dolefully whispered to me, "Jean-Pierre didn't leave me an address to contact him. Last night after I tried to write my address down he abruptly told me he'd look him up some day."

Justin didn't ask and I didn't tell him that Franco had given me an address to contact him. I don't think in our short time in Florence that we'd fallen in love with these guys. I gave Justin some of his own advice. "Look, Justin, it's better to have had a good time than not." But secretly I thought as I looked out the van window at the scenery, Jean-Pierre's saying "I'll look you up some day" was really not a good response if one wanted to keep something going.

On one of the train's regular stops I noticed a group of monks walking toward a van that was waiting for them. The sight of them made me briefly yearn for the monastic life. But then I remembered why I left, and came to my senses.

CHAPTER 32

Nasty Homophobia

Our plane arrived back in New York at 6:32 AM. We were greeted by cheers from Roberto, who had volunteered to get up early and meet us. Since I hadn't really slept on the plane, I was tired when I got back to Austin House. I simply laid down on my bed and fell fast asleep with my clothes on. About six hours later I woke up, showered, and put on some fresh clothes. I met up with Justin and Anthony later in the afternoon. We agreed that the next morning would be the best time to give our report on the international meetings and read off the new program ideas that emerged from our small group sessions. Sally and Debbie filled me in on the latest gossip. I wondered about Carlos and what was going on with him. Around three in the afternoon I started calling people to let them know I was back in Manhattan. Carlos' uncle picked up the phone and said he was at work. I suspected he would be, but I had hoped he might have the day off. Bradley was happy to hear from me but kept talking on and on about his pet project, Shepherds House. Eventually I lied and said I had to be somewhere just to get off the phone.

I was in the library examining some new donated books when I heard a lot of yelling and cursing coming from the sidewalk. I was feeling nosy, so I walked onto the fire escape to see what was going on. Sandra and her husband Nate, who'd been in our program before, were part of the commotion. Nate and Sally were holding Sandra back from having a fistfight with Justin. All I kept hearing from her, over and over again, was, "You sorry faggot, why don't you find your own man. You and everyone like you are nothing but fucking AIDS bitches. You want something up your ass? How about a fucking knife, you sick motherfucker." I walked quickly to the security desk. By the time I got there, William and Sally were asking Sandra not to come into the building until she calmed down. Roberto and I escorted Justin to the outreach office to give him a chance to calm down as well. Justin was so angry, he refused to talk about anything. All he could say was, "Leave me the fuck alone."

I can always count on Sally and Debbie to keep me apprised of what's going on in the building. At the dinner table Sally leaned forward. She knew I wanted her information. She whispered, "Justin was after Sandra's husband the last time they both were living here. It appears Justin didn't really care at all that Nate was attached to Sandra."

Debbie was also sitting at our table. "It gets even more interesting," she said. "I saw Justin and Nate on the roof one time. Nate was playing around with Justin the way no straight man should be with another man." Our conversation was cut short by Mike, who was going from table to table saying hello to everyone. I didn't need Sally and Debbie to explain the rest of the story. Sandra had either noticed or gotten wind of Justin liking her husband, and it disturbed her. I could tell by what I witnessed and the force of her words to Justin earlier outside the building.

The evening took a turn for the worse when I was looking at some literature on the community board. Nate was speaking to a group of guys near the library, trying to assert his manhood. I heard him say, "Yeah, that fucking fag tried to have me, but I made it clear my ass said Do Not Enter. I like pussy. Don't fucking come near me or I will chop what's left of your manhood off." As he and the guys moved into the library for movie night, Nate continued to gay bash.

I'd heard it from Sally and Debbie, but I had to hear it from Justin to find out what was true and what was not. I hoped he would give me the honest truth. I found him in his room and joined him on his way to the roof for a smoke. "Well, well," I said. He lit his cigarette and sat near me on the ledge. I felt his embarrassment over the situation, but after a couple of puffs on his cigarette Justin gave me the whole story. "When Sandra and Nate were living here before, it was because they needed help in staying clean from heavy crack and alcohol use. While Nate was working with me in the clothing room one afternoon, he made a sexual pass at me. You know me, I'm horny twenty-four hours a day. I felt, like, who's gonna know or find out? So we both did the deed, and not only that one time. There were other times in my room."

Justin said he suspected two things. "One, Sandra is very homophobic and listens to Nate's ramblings about how us gays in the building keep coming on to him constantly. And two, I really think this is how Nate handles his bisexuality, by bashing gays in the hope of keeping the spotlight off him in front of his buddies."

"What are you going to do?" I asked "Because, yes, Austin House, I mean, according to our rules and principles we cannot throw someone out for being homophobic. But we can ask them to leave for being unruly or disrupting community life."

Justin, of course, already knew this himself. He stood from the ledge and said, shaking his head, "I don't know. We'll see." As he put out his half-smoked cigarette and tossed it over the side, he said, "Let's both not talk about it again. Just give it a rest."

It was nearly eleven when Carlos called. It was so great to hear his voice again. He avoided my questions about how was he doing by answering each question with a question, which is more than just irritating to me. But knowing his temperament, I allowed him to lead the conversation. I just knew something was up with him, but I gave him time to answer me. Carlos made the whole conversation about me, asking about my trip, where did I go, what did I see, why didn't I send a postcard. As for the postcard, I said I was too busy with meetings, not admitting the fact that I was roaming around with Franco and others and forgot to send him a simple postcard. We looked at our work schedules and set a date and time to meet on Friday night: the corner of West 86th Street and Park Avenue at seven. He never did answer my question about whether something was disturbing him. If there was something, I'd have to wait until Friday to find out.

I thought Justin's situation with Sandra and Nate was going to die down. But I still kept hearing shit coming out of Nate's mouth. During breakfast he was sitting six tables over from me, and yet I could hear him say, "How can a guy kiss another guy's mouth?" Meanwhile Debbie and I were sitting there trying to enjoy our hot cereal. I thought, if a man or woman has to constantly prove their heterosexuality, then there's more to their personal story than they care to tell. Twice before I'd almost gone to Anthony and Mike about Sandra and Nate's constant bashing of gays, especially after hearing Sandra call a singer on television a "no-talent faggot ass." I realized I had to meet with Justin to convince him to help me think of a creative way to deal with these two. Yes, I could have gone to Anthony and Mike about all this, but my mind was made up. These two struck me as the type who'd get louder and nastier if confronted about their gay bashing. I paced Justin's room and then the roof. Finally I turned to Justin and broke into a big smile, a smile he thought seemed very sinister. I pulled two folding chairs together for us to sit. My plan left him speechless. He said nothing at first, but then he asked, "Do all monks have such creative ideas?" Laughing, I said no. We agreed that our plan should go into operation the next evening around six. We both had two big roles to play if we were going to bring it off without a hitch.

During morning meeting, the three of us gave our report on the international meeting in Florence. We distributed leaflets on what the other communities were doing by way of helping the poor. Justin and Anthony described what the lectures were about and answered questions. When I felt the time was right to speak, I presented a copy of new program ideas to everyone. Some on the list we'd already implemented, while others, like weekend passes, we needed to discuss. In closing we answered a few questions about sightseeing and the food in the region.

Anthony and Mike surprised us at the very end of the morning meeting by making an announcement. Reading an official letter from the bishop and cardinal's office downtown, Mike introduced the final decision of the cardinal in the selection of our new administrator: Anthony will become the top priest and administrator, and Mike will be reassigned to All Saints Church here in Harlem. We all looked at one other, not knowing whether to clap for Anthony or feel sad that Mike would be leaving us. In his letter the cardinal said that because of the shortage of priests, he was unable to assign two priests to Austin House at this time. None of us, as far as I knew, preferred Anthony over Mike or vice versa. These two examples of true and faithful priests had restored our community and dealt with the issues surrounding Father Doug. A huge party was then arranged so that everyone could formally welcome Anthony as administrator and wish Mike well in his new assignment.

I returned to work in the outreach office. It was my first full day back at work. I immediately saw the things my fellow workers had done or not done. But I had no complaints. I just rolled up my sleeves and got to work. For most of the afternoon I was nervous about my plan going off. Shortly after 4:30 PM the first part of my strategy went into effect. I spoke to Sandra alone while Justin arranged to meet Nate in private in a small nook at the end of the second-floor hall. Trying to convince Sandra to keep a secret and go along with what I had to say was not easy. She had the impression that I possibly wanted to do her some harm. She asked that Sally be brought in on my little plan, which I had only partly revealed to her. Sally helped me seal the deal by mentioning that she'd known me a long while now and knew I wouldn't be wasting their time. Sandra then did as I instructed and agreeing to meet me and Sally on the third floor at exactly 5:45 PM in order for everything else to come off. Sandra, in her loud nasty way, asked, "What do you mean, for everything else to come off?"

I really wanted to slap this girl in the head to get her to shut up and just go along with everything. Sally moved toward her and said, "Luis wouldn't do anything stupid enough to get us kicked out of Austin House."

When Sandra left, Sally tried her best to get me to tell her what the deal was. I stuck to my guns and proclaimed, "It will definitely be something good for you to witness."

My beautiful plan reached its culmination when Sandra, Sally, and I jumped out of Justin's closet to find Nate with his pants unbuttoned and in a compromising position with Justin on the bed. While Sandra stood there screaming, Justin, Sally, and I slowly excused ourselves and made our way to the roof. We closed the roof door behind us knowing that people were running to Justin's room to see what was wrong. Sally was in a state of shock. She couldn't speak at all and just made little sounds. While she tried to pull herself together, Justin and I played it cool. Sally asked us to please always be her friends, because she may need our help one day.

My plan had worked perfectly. Justin lied to Nate, saying he was leaving the Austin House program for good the next day. This was to make Nate interested enough in having one last fling. To make the other elements of my plan look enticing to Nate, I selected the perfect time for their rendezvous, 6:00 PM, when everyone would be at dinner and no one would see him entering Justin's room. Now as for Sandra, I asked her to lie to Nate, saying she would be out visiting her sister and wouldn't be back until nine. This was an important factor in making Nate more comfortable about going to Justin's room.

Later that night, Justin, Sally, and I fished around to hear if anyone really knew why Sandra had a meltdown. When we compared notes, the only thing we found out from other community members was that they'd had a major disagreement and were sleeping in separate rooms that night.

The next morning, as I was preparing the outreach office for the workday, Sandra walked in and refused to speak to me, instead requesting Roberto to help her find an alternative place to live. Roberto, who had no real clue to what had happened the night before, tried to be of help to Sandra by offering to speak to Nate man-to-man. When Roberto tried to break it down for Sandra by saying, "Only a man knows what another man's real needs are in a marriage," I couldn't stand it any longer. I was bursting with laughter. It was that last line that sent me running into the kitchen for a coffee break. As I left the office, I heard Sandra cut Roberto off, saying, "Just find me another fucking place to live."

Friday afternoon the mail brought a gift for all the volunteers in Harlem. An envelope containing $670 was accompanied by a short anonymous letter addressed to Anthony, Mike, and me. "I want to commend all the hard work your volunteers do, giving a year or more of their lives to the poor. This money is for all the volunteers living in or outside Austin House to have a day of fun." None of us had ever experienced this before. Normally all donated funds went for the work of Austin House. The three of us were surprised that whoever sent the money took the risk of sending cash. I thought the same thing Mike was thinking, why didn't they use a money order? Raising the money above his head, Anthony proclaimed, "It's not how a blessing comes to us that matters. All that matters is that it went from A to B without any problems, thank God." I gathered all the volunteers together in the library after work to read the letter to them. I knew they would be excited. A planning meeting was set for Monday around 7:30 PM in the community room on the fourth floor.

I had just an hour and twenty-five minutes before I was to meet Carlos downtown. I left the others in the library and went to rest, shower, and put on some fresh clothes. I was excited about seeing Carlos. It was like we were going on our first date again.

Seeing him on the corner of 86th Street and Park Avenue, I moved toward him as he extended his right hand. In his Puerto Rican accent he said, "Hey man, what's up?" We hugged, and as usual his lips grazed my cheek when I pulled away. Even though I hadn't send him a postcard, I did have a present for him, a small knickknack from Florence. We walked to Central Park and then south toward the zoo. Carlos was very quiet. He only nodded when I asked about music and the basketball games that were on television the past week. But at one point Carlos quickly looked around to see if anyone was in sight, and then he pushed me off the path and kissed me hard on the mouth. It happened so fast and was so pleasing, it took me a couple of seconds to recover and catch up with him. He'd continued down the path in front of me and was jokingly asking me to keep up. Ten minutes later Carlos sat on a bench and asked me to sit next to him. He hesitated. "I have something important to tell you." His tone of voice told me right away that it wasn't good. Questions flashed through my mind. Is he going back to Philadelphia permanently? Is he moving in with Nancy? Are they getting married? I didn't know what to think.

CHAPTER 33

※

They Took a Chance

Smacking his hands together between his knees and looking straight ahead, it came out. I chuckled, thinking that he was playing around. Then he lowered his head, looked at me sideways, and repeated what he'd said. "Luis, I'm serious. Nancy is pregnant." And as if that information hadn't already numbed me, he commented rather flamboyantly, "We both just took a chance, because we couldn't find a condom."

I had to stand and get some air. It felt like I separated from my body and returned maybe six seconds later. I looked down at him sitting on the bench and finally spoke. "You're a fucking idiot. Something like this was bound to happen without a condom." I was so disturbed by this I wasn't able to look him in the face. I flopped down on the bench next to him. "So what's next?" I asked.

Carlos took his time. "Well, we're moving to her hometown in Pennsylvania. We plan on leaving next week to live with her parents until we get our own place." All the gold in the world couldn't have made me stay with him another minute. What stopped me was his comment, "Yo, just be a man and say what's on your mind."

I stepped toward him. I kept what I had to say plain and simple. I raised my voice, so I was glad no one else was around. "I've always had a thing for you, ever since I first saw you in Austin House. It was not just a sex thing for me. You're able to separate in your head between me and Nancy. I can't do that. And now with this baby issue and moving away, *it really fucks me up inside!* I need a whole heart, not half of one or a quarter of one, but a whole heart. I kept blinders on, thinking you would come around. But no, Nancy gives you what she can physically and emotionally. Then you're able to turn to me for what I can give you. I need someone who'll keep me and me alone in the picture."

Carlos interrupted and stood to come closer to me. He looked around himself, raising his voice while hitting his chest. "Fuck it, Luis. You knew the deal with me. It was no secret. I didn't keep it from you. I told you what my deal was. Look, man," he paused, "with guys I don't normally hang out with one guy the way you and I have. It wasn't about encounters, even though it was fucking great. But yes, fucking yes, Luis, I see you as more than just an encounter."

When I felt my eyes starting to water, I simply started to walk away. I could hear him smack his hands together as he yelled, "Come on, man." But I'd had my "truth being real moment." I never wanted to be a woman or want their physical looks. But I became very bitter and I was jealous of them going off to make a life together.

I spent the rest of my evening in Austin House listening to soft jazz and reading some Native American poetry. When I arrived for work at Shepherds House on Saturday, Mary whispered, "You have a guest in the next room who's been waiting for about thirty minutes." Putting my backpack down near the front door I walked into what was formerly our dormitory. Carlos extended his right hand, but I refused to shake it and asked him to leave. I was cold and to the point, "Carlos, there's no reason for us to talk any further. Nothing fucking positive can come of us talking." Our conversation got heated even though we tried to keep our voices down as we traded insults. "Luis, you're a self-centered bitch who can't accept me trying to make some peace. All you fucking care about is what you're not getting out of the whole situation." My mood softened when Roger came into the room to get something, stopping Carlos from calling me a dick after I'd just called him one. I turned in the direction of the front windows so Carlos couldn't see me smile. Roger apologized for interrupting our conversation and left. I felt Carlos' sincerity when he said he didn't want to leave the city with everything up in the air.

Roger came back to let me know the paint and brushes were on the third floor and asked me look everything over whenever I got a chance and see if I needed anything else. Bradley, meanwhile, started to bring in some construction supplies. And then John, one of the volunteers from the squatters' building down the block, brought me some beeswax for my hair. Beeswax is good for dreadlocks and I've been trying to grow mine back again.

I was impressed when Carlos walked over to Bradley. He reintroduced himself and asked Bradley if he could volunteer to help me paint bedrooms. Bradley was accepting all the help he could get, because our opening date was only three days away. He instructed me to show Carlos where he and I would be working on the fourth floor. Instantly I knew Carlos wanted to continue talking to me while we worked together. I'm not proud to say it, but I still acted coldly in dealing with the fact he and Nancy were going to have a child. Silence was my weapon of choice as we painted our first room. He tried to talk with me about every single thing we liked together. He finally broke me down and out of my silence as we painted the baseboards in the chapel. He'd gotten around to asking questions about God and about the mass, religious icons, and the vigil light. My heart was moved to put my worldly feelings aside and give him the answers he wanted.

With Carlos' help we finished painting four small bedrooms as well as the baseboards in chapel. By the end we were talking as if nothing had happened between us. I was impressed he stayed to work all day long. When I finally noticed the time, it was almost five. After cleaning the brushes I led him to the front stoop. We parted with a handshake but no hug. I suddenly remembered and called after him. "Hey, our opening is on the twelfth of May. Wanna come by and hang a bit?"

Just when I thought everything was going well, he broke the news. "That's the day I'll be leaving Manhattan. We're taking the one o'clock Greyhound bus to Pennsylvania."

I acted as if it didn't faze me one bit, but of course I knew that Nancy would be going on that bus with him. We said nothing about exchanging addresses or phone numbers or keeping in contact. We shook hands and stared at one another for a few seconds. He then stepped back, took his Walkman out of his back pocket, placed the headphones over his ears—and simply turned away. Knowing this was the end, I sat on the stoop and watched him walk west on East 7th Street. The weather was nice, and there was salsa music coming from a building across the street. I sat on the stoop for close to twenty minutes before Mary called me in for dinner.

CHAPTER 34

❦

In Bad Company

Friday afternoon I took the 12:30 PM Long Island Rail Road back to Huntington. I'd accepted an invitation to Joan Gibson's forty-fifth birthday party. Her family and mine have been close for many years, closer than our blood relatives out west. The party was held over on East 8th Street. Walking into the party I laid my gift on the table with the other gifts. I'd remembered after all these years that she collects knickknack frogs, so that's what I'd gotten her. The conversations with old childhood friends weren't to my liking. They seemed to surround who was in jail versus who just got out, or who was fucking whom and who had gotten pregnant in the mix of sneaking around. Seeing so many people being loud and drunk made me feel I didn't belong at this party.

The evening got worse. I was reunited with some of the neighborhood bullies. Even though they were adults like me, they couldn't help but greet me by slapping my hand when I put it out to shake theirs and said hello. On their way past me to get beer, they laughed and playfully called me "faggot." Those in the crowd who overheard this comment smiled and giggled, making me feel like garbage. As I tried to mingle in the large crowd, it became harder and harder to hold a decent conversation. I don't think I'm a snob, but damn, I said to myself, can't people at this party talk about anything else besides drugs, jail, who's fucking whom, or bitches and whores?

The evening got even worse. After wishing Joan a happy birthday I went to use the bathroom on the first floor. I could hear people's voices coming through the window over the tub. I couldn't see them, but I was able to make out the voices of three old family friends. As the wind blew the smell of marijuana in the window, I heard my name mentioned. Then reality hit. "Oh my God, girl. I can't believe that faggot is back in town. Is he going to move his ass back to Long Island?" Then another said, "His family is so embarrassed by him. It took some people months to find out they have a brother, and they sure as hell don't mention it." As I was trying to recover from that last comment I could hear the DJ call people together. My heart was truly broken. As I washed my hands at the sink, everything came to me at once—Carlos leaving the city and the comments I'd just heard—I was almost reduced to tears.

Taking a little time to pull myself together, I stepped back from the sink and realized that the type of love I seek and want in family and friendships was not here.

Then I thought of Manhattan and all it offers. I thought of my friends in Austin House, Shepherds House, and in Europe who have given me that honest love of friendship and were awaiting my return to them. It was appreciating this fact that turned the evening's bad experience into a good reality.

I left quietly while everyone sang "Happy Birthday." Walking north on New York Avenue toward the Long Island Rail Road I made the decision never to torture myself again by mixing with this crowd. And if there were really no way around it, then I'd set a time limit for myself.

CHAPTER 35

End of a Love

I spent the next couple of days trying not to think of Carlos. I buried myself in work, from Austin House to Shepherds House. All of our preparations for the opening paid off, as I knew they would. On the invitations that Bradley, Roger, and Mary put together, it said the opening would go from 3:00 PM to whenever. It amazed me how much people can party, especially those that can go all night. We had people showing up before 3:00 PM bringing gifts and canned goods for our pantry. Some of my friends from Austin House that had never been to Alphabet City came down to visit me and see the building,

Justin and I pulled away from the crowd and retreated to the kitchen area. Before he could even inquire about me and Carlos, I told him all the news Carlos had shared with me. Justin yelled, *"That motherfucker!"* Two nuns at the opposite end of the kitchen stared at us. Justin apologized to the nuns. He had me laughing as he tried to make the sign of the cross over his heart.

We returned to the party. And what came next was really uplifting. It was Ryan and his girlfriend Marissa coming in the entrance. I was speechless. I knew from Ryan's letter to me last month they were coming to Manhattan, but obviously he wanted to surprise me. Ryan answered my question before I could ask it. He'd phoned Austin House looking for me, and William gave him my schedule. And to make a long story short, he called Shepherds House and spoke to Bradley, who told him of our opening party, which led them both to be standing in front of me at that very moment.

Feeling a tap on my shoulder, I turned to face yet another surprise. "Oh God," I exclaimed. It was Phillip. Again I was speechless. I let him do the talking, which by the way he did. Being straightforward, Phillip mentioned that monastery life was not for him after all. He even joked about starting a social club for ex-monks and priests.

Once everyone was introduced to each other, I quickly noticed how right I was in thinking that if Bradley, Ryan, Phillip, Anthony, and Mike all met, they'd really get along well together. For most of the evening, they talked together in their small group, at times talking to other guests at the party but always gravitating back toward each other. They discussed homelessness, social work, inner city programs, and lack of religious vocations.

The evening just kept getting better. Manhattan's socialite Rosalind Hamlin showed up with a small entourage of Broadway actors. Bearing champagne bottles, she and her friends made a memorable entrance. Within minutes of her arrival, Roz had everyone dancing to the jazz music being played.

Hosting all these people—from volunteers and Austin House members to members of the archdiocese and our good friends from the squatters' building—wiped me out. I'm sure Bradley and the others felt the same. After about four and a half hours of giving tours and preparing food, I got some alone time on the back patio. Bradley soon joined me. We thanked God for his goodness and blessings. Sitting on the large rocking swing, he asked if I'd consider staying on in his program. He would help me in getting financial aid through programs if I wanted to pursue a social work degree. We continued discussing this. I told him I had a feeling I was called to be a practical nurse, specifically working with people who have AIDS. Looking past me Bradley had a blank look on his face. Then he smiled and said, "We can talk later." As he excused himself, he tapped me on the shoulder and said I had a visitor.

Looking up I had another "Oh my God." It was Carlos coming toward me to sit on the swing. He had decided to leave the following day instead, feeling that he had to be here for a building he helped put together. Even though I didn't want to give another tour, I perked up when he asked me to give him one. After the tour I informed Justin of my plans. "I'm going to walk Carlos halfway to the subway station at Astor Place." I was truthful when Justin asked me if I was going to be okay. I said no. Before Justin could ask any more questions, I announced, "If anyone is looking for me, I'll be back in twenty or thirty minutes." We were trying to leave, but Justin asked which direction we were going. "I don't know," I replied, "but Tompkins Square Park will definitely be the halfway mark."

The neighborhood sounds, loud music, and people yelling to one another, entertained and briefly distracted me from thinking about what was yet to come. I was powerless over the situation. I could express my emotions, my anger and disappointment. But the reality of it all was Carlos and Nancy are going to have a child. And he has chosen to make a life with her and raise the child. That fact made me glad, because so many kids don't have a father. Call it anxiety or nervousness, my hands started to tremble a little, so I placed my arms behind me as we entered the park, hoping I would calm down. The intensity of the moment left us in silence standing side by side. Finally, facing one another, we both moved in at the same time to hug. For the first time his lips didn't graze my cheek as normal. I wanted a kiss but didn't get the sense he wanted to give me one. Shaking my hand, Carlos backed away, smiled, turned, and walked away. I stood there watching him as he got farther and farther away, disappearing into the darkness of night. I've heard many people say romantic interests can come and go, but it is your first real love you will never forget as time rolls onward. I turned and walked in the direction of the northeast exit of Tompkins Square Park. I stopped in my tracks. Waiting for me were Roz, Sally, Debbie, and Justin. As they moved closer, I could tell Justin had spilled the beans and given them the whole scoop about me and Carlos.

    They all had the wisdom to know I wouldn't be in the mood to really talk. Nothing was said about Carlos as Roz took a bottle of champagne from under her shawl. Speaking softly, she handed it to me. "Hey, babe, you look like you could use this." So I swallowed a big gulp of champagne and almost choked to death. I wanted to wallow in sadness, but seeing friends like these show up, friends who knew the situation, lessened my sadness. It was comforting to know I had such a good support system. Within minutes we all had a buzz on from the champagne. We sang Broadway show tunes, not caring who the fuck was looking at us, and walked back to Shepherds House.

978-0-595-44724-4
0-595-44724-4